BREAKING FREE

FULLY INVESTED BOOK 2

KB ALAN

DEDICATION

For Dad: research partner, knowledge guru, best guy.

ABOUT THIS BOOK

Breaking Free

When Janelle comes to Wildlife Ridge for her best friend's wedding, she's not expecting to fall for the little town. Or it's newest resident. But Aaron Romero is full of charm once he comes out of hiding and he's set his eyes on Nell.

Aaron's happy in his new home, working on his art and ignoring the town outside his gate. Until his car breaks down and Janelle and her grandmother stroll over for the rescue. Now he can't get her out of his mind and he's willing to brave the whole town and a wedding to see where things might lead.

To join KB Alan's newsletter, visit www.kbalan.com/newsletter

When Janelle had been told her best friend Rose's wedding would be in mid-April, she'd foolishly assumed that meant a decently warm, sunny day. The fact that she'd spent most of her life in California, with frequent trips to family in Hawaii, had clearly skewed her perspective on April weather.

No matter how much she checked her weather app as she packed for her trip to Wildlife Ridge, Colorado, her brain had a hard time accepting that she needed to be prepared for rain, snow, *and* sun. Giving in to the inevitable, she called her mom and asked if she could borrow her parents' big suitcase. A wedding event wasn't the time to not have the right clothes, and Wildlife Ridge didn't have any clothes shops that she could recall. It was a charming and tiny town, and she was looking forward to returning, but she wasn't planning a shopping spree.

She checked her watch. Her parents lived in Westwood, less than five miles from her house. If she tried to make the drive during commute times, it would take about forty minutes. But right now, on a Wednesday afternoon, she bet herself ten dollars that she could do it in fifteen.

Grabbing her purse, she locked up her guesthouse and walked

the half block to her car. She liked her little rental, but the one thing she would change, if it wasn't stupid expensive to do so, was her lack of a parking spot.

Weaving in and out of traffic with the ease of someone born and raised in Los Angeles, she quickly pulled into her parents' driveway and checked her watch. Fourteen minutes.

"Yes!"

She pulled out her phone and made an entry in her budgeting app, pulling ten dollars from her discretionary category and moving it into her treats category. Then she frowned. The stupid category was up to one hundred and eighty dollars.

She had a…well, could you call it a bad habit? Maybe. She had a habit of letting the treats category fill up and not actually treating herself to anything. Now that Rose had moved away, she and Naomi had fewer excuses to celebrate with dinner at a nice restaurant. She made a mental note to decide on something special for herself once she got home from the wedding weekend.

When she walked into the house, she smelled incense and stuck her head around the corner into the den. Her parents were there, in front of the open butsudan, eyes closed, chanting.

While she'd fallen out of the Buddhist habits she'd been raised with, seeing her parents in their peaceful moment made her happy and a bit nostalgic. They'd had the same butsudan, the alter where they kept the gohonzon and offerings, since she was a kid, and the same routine. Plus, it meant that they'd also bet she'd be at least twenty minutes in her drive, giving them enough time to go through their process, and they had lost.

Grinning, she jogged up the stairs. When she got to the top, she stopped, turned round, went back down, turned around, and jogged back up, panting a bit as she reached the top. She'd read this was a good exercise technique for people who didn't want to specifically plan a time in their day for working out. Every time she encountered stairs, she was supposed to do them twice.

So far, she had discovered that there were actually very few staircases in her day-to-day environment. Who knew?

She pulled the suitcase out of the closet and headed back down. Was it cheating to leave the suitcase at the bottom on her return trip up? There hadn't been a rule about what she was carrying. Panting more substantially by the time she got back up, she turned and walked down, smiling at her parents as they stepped out of the study.

They exchanged hugs and moved to the living room to chat.

"I'm sorry I missed dinner last night, my boss decided to go to Mumbai and it was a bit of a scramble at the last minute."

Her mother frowned. "That boss of yours."

"True, but I got a raise last week, so I can live with his bad time management for a little longer. And, this means he'll be otherwise occupied for at least a few days while I'm in Colorado."

"That's good. Your grandmother is excited to be joining you."

"Rose loves her, and it'll be fun to have her there. And I know she's really looking forward to going to the war memorial in Denver."

"Honey, are you sure you don't want a ride to the airport?" her father asked.

"Thanks, Dad, but no reason to drag you out to LAX. The company has a contract with a valet service. It's one of the few company perks that I can actually use once in a while."

Her dad's lips twitched. "Getting fancy on us."

She rolled her eyes at him. "Yeah, that's me, next thing you know I'll be ordering a car service and sipping champagne while they drive me to my chartered jet."

He leaned in and kissed her cheek. "Go big, buy the jet yourself."

Laughing, she hugged them both again and headed out.

With the larger suitcase, packing was much easier. She just threw in two-thirds of her closet and called it done. She ate a light dinner and set her alarm. She needed to be at the airport earlier than normal in order to meet her grandmother's arrival. They would have time for lunch before catching the flight to Denver.

The drive to the valet service was easy, and she only had to pause at the curb for a moment as the driver jumped into her passenger seat. She gave the young man her company's corporate info as she drove the rest of the way to the airport, and he filled out the form on his tablet. He was out of the car and waiting for her to pop the trunk by the time she'd shifted into park and detached her car key from the rest.

He had her suitcase on the curb and her receipt ready for her by the time she's made it to the back of the car. Nice and smooth. She hoped the rest of her trip managed to go so well.

Three hours later, she and Grandma were settled into their seats and ready to go. She texted the update to Rose, who responded with a series of emojis that made Grandma laugh.

"How come you didn't fly out at the same time as Naomi?"

Naomi, third best friend in her and Rose's trio, had left two days earlier. "She was going to travel around and scout some rental properties she's thinking of buying."

Janelle didn't add that she hadn't been about to let Grandma make the full flight from Hawaii to Denver on her own when it was simple enough to coordinate the layover with her own flight from Los Angeles.

"I'm just amazed at what that girl has accomplished. How many buildings does she have now?"

"She has the triplex she started with, the one you visited. She moved out of that two years ago and bought a four-unit building, but so far that's it. She's decided that it's silly to only invest in Los Angeles when she can get so much more for her money in other markets, so that's what she's looking at now. She liked Colorado when she was visiting Rose and figured she might as well look around. She has the money ready to invest somewhere cheaper, now, or she'd have to wait another year to be able to invest here."

"Smart girl. I'm so proud of all of you, making your way on your own, not waiting for a man to get your life started."

The plane started to taxi and Janelle held her grandmother's hand. "Do you regret marrying Grandpa so young?"

Grandma pursed her lips. "No, but it's a different time now. I worried about your mother when she followed suit and married even younger than me. But that girl met your father and knew what she wanted and wasn't going to waste any time getting it."

"She had me when she was only twenty."

"They were here in California by then, and she told me the only time she got weird looks was when her hands were swollen in pregnancy and she had to take off her wedding ring."

"That, and people asking her if she was the nanny when she would take me to the park."

Grandma looked at her solemnly. "She told you that?"

Nell gave her a wry smile. "She said I was a super-white baby, didn't start getting my color until later. And there weren't many other half-Japanese, half-Hawaiian natives in the neighborhood."

"She told me she hoped California would be more progressive with a mixed marriage, but sometimes she wondered if she should have talked your dad into going back to Canada. But..."

Nell and her grandmother grinned at each other as they both mock shivered. "Cold," Nell agreed. "And here we are, heading to Colorado. Have you ever been to the mountains?"

"Your grandfather and I took the kids to Park City, Utah, when they were in high school. Your uncle begged and begged for the chance to learn how to ski, and the girls said they would try as well. He took a couple of lessons and did okay, but he never asked again. Your mom did fairly well, and your Aunt Linda was too busy flirting with all the boys to give it a proper try."

Nell grinned again at her grandmother as the flight attendant came by to offer them drinks. They relaxed and chatted for a while, until a nicely muscled Latino man moved down the aisle towards them, presumably on his way to the bathroom.

Grandma nudged Janelle's arm. "You haven't told me about any dates lately. You could go stand in line for the restroom, you'll have a few minutes to chat, see what he's like."

"Ah, come on, don't you have enough grandkids by now?"

Grandma put her hand on Nell's arm. "It's not that, my darling. It's that I want to see you happy."

"I *am* happy. And maybe I'll get married and have kids, maybe I won't. But I promise you, I'll be happy either way. I enjoy my life. Dating is fun. But I haven't met anyone that...I don't know, makes me excited to see them after the first date."

"No quiver in your loins?"

"Grandma!" Nell laughed. "I mean, I'm not saying I'm not having fun now and then, but no, I haven't found anyone who makes my loins quiver with excitement at the idea of seeing them."

Grandma frowned. "But you're happy? Working a job you don't like, playing with cars in your spare time, and having occasional fun with dates?"

"It's not my job I don't like, just my boss. The work is fun. And the cars are fun. I sold that Porsche I fixed up for a nice profit, and I had a great time doing the work. I know I'm thirty-six and you already had all three of your kids by my age—"

"No, don't go by that, it was a whole different world for women. My mother got married at the end of the war, and she was twenty; her parents were afraid she was already too old. But she insisted on waiting for my father to come home."

"And you got married at twenty, too. Did you think you were getting too old?"

"No, I just felt ready."

"And you found a Hawaiian boy, who wasn't Japanese. Were you worried about bringing him home?"

Grandma smiled, her gaze going fuzzy with memory. "No, it might have been different if it hadn't been for the war, but after...I guess they didn't hold on to many of the old traditions. I can't even speak Japanese anymore. I wanted my children to learn, but it wasn't taught in the school, and I didn't know it well enough. I tried to get my mother to speak it to them, but it didn't really take. I'm glad your father taught you his French."

"Me, too. And mom followed tradition and got married at twenty."

"She was ready to get off the island. Which was funny, because your father wanted to stay."

"And surf."

Grandma laughed. "Yes, and surf. That's why he'd come, after all. But your mother was smart enough to know he wouldn't want to stay forever, and once he was ready to go, she would have her chance."

"Couldn't she have gone away for college?"

"Yes, but—and you must never tell her I told you this—she was too afraid to go off on her own. She didn't have your independence. With your father at her side, she was ready to dare anything. But on her own, she would not have left the island. At least not for several years."

"That's okay, she made it work."

"She did, yes, and he was a good match for my oldest. He lets her be brave, and she not only gives him family, but the need for family."

"Yeah, his parents weren't nearly as awesome as you and Grandpa."

"Well. Few are."

Janelle laughed. "And at least two of my cousins upheld the tradition of marriage at twenty."

"Ah, those two. They both should have waited. Maybe not as long as you, though."

Grandma's phone beeped and she picked it up to check the message. Janelle leaned over as she sighed.

"What now?"

"Your aunt received koden from her old neighbor and she's deciding how many stamps to send in the thank you card."

Aunt Linda's father-in-law had passed away several weeks before. The Japanese had a tradition of koden, which meant sending money to grieving families when they experienced a loss. For reasons that weren't clear to Janelle, Japanese American families on the mainland had then added to the tradition by sending postage stamps in their thank you cards. The number of stamps was determined by how much money had been sent. That amount of money was also important, to avoid giving insult. Grandma Yuki had a list of how much she'd sent, who she'd sent it to, how much she'd received, whose loss she'd received it for, and the corresponding number of stamps. Janelle found the whole thing fascinating, but was kind of hoping it would die off with her generation.

"Sometimes I wish this stamp tradition had been kept to the mainland," Grandma grumbled as she waited for her daughter to respond. "This wasn't something my mother had to deal with."

"But then you wouldn't be able to help Aunt Linda with her family and neighbors in Michigan."

Grandma gave her the side-eye. "Cheeky."

Janelle just grinned as the phone beeped a response.

Grandma typed out another message and hit send, then leaned back, looking pensive.

"You didn't know him, did you?" Janelle asked, gently.

"We met at the wedding, many years ago." She reached over and patted Janelle's arm. "I'm okay. Sometimes I forget how old I actually am. I don't feel like I'm seventy-four, but then someone from my generation dies, and I remember that I won't be around for much longer."

"Grandma!"

"Shush, it's a fact of life. But I want to be there for your special moments, and your cousins'. I want your mom and your aunt to be able to ask me how many stamps to send, or how much koden is appropriate, even if they argue with my opinion."

The very idea of her grandmother not being around made Janelle's heart ache. She loved the woman with her whole heart and knew that Grandma's loss would be devastating for the family. To not be able to send a photo of her and Naomi trying on outrageous dresses in Beverly Hills, as she'd done last week, or just to call and get the latest news on life in Hilo. She was suddenly happier than ever that Grandma had decided to come to Colorado for Rose's wedding.

Nell closed her eyes, her mind going back over their earlier conversation. As she'd said, she wasn't opposed to the idea of marriage, not at all. It was just getting harder and harder to imagine falling in love, wanting to tie herself, her future, to a man, but if she did, the idea that Grandma might not be there to see her married was too horrible to consider.

But here she was, on her way to a wedding. Seeing Rose and Ethan together had made her heart tingle in a way that her loins had steadfastly refused to do for ages. It made her incredibly happy to see them in love, and she had no doubt that theirs would last.

JANELLE GRINNED AS NAOMI, meeting them at luggage claim, picked Grandma up in an enthusiastic hug.

"Grandma Yuki!"

Grandma's expression tried to maintain stoic, but she lost the battle and offered a wide smile. "I've missed you, too, Naomi. You didn't come to the island last year."

Naomi carefully lowered the older woman to the ground and stepped back. "I wanted to, but the timing just didn't work out. Next time."

"Good. Now, where are our bags? I'm anxious to meet this Ethan our Rose has decided on, make sure he's good enough for her."

Janelle waited until they were settled into the rental car, then leaned forward from the backseat. "So, how are the plans going? Is it crazy yet? Has Rose morphed into a bridezilla? I can't imagine it."

Naomi scoffed. "Of course she hasn't. She's being chill, though now that we're three days out, things have sped up a bit. For tonight, they're staying in for a quiet dinner while we get settled in. First thing tomorrow, it's on. There's a list of things for each of us."

"And tomorrow is the bachelorette party."

"Yes. Anna has ordered the stripper, the decorations you shipped are in a box in Ethan's office that he swears he hasn't opened, and one of us needs to pick up the desserts at the bakery while we're running around doing other things."

"Whew," she said quietly, seeing that Grandma's eyes had closed. "Sounds like everything is coming together."

"Yes. Cal and Jin, Rose's friends, had a nice dinner delivered from that restaurant we went to, Monarch?" She met Janelle's eyes in the rearview mirror.

Janelle nodded. She definitely remembered their night out at the fancy restaurant when they'd come out to meet Ethan.

"The guys gifted it to them so they could have one last quiet night in before all of the craziness happens. Ethan was going to insist on driving to pick you up tonight, because it was snowing and I'm not exactly experienced with that. But it finally stopped and I convinced him I could handle it and he and Rose should have their night."

"When do Jennifer and Brad get in? They're staying at the same B&B as us, right?"

"Yes, and so is Pablo. All of them get in tomorrow early afternoon. Jennifer and Brad will wait for Pablo, and they're sharing a car to get here, then Pablo and Brad will go away and leave the B&B to us for the bachelorette. We're taking over the whole place for the party since it's all just us."

Ah, Pablo, another friend from their old college group, one she hadn't seen in a few years. So much of the group had scattered after college, it wasn't unusual for them to only meet up at weddings. "I kind of wish Jennifer and Brad were bringing the baby so we could see her, but it's nice they'll be able to have this time away, too. Cammie's so cute, though it would have been weird to have a four-month-old at the bachelorette. And, wow, I haven't seen Pablo in years. I guess since Samantha Carney's wedding."

"Didn't he hit on you at her wedding?"

"Yes, but he was drunk."

"And you were there with…" Naomi squinted at the road ahead. "Derek. No, Darnel."

"Yep, Darnel. We'd been together six months, but only lasted three after that."

"He wanted to go to grad school in Nebraska."

"I told him I wasn't interested in Nebraska, but really it was more that I was tired of him moving from school to school rather than actually getting started in anything. I mean, if he'd had a realistic end goal, I could understand, but I really think it was just easier for him to keep being a student than to start paying his student loans."

"You were not wrong, my friend." Naomi glanced at her mirrors and moved lanes to pass a semi-truck. "Pablo seems to be coming single, and he was fairly attractive, as I recall. I want to say I've heard he's a veterinarian now?"

"I think I heard that, too. But, I mean, come on. He's a guy who hits on women who are in relationships."

"Fair point."

When they were an hour out, she called the pizza place in Wildlife Ridge, City Pizza, and told them when they expected to arrive at the B&B, prepaying with her credit card, including tip, and asking that the pizza arrive before they did. It had been a long travel day for Grandma, and she'd already told Rose that they would just head straight to the B&B and see her bright and early in the morning.

When she'd hung up, she sat back and watched the road race past for a few minutes. She'd been so excited, but also sad, when Rose had been the first of them to make a move, literally, by leaving Los Angeles and going to Colorado. Her plan had been to see if living there, in a lower-cost-of-living town than LA, would work, but really as a starting point to being able to live anywhere in the world. She dreamed of traveling while still supporting herself with her computer business. But she'd ended up falling in love with Wildlife Ridge, as much as she'd fallen for Ethan.

Still, she and Ethan were going to travel. Instead of a honeymoon, they were beginning a six-month stay in Spain. They'd bought a fixer-upper house in Wildlife Ridge that they were going to work on once they returned.

Janelle wanted to travel, but just for vacations. She wanted to find somewhere to settle down and be comfortable in her own place. Not that she wasn't comfortable in LA. Exactly. Sort of. She liked being able to go to museums once in a while, liked that there were restaurants galore, but really, she was kind of a homebody.

Those were once-in-a-while activities for her; there was no need to live in a big city like Los Angeles when you didn't love going out to the theater or a fancy restaurant or a concert three nights a week. And it definitely wasn't worth the traffic and crowds.

She'd taken a couple of vacations to small towns, hoping to find one that felt like home. So far, she had liked one, been annoyed by another, and had been indifferent to the third. The one she liked, in Eastern Washington, was a possibility, but she wasn't really sure it would hold up for the long term.

But, then again, she wasn't making a lifelong decision. If she moved once, she could do so again.

Naomi and Grandma were having a murmured conversation, and Janelle realized she'd let her eyes close. She opened them to find that they were approaching Wildlife Ridge. Time to stop worrying about her future and start enjoying her time with friends.

One side of the highway was mountain, and the exit to Wildlife Ridge branched off the other side, nestling into a small valley that was backed by more mountains that she couldn't really see at night. It was more of a feeling of their looming presence and a lack of light.

But the town was lit and inviting. Main Street was where nearly all of the businesses in this town of less than twenty-five hundred people were located. There was only the one gas station first thing off the exit, one two-story strip mall and then several restaurants, including a couple of fast food joints, a Starbucks, and other miscellaneous shops.

She remembered a library, a Masonic Temple—she wasn't exactly sure she knew what that was—and a sheriff's station from her previous trip. The elementary school, and the junior and senior high school were just off Main Street, as were several small neighborhoods and a couple of apartment buildings.

Very quickly they passed the end of Elk Street, a one-way road that they wanted to be on. Only a few yards down, they were able to turn left onto the street. Elk Street made a giant cul-de-sac and came back around to Main. The space formed by the road was a giant lawn dotted with several trees, a little amphitheater, and Town Hall. This is where the wedding would be held.

When they had completed the loop and were most of the way back to Main Street, they turned right onto Glaring Road and made their way to the Columbine House B&B.

She'd made the arrangements for their stay and for the bachelorette party with Bob Bares, the owner, who was quick to come to the door to greet them and help them with their bags. She was very glad to see that the photos online hadn't done the beautiful house justice, and their rooms were excellent. Let the wedding weekend begin!

CHAPTER TWO

The day of the bachelorette party started with a lovely breakfast and a short drive to Rose's apartment. The building —owned by Ethan, Janelle had learned—was a well-maintained brick building near the other end of town. They parked in the small lot and held the door open for an older gentleman who was heading their way with his dog.

"Hello, Mr. Brown," she greeted. They'd met on her last visit. "How is Charlie doing today?"

The dog in question wagged his tail enthusiastically as she rubbed his head.

"He's doing well enough. Already jealous that he won't be at the wedding with the rest of us."

"Aww, I bet he'd look cute in a little suit," Naomi said.

Mr. Brown gave a dismissive sniff, but she could see the smile trying to curve his lips. "I can't imagine. You ladies have a wonderful day." And he tipped a pretend hat at Grandma Yuki.

"Grandma Yuki!" Rose cried out as she opened her door and pulled Grandma in for a hug. Janelle had to laugh. Her friends had spent a couple of spring and summer breaks with her, visiting Hilo. "I'm so, so glad you came. I've missed you."

Grandma fluffed Rose's hair and smiled. "Look at you, beautiful girl. I don't know if it's the mountains that agree with you or the man, but I approve."

Rose blushed and ushered them inside before hugging Janelle.

Grandma handed her a package. "I brought you some of my lilikoi jelly."

Rose squealed. She was definitely a fan of Grandma's passion fruit jelly.

"I'm so glad you're here," Rose said, turning to Janelle. "I know it's a given, but I'm still glad. I have a secret plan to convince you that Wildlife Ridge is everything you've been looking for in a small town."

Janelle rolled her eyes. "It's a lovely town, I have nothing against it. But it's a little more expensive than I'm looking for."

"And that's not really how secret plans work," Naomi added.

Rose waved that away. "I can pretty much guarantee you could retire today and live here without ever earning another penny, but, knowing you, you would be working within a week."

"A month at the most," Naomi agreed.

"Three weeks, at the top," Grandma added.

They moved to the living room and sat as Janelle tried to decide if she should be embarrassed, impressed, annoyed or...well, they weren't wrong, so...

"The crazy part is, I think Tony has learned to read my mind. Every time I run my numbers at home and think, okay, these look good, I'll give it six months to tie up my life and then I'm out of here, I swear to you he gives me a raise within a week."

"I think it's because you no longer worry about upsetting him, and you just do what you know needs to be done, rather than listen to anything he says," Naomi told her.

"Oh, I listen to him. He's good at some of what he does, that's why he was so successful, building that company from scratch. I've gotten a lot better about knowing what to ignore, though."

"Which has subconsciously changed your attitude and probably even made you better at your job. At least he recognizes that, so you're right, he can't be too much of an idiot," Rose pointed out.

"No, but he is, sorry to say Grandma, still an asshole."

They all laughed and jumped into the wedding plans and, before too long, Janelle and Naomi had their first assignments. Knowing that her grandmother would want to take a walk, she volunteered the two of them to take Rose's wedding cake topper over to the house of the woman who owned the bakery. It was just down the street and wouldn't take them too long, but they'd get to see a little bit of the town.

As they headed down the hall to the stairs, they ran into Ethan. Rose enthusiastically introduced Grandma to her fiancé and they chatted for a little while before the bride checked her watch and got the group moving again.

"We'll meet up for lunch at my mom's house," she reminded them as they all split off at the steps of the Salmon Springs apartment building.

"It's nice to see her so happy," Grandma said as they zipped up their jackets and turned right.

"Isn't it?" Nell asked. She took a deep breath of the crisp, clean air. The mountains rose tall around them, blanketed in a sea of green trees. The sky was a bright blue with wispy white clouds adding a touch of character. The snow was piled up at the curb and on the edges of the sidewalks, but the road had been plowed and the sidewalks shoveled, so she wasn't worried about their safety. And it was beautiful, still fresh and white, giving the town a clean and sparkly décor.

"It's such a different beauty than my islands, but quite incredible."

"Yes. I've been thinking about that, if I can move anywhere, which is the idea, right? Do I want beaches or mountains? Desert or forest?"

"And have you decided anything?" Grandma tucked her hand into Janelle's arm, careful not to knock the box with the cake topper.

"No, not yet. I love Hawaii, but I don't want to live there. I'm happy with my regular visits to see you."

"There are other coastlines."

"True, but a lot of them are very expensive. And the weather isn't always the greatest. I mean, I am very much not interested in hurricanes."

"That does remove a number of the cheaper options."

"That's Rose's parents' hardware store," she said, gesturing across the street as they paused for a woman and her two dogs to walk by on the sidewalk.

"I bet they never even thought to hope that she would move back here for good."

"I bet you're right."

"Rose said they went to Denver to see a play, and that they've both been spending more time at the store together. The schedule is supposed to be that they work different days, but it seems like that's not been happening. Rose said the word dating, and her mom didn't object, but Rose didn't push for details."

"It would be lovely if they find their way back to each other."

The elementary school was on the other side of the hardware store. On their side of the street was a sports field and then a side road called Toad Lane. It hadn't taken Janelle long to realize that much of Wildlife Ridge was named for, well, wildlife, of one sort or another. She hadn't quite decided if it was cute or annoyingly cutesy. She'd met Ian Rabbit, who'd told her that he was a descendent of the original family who had settled the town, and had decided that they didn't want to name it after small prey.

Speaking of cute, they stopped in their tracks as a car approached, giving a friendly toot of its horn as the driver waved at them. They turned their heads and watched as the car, painted to look like a snake, drove by. They looked at each, blinked, and resumed their walk.

Beyond Toad Lane was a small block of houses, one of which belonged to the baker. According to Rose, the woman wouldn't be home, since she was at the shop, but had requested they leave the box on her porch.

As they neared the corner of Toad Lane, she could see a man standing in front a black Lexus RX 350. The driver's-side door was open, with the man—she assumed the driver—standing there, arm raised, cell phone in hand, in the classic position of someone trying to get cell service. He cursed and dropped his hand, rubbing his other through his short dark brown hair in obvious frustration.

"Car trouble?" Grandma wondered.

"Maybe. Or maybe something else," she said doubtfully. Only because, as her grandmother well knew, if she really thought it was car trouble, she would have to walk down there. She just couldn't help herself.

And why was she hesitating?

Because he was a handsome man in her age bracket, that's why.

Disgusted with herself, she turned the corner and headed his way. If he'd been a woman, or a middle-aged man with thinning hair, she wouldn't have thought twice about it. But sometimes displaying her knowledge of engines to men went badly, and when they were of the attractive sort, it was somehow more annoying.

Besides, she was one-hundred-percent sure grandma had also noticed the level of handsome the man possessed. Oh boy.

AARON KNEW that he was disproportionately aggravated with the situation at hand. He was about a mile from his house. He was a fit guy, and it was a beautiful spring day; there was nothing troubling about walking a mile. Two, even, if he ended up having to walk back to meet the mechanic, if he could call one out.

He had nothing pressing on his agenda. Having completed his business in Denver yesterday, he'd enjoyed a late supper with a couple glasses of wine and decided to stay the night and drive home in the morning. His schedule was his own, and there was not one single thing that needed to happen in the next two hours.

So, the fact that his car had simply stopped, after driving for nearly two hours and taking him ninety-nine percent of the way home, shouldn't really be that big of a deal.

What *was* sticking in his craw, though, was that part of yesterday's business had included leaving his car at the dealership for regularly scheduled maintenance. He was not a car dude, had no love for them, no care for how they worked, but he respected their utility and did his part by making sure that he followed the manufacturer's recommendations for regular service. And yet, here he was.

He checked his cell phone one more time, but it still read "no service." Lowering the phone, he saw movement and looked towards Dragonfly Road, where he saw two women walking towards him. The older woman was hard to pin down. Sixties? Seventies? Eighties? She had gray hair that cut off at her chin and sparkling eyes that showed she recognized a man who was annoyed with life over a minor setback.

The younger woman had dark brown hair that flowed past her shoulders, features he couldn't begin to pin down—though he thought chances were good she was related to the woman at her side—and a more schooled expression on her face.

He hoped he wasn't staring, but she was hard to resist. Sweet button nose, comfortably curvy body, and, he could see as she got closer, beautiful brown eyes that had the song running through his head.

"Having trouble with the car, the phone, or both?" she asked.

"Both. Thanks for asking. I'm Aaron Romero, I live up the street a ways."

"No problem, let's see if we can help. I'm Janelle Bouchard, and this is Yuki Anakalea. Grandma, do you want to see if your phone has service while Aaron pops the hood?"

He blinked and turned towards the car. He'd never opened the hood and wasn't actually sure where the button was. Hoping for the best, he leaned in and searched the area below the steering wheel, next to the door. Spying what looked like the likely lever, he gave it a quick pull and heard the satisfying clunk of the hood releasing. Whew.

Sweat popped out on his brow. Would she expect that he'd have some clue what he was looking at? Surely not, else he would have opened the hood before she'd come over.

Walking to the front of the car, where she'd already lifted the hood, he saw she didn't hesitate to reach in and nudge this and wiggle that.

"I do have service," Grandma said.

Aaron turned to face her. "Fantastic. I'm almost certain there's a mechanic in town. Are you able to look up the number?" He moved closer so he could see the screen of her phone. She'd already accessed Google maps and was typing in *mechanic*.

She angled the phone so that he could see as the map appeared, and he nodded when she pointed to Bighorn Automotive, which was just over two miles away.

The sound of his engine had his head jerking up.

Janelle hopped down from his driver's seat, where she'd apparently gone to push the ignition button. She smiled at him. "Good to go. Did you get serviced recently?"

He blinked, tore his gaze from her lips and focused on the question. "Yesterday, actually."

"That makes sense. They didn't tighten the connection to your battery, and it jiggled itself loose while you were driving. If you have any tools in the car, I can tighten it down. If not, just make sure you tighten here and here," she pointed. "Otherwise, swing by the garage and they can do it for you easily."

"Wow. That's amazing, thank you so much." He noticed she was holding her hands away from her body. He didn't have tools, but he did have napkins. Grabbing a couple from the center console, and a half-empty bottle of water, he offered them both to her.

"Oh, great, thanks!" She dampened the napkins and wiped her hands clean.

"I really appreciate your help, you saved me at least an hour's aggravation."

"You can buy her a drink at the wedding, as thanks," Grandma suggested.

He searched his brain, trying to make sense of her words.

"We're in town for Rose Chapman and Ethan Woodford's wedding on Sunday. They both live here?" She made it a question.

"Ah, okay. I'm afraid I don't know them, so won't be at the wedding." He reached for his wallet. "Let me give you—"

"No," Janelle said with a frown.

"That's okay," Mrs. Anakalea said over them. "They've invited the whole town. If you live here, you're invited. And a drink and a dance will be a very nice thank you to my granddaughter. The wedding is at seven-thirty in the town square. Unless you'll be busy on Saturday night?" Her tone clearly implied that he would be incredibly rude if he did, in fact, have plans on Saturday.

"Uh, no, no plans. But, really, I've never met either of them, I can't come to their wedding."

Janelle smiled. "They really *have* invited the whole town. They're getting married in the town square—which is the big park in front of Town Hall, if you weren't sure—and since it's basically a giant open lawn, they figured they might as well invite everyone. And they mean it; they have a lot of ties to this town, they enjoy the community."

"That's very…nice," he settled on after a short internal debate.

"Wonderful," Grandma said, handing her granddaughter a small box she was carrying and taking her arm. "We look forward to seeing you there. Don't forget to follow Nell's instructions about what needs to be tightened." And with that, she led Janelle back to Dragonfly road.

Janelle looked over her shoulder at him. "Have a great day!"

And then they were gone.

He stood watching as they reached the corner and turned right, heading towards the houses, away from Main Street. He felt kind of stunned, but couldn't really understand why.

With a little shake of his head, he dropped the hood. As he drove the short distance to his driveway, through the gates, and on home, it occurred to him that the only tools in his house were those related to hanging artwork.

This was the kind of situation his family would be disgusted with him for, for not having the tools and wit to have handled himself. As a teenager, he'd come to the realization that he could force himself to do the little things that his family expected of him to fit in, therefore making his daily life easier by pretending to be more like them, which would ultimately make him miserable. Or he could be himself, and be miserable because they'd make his daily life vary between irritating and downright hostile. Just being left alone and happy was not an option.

At the end of the day, he'd decided that if he was going to be miserable regardless, he'd rather do it by being himself than by faking it.

But his family was long gone. He was a successful man in his thirties, and adding a wrench to his small toolbox would not mean he was a pretender. Then again, he'd gone this long without needing the stupid thing, so why bother?

It only took five minutes to throw together a turkey sandwich and grab a glass of soda water. With a little bit of distance from the car and its hidden layers of childhood trauma, it was obvious to him that there were two very simple solutions available. Drive to the mechanic and ask if they could tighten the bolts quickly, or even just loan him a wrench for five minutes. Or go to the hardware store and buy the damn thing himself.

The problem was that because he knew small towns and how quickly any kind of facts, speculation or even unfounded gossip quickly became common knowledge that grew a life of its own, he'd avoided the town completely. One of the reasons he'd taken the Lexus to the dealership in Denver, rather than have it serviced locally.

Though he'd moved here a year ago, he'd lived in this town only by the strictest of definitions. He did live within the town's borders, but he didn't go to the grocery store, coffee shop or restaurants, bookstore or parks.

It hadn't been a conscious decision, but, he acknowledged to himself now, a protective measure. The last small town he'd lived in had been hell. He'd kept to cities for years after that, but they had eventually worn on him and when he'd seen the listing for this house, tucked into the mountains at the very outskirts of the tiny town, he'd been curious enough to look into it.

When he'd decided to buy, he hadn't specifically thought to keep apart from the town and its citizens. It had just happened. And now he needed to consider that it was time to dip his toes into town life by going to visit either the garage or the hardware store.

And then possibly follow through by attending the wedding of two strangers.

He could easily absolve himself of the obligation by figuring out where Janelle and her grandmother were staying and sending them both flowers and wine as his thank you for their help. Or, he could do as Mrs. Anakalea had requested.

A low ding toned through the house, and a buzz issued from the phone in his pocket. He pulled out his phone and accessed the security app. It notified him that someone was at the gate at the end of the driveway.

Clicking in brought him video of Janelle in a pickup truck, smiling at the camera. In her hand, she waved a shiny tool. A wrench, he thought. Though he might be reading way too much into the small image on his screen, it occurred to him that her bright smile lacked the calculating artifice he'd come to expect in any beautiful woman who smiled at him. An expectation that, once realized, had disgusted him both for how frequently he'd witnessed it and for its cynicism. The realization had led to his fourteen-month-long no-dating policy.

Without bothering to activate the speaker, he buzzed her in and opened the roll-up garage door.

CHAPTER THREE

It was only as she drove the borrowed truck up Aaron's driveway and watched him exit the gorgeous house, hands in his pockets, face unreadable, that it occurred to Janelle the quick favor she'd thought to offer could very easily be construed as an excuse to see the handsome man again. And that handsome, rich—she assumed—men were probably approached by manipulative women all the time.

It was something she'd seen happen to her boss many times. The pessimism of the thought had the smile dropping from her face. It didn't matter if other people used favors as a manipulation tactic. That wasn't her, and if he thought it was, that was his problem, not Janelle's.

She let the smile reform as she hopped out of the truck.

"I had just enough time between wedding errands to grab Ethan's wrench and truck and swing by. I promise, it will only take two minutes. When I told Ethan you said your house was just up this street, he said you were most likely the guy who bought the place that the old sawmill owners used to have, and told me to just look for the gates. I hope that's not too…stalkerish."

"No more so than the fact that I knew if I decided not to go to the wedding tomorrow, it wouldn't be hard to figure out where you and Yuki were staying and send some flowers as a gesture of appreciation," he assured her. "Small town life. And this is extremely kind of you, thank you. Let me back the SUV up."

He quickly did so, then pulled the hood release lever as he exited. "So you're involved in the wedding preparations? Does that mean you're in the wedding party?"

He lifted the hood as she moved to join him. She stood close, purely by necessity, and reached in with the wrench. "Rose is one of my best friends, so yes to both of those." A few quick twists and, as promised, she was done. She stepped back and watched as he lowered the hood and let it close with a solid thud.

"You should absolutely come if you'd like to meet some of the town. I haven't spent a ton of time here yet, but so far, everyone has been pretty cool, and you might have a good time. But please don't feel like you need to do it to make Grandma Yuki happy."

"I hadn't quite decided," he admitted, then gestured into the house. "Would you like a drink, or—"

She cut him off with a wave of her hand. "I appreciate it, but there's still lots to do before we break off for the bachelorette party tonight."

"Sure. I won't keep you. Thank you again. It was very thoughtful of you to take the time for this."

"An easy enough two minutes. If I don't see you on Sunday, I'm sure I'll see you around some visit." She flashed him a smile and walked to Ethan's truck.

There. She felt good, having done the favor, and she'd shown that she wasn't a woman who'd simper all over a handsome, rich man. Not that she cared—much—what opinion he'd formed of her.

Well, okay, she did care about that. She couldn't help herself.

With a little sigh, she backed the truck up, and headed for her next task.

"Nellie!"

Janelle smiled at Rose as she walked into the B&B's living room with a tray full of nibbles. Her friend was well buzzed and clearly enjoying her bachelorette party. Starting the evening off with pink champagne Jell-O shots had warmed things up, and the group of disparate friends were chatting away like they'd known each other forever.

Rose was decked out in a BRIDE banner, fuchsia veil, purple penis earrings, and a very colorful condom wrist corsage. Janelle hadn't imagined that such a thing existed, but Naomi had sent her photos while they'd planned the event, and the mix of shocked embarrassment and hilarity on Rose's face when she'd first seen it had been worth the effort of getting it.

The room was a sea of white and silver balloons, and she gently kicked a couple out of her path as she made her way to the coffee table to set the tray down. The decorations were much more coordinated than the bride's outfit, with a requisite photo-ready background against one wall that currently had two takers wearing pink boas and holding inflatable champagne bottles that they pretended to drink from. She recognized them as Pam and Anna, from town. Cal and Jin, two married guys who owned the antique store, and who she'd met on her previous trip, were taking the pictures and laughing along with the ladies.

Jennifer, after showing off a hundred pictures of baby Cammie, was relaxing beside Erin, a pharmacist Janelle had met on her last visit.

"Nellie," Rose repeated from around a mouthful of pig in a blanket. "Ethan told me that you met our mystery neighbor." She leaned forward, eyes wide. "Hardly anyone has met him. You have to tell us everything."

"Do you mean Aaron?"

"Yes, his name is pretty much the only thing we've learned about him all year," Rose said.

"Jin saw him at the gas station a couple of months ago," Cal reminded her.

"Yep, he's young and hot and drives a brand-new Lexus," Jin said.

"He stopped to let me cross Main Street a couple of weeks ago," Anna added.

Janelle had to laugh. "Well, we did meet him, and Grandma invited him to your wedding. I'd say there's a fifty-fifty chance he'll show."

Grandma had hung around for the dinner, taken photos of the group doing their Jell-O shots, given Rose the penis earrings and then retired upstairs.

Cal reached past Rose to grab a pig in a blanket as well. "Tell us everything. Does he smell good? And rich?"

She snorted. "Are we assuming rich because of the house? What if he's mortgaged to the hilt? And what does rich smell like?"

Anna picked up a balloon off the floor and sat down in front of Cal's spot on the sofa, leaning against his legs. "I'm guessing he's an actor who wants his privacy. Why else would he not even buy his groceries here?"

"Who are we talking about?" Jennifer asked.

Pam snorted. "Honey, this here is small-town entertainment. A man moved into the biggest house in town, then had the nerve to just stay inside. He doesn't come into any of the businesses, order food from the restaurants, nothing."

Naomi shook the bowl of parmesan-thyme popcorn with browned butter, then took a handful. "What makes everyone so sure it's just one person in the house?"

Rose froze, her glass two inches from her lips, her eyes going wide. "I'm sure someone told me that. Who told me that? How would they know?"

Janelle drank her wine and ate a pig in a blanket while the locals debated where that information had come from. She knew that at some point, they would remember she'd actually interacted with the guy and return to her for answers. She debated her options. She could tell them the truth. She could tease them. Or...

She checked her watch. They had forty-five minutes until the stripper was scheduled to arrive. Perfect.

Standing, she raised her voice. "Time to pin some penises!"

The conversation immediately switched to cheers and whoops. Naomi grabbed the large poster and unfurled it with a flourish. The extremely buff man had his hands over his—apparently—missing member. Janelle pulled out the sticker penises and waved them around. They were all sorts of colors and designs, and the crowd did some more whooping and hollering. Pleased with her successful diversion, Janelle helped Naomi tape the poster to the wall.

They used a sleeping mask as a blindfold and spun Rose around several times before aiming her at the poster. Janelle supported her friend as she wavered a bit, then tripped forward, penis sticker held outstretched. Naomi snapped pictures and the crowd cheered as Rose stuck the purple polka-dot penis to the model's left pectoral.

When they'd all taken a couple of turns and the poster looked like something from a horror movie, she checked her phone. The stripper had texted to say he was on time. She looked around for Rose but didn't see her. Grabbing a few empty plates and glasses, she headed for the kitchen, poking her head into the dining room as she passed. She spied Rose on the phone, a besotted look on her face.

It didn't surprise her at all that her friend wanted a few minutes with Ethan. She set the dishes next to the sink and pulled the last batch of Jell-O shots from the fridge, filling up a tray. Leaving it on the counter, she went to the dining room doorway. Rose smiled at her and held up a one-minute finger. She spoke into the phone, then tapped the screen and motioned Nell into the room.

"I'll assume, by the foolish grin on your face, that you were speaking to your fiancé?"

"It's obvious, is it? I had to send him a picture of the penis poster. He called to ask me how drunk I was, as he couldn't quite believe what his eyes were telling him."

"Are they having a good time?"

"He says they are. Jackson's brother got drunk and tried to goad Jackson into a lap dance at the strip club, but they shut him up quickly, and Ethan says Jackson is doing okay. They're at a friend's house now, just started poker. Ethan sounded happy and a bit tipsy."

Jackson's wife Alyssa, Ethan's sister, had lost her battle to cancer six months before. Ethan had told Jackson that he could participate in the wedding as much, or as little, as he was comfortable with. Jackson had insisted on keeping his role of best man and had planned the bachelor party. From what Janelle had learned of Alyssa, she would be very glad to know that her husband was living his life, and celebrating her brother's marriage.

"Did Ethan get a lap dance?"

"I told him he could as long as she was wearing underwear and he didn't touch."

"Do we get to see pictures?"

Rose laughed and hugged Nell. "Let's wait and see what our own pictures look like before we bring that into play."

The doorbell rang as Janelle grabbed the tray from the kitchen and headed back to the living room. "Perfect timing. Let's meet Travis!"

LATER, when everyone else had left, it was just Rose, Naomi and Janelle sitting on Janelle's bed, as they went through the photos. The stripper posing with the whole group while still fully dressed in a very nice suit that turned out to be a tear-away. Jin in a teal boa, pretending to unbutton his own shirt. Pam and Rose dancing with Travis when he was down to his underwear. Naomi using the glitter body paint—that Travis urged her to apply anywhere—to draw a sparkly bumble bee on his super-toned abs. Travis sitting on Nell's lap and using his hands to encourage her to test out the muscles in his thighs. Cal giving his own fully clothed version of a lap dance to Rose, who looked like she could barely breathe, she was laughing so hard. Erin and Rose volunteering to act as poles for Travis to dance around, his hand on Erin's shoulder, his ankle on Rose's. Mm, the dexterity!

They'd been very impressed with Travis' professionalism, rhythm and, well…everything. The pictures didn't quite do the evening justice, but they were excellent reminders of an amazing night.

"Happy?" Naomi asked Rose as she put her phone down and leaned back against the headboard.

"Very. This was a wonderful night, thank you both so much." She sniffled. "You're the two best friends I could have ever asked for. I don't know where I'd be right now if we hadn't been there to support and encourage each other. I'm so thankful for you."

Janelle gave her a big hug. "You would be doing amazing things, for sure, maybe just not quite so amazing as with your two best girls along for the ride. But you would have found your way to Ethan, and I'm so, so glad you've met the man who doesn't need to make you happy, because you were already there, but makes every day even brighter and more amazing because he's at your side."

Tears were flowing from all three of them now as Naomi wrapped her arms around them both. "You are one of the most special people alive, so it only makes sense that you attract awesome people to you."

"Well, there've been a couple of losers as well." Rose hiccuped out her laughter.

Naomi grabbed tissues. "That was just so you could appreciate the awesome people more. Wouldn't want you to take us for granted."

"Oh, right, that makes sense."

They dissolved into giggles.

"I hope you guys find this," Rose said, when they'd calmed down. "I know you're responsible for making your own lives happy and fulfilled, and you've done that, and are continuing to do so, but I really, really hope you find someone who…how did you say it, Nell? Makes your days even better."

Nell had to admit that was a nice idea. In the last couple of years, she'd dated frequently but rarely allowed it to progress to a relationship. And the few that had, hadn't lasted long.

Bizarrely, a quick image of Aaron walking out to meet her car, hands in his pocket, casual sexiness exuding as he waited for her to speak, flashed through her mind. A little shiver danced through her belly and she immediately hopped off the bed.

"Let me show you the dress I got for the rehearsal dinner."

CHAPTER FOUR

Aaron liked to work on the weekends. That way, he could schedule necessary errands and appointments for weekdays and not feel guilty that he was slacking. Which was why he'd done his trip to Denver earlier in the week. He typically worked five days a week, even though he didn't actually need to keep to a strict work schedule. Most of the time he didn't do things that might typically need to be done on a weekend, unless he was seeing someone who did work a Monday-through-Friday job. At those times, he adapted.

It had always worked as a pretty good sign of when a relationship was nearing its end, when he started to resent making those compromises. So, working on a Saturday was normal. Considering taking Sunday off to go to the wedding of people he'd never met was definitely not normal.

The studio was one of the reason's he'd been so pleased to find this house. He could have added on, if there hadn't been an adequate space, but that would have meant annoying construction, dealing with people in his house, the inevitable delays. Instead, the room had an amazing view of the mountains and let in fantastic lighting. There was a walk-in closet that he'd filled with shelves for his supplies and still left room to prep and store plenty of canvases.

The walls had been painted a pale cream, but he'd taken a day to change them to a warm yellow, almost gold, with a much lighter yellow trim. The room had several easels, all empty at the moment, and two lounge chairs with a small table between, though he had no expectation of another person joining him for a seat. It had just seemed unbalanced to have a single chair. And a workbench with a sink taking up the length of one wall.

He stepped into the studio, the smells of paint and paint thinner always appealing to him. He pulled out one of his prepped canvases and placed it on an easel. It was twenty-eight by thirty inches and already had the gesso the way he liked. It was ready to go. Pulling out his phone, he set it to Do Not Disturb mode, then activated one of his playlists. A hard, thumping beat came from the sound system.

Consulting his notes to confirm what the client was looking for, he started to squeeze out his colors. The smell of oil paint was a familiar comfort. Taking up a brush, he began.

This particular client was looking for abstracts with a specific color scheme. They were to go in a large office building in St. Louis. He'd be having prints made, but the client wanted the original paintings as well. A nice commission for sure.

He started to paint, losing himself in his work, letting the lines and swoops flow without much conscious deliberation. It wasn't difficult work, as long as he kept some part of his mind attuned to the objective, the client's request. Commercial art paid his bills quite well and offered him a fair amount of freedom. Sometimes he had specific requests, as with this job. More often he could paint whatever he liked, as long as he kept the market in mind. His paintings were meant for office buildings and banks, as well as retail stores, so people could decorate their homes with prints that looked like oil paintings.

Stepping back, he gave the work in progress a critical look. One of the shades of blue wasn't quite to his liking, so he re-mixed some color and brushed it on. Stepped back again. Better. Checking his watch, he saw he'd been at work for several hours. He was pleased with his progress and had reached a good stopping point.

He cleaned his brushes and put the materials away. Past girlfriends had told him that for an artist, he was awfully anal. Whatever.

Next, he pulled out another canvas, already prepped. This one was a bit larger, and he had been thinking acrylics instead of oils. He gathered the materials he wanted, closed his eyes for a minute to pull the image that had been gathering for a week or so to the front of his mind. Bright flowers, windblown and slightly bedraggled against the background of a stormy sky.

Just as he opened his eyes, a figure popped into the image. A woman, face turned up into the rain. The face he'd seen yesterday…

He closed his eyes again, picturing the lovely features of Janelle Bouchard. She had a strong body and soft features. Hair that looked slippery and invited a man's fingers to run through the strands. He remembered perfectly shaped eyebrows and delicate fingers that looked almost absurd, considering how competently they handled the wrench.

He shook his head. No, his stormy bed of flowers didn't need a garden princess. That wasn't the look he was going for.

Pulling out his phone, he brought up his playlists. Debated. His finger hovered over a list he didn't use often, but sometimes it was just right. He selected KPOP and let the music fly. He picked up the brush, added color, and began to paint.

Sometimes he used reference photos, but for this sky, he needed only his memory. Southwestern Ohio could produce some beautiful stormy skies, and he'd seen plenty of them. His brush paused for a second…because sometimes those storms were deadly. But he shook it off.

Again, he lost himself in the painting until his stomach protested. He stepped back and checked his watch. It was well past lunchtime, heading into the early dinner hour. Casting a critical eye over the painting's progress, he slowly nodded his head. He hadn't gotten as far as he had with the commercial piece, but that was okay. Making the commercial art was like drinking a good beer with a burger. Creating fine art, as his agent insisted he call it, was more like drinking a very nice whiskey after an excellent meal. Except for when it all went terribly wrong, of course.

He turned the Do Not Disturb setting off on his phone and switched the music to Frank Sinatra while he cleaned up, then went downstairs to the kitchen, humming along as the music switched to the downstairs speakers. Opening the freezer, he shuffled through the meals that had been delivered two days ago. There was a pork chop deal that had looked pretty good. He found the right package and opened the large bag to pull free the separate smaller bags and the recipe card.

A quick read and he was ready. He turned on the oven and set a pot of water to boil. Opening the fridge, he perused his beer options and chose a hefeweizen. A delivery service, separate from the ready-made-meals one, brought him groceries once a week. He told them what he wanted, and he'd developed enough of a relationship with one of the drivers to give her some leeway to have fun with the beers. The bottle opened with a satisfying *snick* and he took a long pull. Very nice.

The music dimmed and his phone rang. He frowned. He wasn't expecting any calls.

The screen showed that it was his best friend, Carole. Answering, he set the call to speakerphone, then checked the water. Almost boiling, if he was any judge. And he'd become a fair judge about the heating up of water.

"Hey CC."

"Hi Aaron. How're you doing?"

"Just cooking dinner."

He removed the two small twice-baked potatoes from their vacuum sealed wrap and put them on a sheet pan, ready for when the oven beeped.

"First of all, it's, like, four your time," she said, amusement coming through clearly. "Secondly, don't call that cooking."

"Hey, I'm even using the oven this time."

"Are you boiling water?"

"Yes."

"My statement stands."

He smiled. "Whatever. What are you doing?"

"Calling to find out why you haven't RSVPed to Aubrey's birthday party."

He checked the water again. Just getting there. He'd let it go another minute since he had the feeling he'd be on the phone for a while, anyway.

"Because it's in California and I'm in Colorado?"

"And yet, you didn't respond with a no."

"Would that have worked?" The oven beeped so he stuck the tray with the potatoes on it inside and set the timer.

"Did not responding work?" she countered.

"Apparently not."

"Are you really saying you can't be bothered to get on an airplane for your goddaughter's first birthday?"

"I'm fairly certain she won't remember the party, or me being there. Or not being there."

He grabbed the tongs from the drawer next to the stove as he heard happy baby babbling come through the speaker.

"See, she says you better be here or else."

"Well, then, tell her I booked my flight yesterday." Picking up the bag that held the pork cutlet, he gently lowered it into the roiling water. Then did the same with the bag of honey-glazed carrots.

"Grrrrr. How hard would it have been to RSVP?"

"Like we weren't going to talk on the phone sometime this week, anyway?"

"Well, yeah, but we could have done it yesterday when you called to RSVP!"

He laughed. "The party's isn't even for, what, four weeks? Besides, I had car trouble yesterday, it threw my schedule off."

She scoffed at that, but relented. Having been his girlfriend briefly in college, she knew how much he hated to deal with car stuff. "Yes, four weeks, so fine, I'll take that pathetic excuse. What else is happening in your world?"

"I was invited to a wedding for tomorrow. Two people I've never met. Apparently the entire town is invited."

"Holy cow, the town really is that small?"

"Evidently. It's being held on the town square, so they just went ahead and opened it up to everyone."

"So you've finally interacted with people in town?"

"Sort of. Not really. A couple of women helped me with my car. They told me about it, but they're just visiting for the wedding."

"You have to go."

He snorted.

"No, really! It's the perfect way to meet everyone."

"I don't think perfect is the word that I would use."

"Listen, you have to—wait. You didn't say no. Are you actually planning on going?"

She'd always understood him way too clearly.

"Probably. I owe a favor to the two ladies, and it was suggested that buying them drinks at the wedding would be appropriate."

"Well, there you go. What are you taking as a wedding present?"

"Shit."

"It's okay, this kind of situation you don't have to go too crazy. You can do a check in a card, but only if it's an actual wedding card. Or you can do a very nice bottle of wine, if you're reasonably sure they're not abstainers. Or a case of decent champagne. But you should really do the wedding card, the check, and one of the other options. You're rich, use the money for good."

"Hm." He actually had all of those things, except for the card. "I think that could be seen as being pretentious."

"I disagree."

He'd have to give that some thought. Of course, if he'd met any of the people in town, it would be easier to determine. Oops. "I have some cards that were run from one of my paintings, but they're blank inside."

"What's the painting?"

"Irises."

"Sold."

"Cool. Thanks for the assist."

"You're welcome. I'm glad you're going. I like the idea of this town for you, but only if you actually live there. And I'm glad you're coming to the party. We've missed you."

"Yeah, me too." He added the bag of sauce to the pot of water. He'd flown out to see the little family two weeks after Aubrey was born, but hadn't seen them since. "I was afraid to come visit. Beth was getting pretty moonie-eyed last time I was there, I don't want her to fall for my charms and leave you behind."

The girlish laughter that filled the room made him smile. Beth liked him, else he never would have been selected as godfather, but she was madly in love with CC and had zero attraction to men.

"Yeah, that'll happen. Let me know how the wedding goes."

"Yes, ma'am."

"Enjoy your so-called dinner."

"Hey, you can knock the idea that I'm cooking, but the dinner itself is excellent."

"Whatever."

Smiling, he ended the call and the music turned itself back up. He'd just taken a drink from his beer when the timer sounded. Perfect.

He turned it off then used a pot holder to retrieve the potatoes and set the pan on the counter. Using the tongs, he lifted the bag of meat from the water and poked at it with his fingers. Seemed about right. It had been cooked before being flash frozen, so the boiling water was just meant to heat it through.

Plopping the meat onto the counter, he quickly followed with the sauce and the carrots. He turned the burner off and dumped the water into the sink. He got a plate from the cupboard and frowned. He'd forgotten to stick it in the warmer. Ah well, he'd survive.

He opened up the plastic bags and plated the meat and carrots, added the sauce to the meat. He plunked one of the potatoes down and studied the results. Not bad.

He carried the plate, cutlery and his beer to the dining room. Tasting the pork, he approved. CC teased him, but mostly because she thought that instead of figuring out how to eat well when living on his own, he should be out there, finding someone to share meal times with. He'd pointed out that there was no guarantee this theoretical woman would be able to cook any more than he could, but she'd just frowned at him. Not the point.

Eating alone didn't bother him. He didn't even mind eating alone in restaurants. He wondered what Nell and Yuki were having for dinner, and how big of a group they were with. Weddings brought friends and families together, he knew. At CC's, he'd been one of the groomsmen. It was probably the last time he'd felt lonely, actually, and he'd been surrounded by people. Usually he was fine in a crowd, but that...had been different. He frowned. Maybe going to the wedding tomorrow wasn't a great idea.

Then he pictured Janelle's face. And Yuki's. And reminded himself that unlike CC's wedding, he'd be able to leave at any time. Settled again, he opened up the book he was reading on his phone. Only a couple of chapters in, so far he was enjoying it. Within seconds, he'd been pulled back to the WWII soldiers, cut off from their unit, and encountering a paranormal evil they never could have anticipated.

NELL WOKE up in a happy mood. The bachelorette party had been a success, the bride and guests had all seemed to enjoy themselves quite a bit, and no one had gotten drunk enough to throw up.

She caught up on social media for a while, pleased to see that she approved of all the photos of her that appeared. She couldn't wait to show a couple of them to Grandma.

The plan was to take it easy this morning. Rose had spent the night at the B&B, so they were going to have a lazy breakfast, finish up any last-minute details or errands that might need their attention that afternoon, then get manicures and pedicures. The rehearsal wouldn't take more than a few minutes, then dinner and an early night.

She did the shower-and-prepare-for-the-day thing, then headed downstairs to meet everyone for breakfast at the appointed time.

Instead, she found Ethan in the living room, chatting with Rose, Naomi and Grandma.

Rose bounced up. "Since we're so on top of things and only have a couple of minor details to deal with this afternoon, instead of breakfast, Ethan is surprising us with a picnic brunch." She was beaming, clearly pleased with her fiancé. "It's supposed to be a clear day, in the high sixties. Mom and Dad will be there, all of the out-of-town guests are invited, and we can just chill and hang out."

"Sounds perfect," Naomi said in approval.

Within the hour, they were set up next to Darla's Duck Pond, on the far side of Ladybug Park. There was a playground in the park, which was currently hosting three kids and two squealing toddlers. There were also tables and grills, but the wedding party had chosen to set up by the pond instead. Ethan told her there was ice skating in the winter and fishing the rest of the year. It wasn't big enough for boats.

They laid out thick blankets and some camp chairs and a folding table piled high with food and drinks, plates, cups and cutlery.

Ethan and George, Rose's father, made mimosas and handed them out, and they fell upon the food like people who had...well, partied all night. Stories from the two events began to flow, and Nell nearly spit out a bit of scrambled-egg-stuffed croissant at a story involving Ian Rabbit and a bad poker decision.

A small group decided to try out frisbee golf, as there was a course set up throughout the park. George had promised to show them where to get the equipment and how to play. She was mildly curious, but feeling way too lazy to join in right now.

She had her head on Naomi's thigh and her eyes closed as she listened to the conversation around them.

A man Rose introduced as Ben came by and she talked him into having a mimosa.

"Grandma Yuki, how did you meet your husband?" Rose asked.

Rose and Naomi had never met her grandfather, who'd had a heart attack when Nell was in high school, but they'd seen photos and heard some stories.

"Ah, well, let's see. That was in nineteen sixty-five. I had graduated high school, but of course I was still living with my mother. I'd been working at a hotel since I was sixteen, and wasn't in any hurry to settle down. It was the sixties, right? A woman didn't have to get married to have worth."

"Amen," Ben said, raising his glass to Grandma. She guessed Ben was about the same age.

Grandma responded with her coffee, then paused to take a sip. "And then Moses Anakalea walked into the hotel. He was from the big island, in town on business. He was older than me, twenty-four to my eighteen, and I thought he was very mature and sophisticated. He invited me to dinner before I'd finished checking him into his room."

"And you accepted," Rose said.

"No, of course not." Grandma lifted her chin. "I knew he'd booked the room for four days. If he wanted me, he would keep asking. And he did. I said yes to dinner on the third day."

Janelle smiled as Rose and Naomi laughed in delight.

"He asked me if I would move to the big island. I told him no. My father had died three years before, and my mother needed help paying the rent."

"You were in Honolulu, right?" Janelle asked.

"Yes, and I was the oldest. My brother is two years younger, and we wanted him to go to college. Moses began to court me. He would send me letters and call. When he called, he would always talk to my mother as well. I would say he courted her almost as much as he did me. When he came to visit, he would always make sure there was time for at least two dates, one with just me, and one with me and my mother."

"And what did she think about that?" Rose's mom, Francine, asked.

"She was skeptical at first, but he won her over quickly. My husband could be very charming, which is why he was such a successful salesman. If he'd been full of himself, I would have shown him the door."

"And he asked you to marry him on the six-month anniversary of the day you met," Nell said.

"That's right. He had built a house, with a mother-in-law unit, just outside of Hilo. He brought pictures and even a floor plan, along with the ring."

Ethan grinned. "The way to a woman's heart?"

"By then my brother was graduating and ready for college. Moses wanted a family, and I did as well. We wanted to start right away, and with my mother there to help, everything was perfect."

"And did everything stay perfect?" Rose asked.

"No relationship is ever perfect, of course. But we had a marriage that was better than many. We complimented each other well, supported each other. Which isn't to say we didn't fight. We once went a week without saying anything more than 'please pass the salt'. Of course, I have no idea what the fight was about anymore."

She sipped her coffee. "If I had to narrow our success down to one thing, I would say that in addition to simply loving each other, we respected each other. So, even when we were mad, even when we were convinced that the other person was wrong, we showed respect."

Nell saw, out of the corner of her eye, Rose's parents making eye contact. It seemed a private look, so she focused on her grandmother.

"He died young," Nell said softly. "Only sixty-eight. Do you think you would ever date again?"

"I would never say never, but I've not been tempted yet."

Rose asked Ben about his marriage. Apparently, he'd retired to Wildlife Ridge a decade ago, after his wife had died. Nell listened, but she was distracted by the idea of her grandmother dating. She made a bet with herself that Grandma would dance with at least two men at the reception tomorrow. Eligible men, not Ethan, or George Chapman, she amended as she watched her grandmother listen to Ben.

CHAPTER FIVE

Aaron was halfway to Town Hall before he realized it was kind of ridiculous to have driven. It was a six-minute drive. Dozens of people in their wedding best were walking along Main Street as he slowly drove past. He parked in the lot behind Town Hall, walked past that building and a small amphitheater, wondering why the wedding wasn't set up on the stage. Instead, he arrived at several rows of chairs laid out, with a gazebo at the front. He was glad, because he could take a seat in the back row without walking past the assembled guests.

He wasn't the most social of individuals. Hence the hiding at his house for months, making no effort to meet or engage with the community. As a teen, he'd learned that trying to conform to what his parents expected of him was going to destroy him. So he'd stopped. And he'd taken it too far, in that typical teenage way. Become an antisocial art geek. In a bigger city, he probably would have found at least a couple of people to bend with in that way, but in his small Ohio town, he'd been the outcast. And so he'd embraced it.

As he'd prepared himself for college, for life out of that house, out of that town, out of that life, it had slowly begun to dawn on him that he could make an active choice in who he wanted to be in the future. While he still wanted to be true to himself, he didn't have to be alone and "misunderstood". There were other people out there like him, he knew that. Just being able to take art classes in college would afford him plenty of opportunities to meet people he enjoyed, he assumed.

So he started college with that frame of mind. And he watched those around him, people who seemed to socialize without effort. He found two types. Those who were confident and knew no wrong, regardless of the topic. They would state their opinions as fact, and believed fully that they always knew the best course. They were surrounded by others who agreed with them always.

Then there were those who were confident, but surrounded by other thinkers and always willing to listen and learn. Instead of sycophants, their companions, whether introverted or extroverted, were encouraged to voice their opinions. Debates were considered normal, not mutinous.

He also, slowly, realized that often the folks who seemed the most confident, were actually the most insecure.

His freshman year was a revelation, and he'd worked hard to make himself a man he was proud to be, instead of the rebellious teenager who'd been on the right track, but whose main goal had been to show his parents that he didn't need their approval.

Which brought him to being the person who could walk into a wedding full of strangers, feeling confident in who he was and that he could navigate the event, and maybe even start some friendships. There was still, of course, the unease of being on his own, but he knew that wouldn't last long.

He dropped his gift off at the designated table and took a seat in the last row of chairs. He guessed there were about sixty people present. A woman was playing guitar off to the side, the music drifting over the murmuring audience. A trio sidestepped into his row and a man held out a hand. "I'm Ron Bakshi, and this is my wife, Sandy, and our daughter, Dara." The ladies waved and took their seats.

"A pleasure. I'm Aaron Romero."

"Glad to have you here. We came to Wildlife Ridge about twenty years ago, just after Sandy and I married. So we've known the bride and groom a long time. We're so glad to have Rose back in town."

"I take it you like living here, then?"

"Absolutely. I was able to get a job as a park ranger, over at the Beddow State Park down the highway. They'll have to kick me out of there if they ever want me gone."

"It's always great to hear when someone loves their job."

"I'm a manager now, so I don't get to run around the park all day, like I used to, but it's always there when I want to step outside. Are you here for the bride or the groom?"

"Actually, I've never met either. I was told the whole town had been invited, and I moved here last year, figured it was time to meet people."

"Oh, wow, that's great! Where did you move to?"

"The end of Toad Lane, over past where the kids leagues play sports."

"Sure, we heard someone had moved into the big house behind the gates. I'm glad you came out."

"Thanks," Aaron said, as the couple in front of them turned around in their chairs, clearly having overheard.

He spent the next five minutes exchanging names and pleasantries with half a dozen people in the immediate vicinity. He discovered that his house had belonged to the same family that owned the sawmill a couple of generations back, but had been sold when the mill started to decline. He hadn't actually known what the industrial looking building right off the highway was, only that it seemed to emit steam twenty-four hours a day. He really needed to learn more about this town.

Finally the music changed tempo to indicate that the wedding was about to begin. Two Black men and a white woman had made their way to the front of the gazebo.

"That's the mayor, who's going to perform the ceremony, then Ethan and his brother-in-law, Jackson," Ron said in a low voice.

Aaron nodded.

Everyone turned to look over their shoulders. There was a small white tent that he'd walked past without paying much attention, about twenty feet behind his row. A flap had been opened, and Janelle and a Black woman stepped out. They wore flowy dresses and flowers in their hair, and looked as bright and sunny as the spring day.

They slowly walked up the aisle together, arms linked at the elbows, until they reached the front and took up positions on the opposite side of the mayor as the men.

The crowd rose and fully turned to the back to watch the bride make her way to her groom. Aaron watched the groom. If the look of pure love and happiness on the man's face was enough to go by, then he'd say this marriage was going to go the distance.

JANELLE HAD ALREADY SEEN Rose in her wedding dress, veil down, flowers in hand, but she still teared up again when her friend began her slow walk down the path to Ethan. Beside her, Naomi sniffled, and Nell was glad the other woman had made sure they both had a couple of tissues tucked into their bouquets, just in case.

The dress had simple straps, a sweetheart neckline, and a fitted bodice that flowed down to a subtle lace skirt, with slits at the thighs and a small train. Her high-heeled sandals had chunky heels that navigated the lush green grass well while still looking elegant.

She held a bouquet of roses in sweet spring colors, as did Naomi and Janelle. They also wore matching headbands of the mini rose-buds. They had matching soft, flowing slate-blue sundresses with wide straps. Janelle felt pretty and was fairly bursting with the romance of the day.

It was late enough that the sun had lost its bite but still early enough for the light to dazzle against the mountains that surrounded the little town. The three of them had little faux fur wraps ready for the cold. She was surprised she didn't need it now, but the excitement was keeping her warm.

Janelle and Naomi stood in a white gazebo, along with the mayor, who was conducting the ceremony, Ethan and his brother-in-law, Jackson. Soft lights wrapped around the gazebo and branched off over the seating area, which would become the dance floor later on.

For now, she watched as Rose glided up to the gazebo, her gaze solely on Ethan as he waited for her, identical looks of love on their faces.

Janelle sighed and Naomi sniffled. They shot each other quick grins as the bride and groom turned to face the mayor. Janelle caught Rose's mom giving her dad a squeeze. She was glad the two had found their way to being friends again, for their sake as well as Rose's.

Some movement at the back of the rows of chairs caught her attention. Her breath caught when she saw Aaron watching her. Well, he was probably watching Rose and Ethan. *He'd come.* She felt a little sparkle of excitement in her stomach.

The mayor was getting to the good part, so she returned her attention to the "I dos". Ethan lifted Rose's be-ringed hand to his lips and laid a gentle kiss on the knuckles, then slid his other arm around her waist and pulled her in for long kiss that had the crowd cheering.

When they broke apart, both were flush and smiling. The cheers intensified and Janelle joined in with a whoop. She was glad to see the genuine happiness on Jackson's face. She knew both he and Ethan must be hurting at Alyssa's absence, couldn't imagine the pain of the loss that was only six months old. She hoped Jackson would find real happiness again.

She and Naomi each took one of his arms, and they followed Rose and Ethan down the aisle. She glanced over to where she'd seen Aaron—and found his gaze on her, a slight smile on his lips. She gave him a little nod, and his smile grew bigger.

He'd looked good in his slacks and shirt the other day. He looked amazing now in a slim-fit suit, polished and sophisticated. But she thought he would look even better later in the evening, when he took off his tie, his jacket, started to look a little disheveled. Yum. She hoped he'd stay that long.

The music started while they took some photographs. She stood with Naomi and Jackson while Rose and Ethan posed with Rose's parents.

"Are you enjoying working and living in the same town again?" she asked. "No more commute?"

"Yes and no. I usually enjoyed the drive. I was never good at sitting and reading, but I got into the habit of listening to audio books on my commute. I miss that."

"Have you considered getting a dog? I have a friend who walks her dog and listens to audio books."

He pursed his lips. "That…might work."

They were called in for pictures, so Janelle put her arm through his again and they made their way forward. When they reached the couple, she threw her arms around them both and squealed. "You're married!!!!" They laughed.

"We totally are," Rose agreed. "It's crazy and awesome and scary and amazing and I'm *so* happy!" she gushed.

Janelle laughed again. "You're adorable. Let's take pictures."

They did serious pictures and silly pictures. Elegant ones and fun ones. The sun was setting and the photographer worked hard to get the shots in the beautiful light. By the end of it, she was almost crying from laughing as she and Naomi tripped off to find a table. Almost immediately, she spotted Grandma and veered Naomi in that direction. She was completely unsurprised to see Aaron sitting at the table, along with Cal and Jin.

She smiled a hello as Grandma introduced Naomi and Aaron, but was interrupted from saying anything when Ethan jogged up.

"We need you guys back for a couple more pictures with Grandma Yuki." He held an arm out to Grandma. "If you will?"

Her grandmother was clearly touched and rose to take his arm.

She spoke to the table. "We'll be back shortly, I'm sure. Please excuse us."

A couple more photos and they headed back to the table. Janelle leaned down to speak softly to Grandma, so only she and Naomi could hear. "I see you've made another conquest."

Naomi snorted. "None can hold out against a determined Grandma Yuki."

Grandma sniffed daintily. "I have no idea what you mean."

She was smiling as they rejoined the table.

CHAPTER SIX

Aaron found he was staring at Janelle's smile. Again. From the moment the wedding had started, he'd been captivated by that smile. Or her laugh. There was just so much joy in her. He wouldn't claim that she was the reason he'd come, but he could say that she was the reason he was glad he had.

Mrs. Anakalea—who had quickly insisted he call her Yuki—had grabbed him as soon as the ceremony was over, and he'd escorted her to a table where they were joined by Cal and Jin, who introduced themselves and told him all about the bachelorette party, and pulled out their phones to show pictures. His favorite was one of the three best friends, arms around each other, feather boas about their shoulders, brightly colored loose feathers flying around their faces as they all laughed.

Cal and Jin had sat to one side of Yuki, and he on the other, so Naomi and Janelle took the remaining seats, with Janelle next to him and Naomi next to Jin. The lights strung overhead had come on while the photos were being taken, but it wasn't yet fully dark.

A server quickly arrived to pour them water and drop off a plate of bread. Everyone except Janelle took some and buttered their pieces while Naomi told them about the rehearsal dinner the night before.

"There wasn't really much to rehearse," she said. "Mostly it was just nice to have a dinner together, Rose's parents, Jackson, us and Grandma Yuki. Jackson made a little speech about how pleased he was for them, and how he knew Alyssa was watching and had never wanted anything but to see Ethan this happy and blessed, and oh my god, I nearly lost it."

Janelle leaned into him. "Jackson's wife, Alyssa, passed away last year from cancer. She was Ethan's sister."

"I'm sorry, that must have been terrible. Did Rose know her?"

"She knew her from when they were kids, but she just moved back to town earlier last year. When she reconnected with Ethan, Alyssa was already relapsed and pretty sick, but they were able to spend a lot of time together. Alyssa helped with a lot of the wedding plans. I can't even imagine what it's like to lose a sibling like that."

She shuddered next to him, and he wished he knew her well enough to put his arm around her.

"It all depends on the relationship they had. I'm sorry he lost her, but I'm glad that they were close while she was alive."

"I guess that's true. Not all families are close."

"You don't have any siblings?" he asked as the waiter brought them salads.

"No. I have a lot of cousins, and we're fairly close, but I live in California and they live in Hawaii and Michigan."

"That's quite the difference."

She laughed. "Yeah, we don't go visit the cousins in Michigan, they come to us or we meet up in Hawaii. By their choice, so they have reasons to leave in the winter."

"Not much of a skier?" he asked.

"I haven't tried, though I'd be willing to. But I'm more likely to hang out in a cozy cabin next to a fire, watching a movie. Just like I know how to surf, but to be honest, I'd rather be under an umbrella with a good book than getting beat on by waves and swallowing saltwater." She forked up a bit of salad and dabbed it in her vinaigrette, which she'd left to the side. "What about you?"

"I ski about once a year, and then remember that I'm not much of a sports guy. I was thinking of trying some hiking when the weather's better."

"Rose was telling me the state park nearby has some great trails. I was here in the winter, and it was beautiful, but now, in April, it's just so stunning every time you turn around."

"It absolutely is."

She smiled and tuned back into the conversation that was going on around them. Naomi was checking her phone with a frown. "Dang, the offer I made on that triplex was countered too high. I'm going to say no. But the agent has another one in Bell View that looks interesting." She scrolled her screen up. "Except he can only show it to me tomorrow morning. Ah well, I'll have him do a video. You can see a lot from those."

"You should go if you want to see it. Better to see in person. Grandma and I can get another ride to Denver."

"Don't be silly, I said I'd take you and I'm happy to do it."

"You two fly out in the morning?" he asked.

"We're going to a museum that's having an exhibit we want to see. We have a late-afternoon flight, so if we head out in the morning, we should have enough time to do the museum, grab some lunch, and get to the airport nice and early."

"I can take you."

She opened her mouth to object, he was sure of it, but Naomi spoke first. "Wow, are you sure? We wouldn't want to drag you all the way out there. And I'm sure the virtual tour would give me a good idea about the property."

"I drive out there all the time, it wouldn't be a problem. And it would be a more fitting thank you to Janelle than the drink I haven't bought her at this open-bar event," he added with a chuckle and a tip of his head to Yuki.

Again, Janelle opened her mouth, but this time it was her grandmother who beat her to speaking.

"That's extremely kind of you, Aaron. We would appreciate it very much."

Janelle's mouth closed, and she glanced over at her grandmother before turning back to him. "Thank you."

"My pleasure. Why don't you text me the address where you're staying, and that way you'll have my number if you anything comes up."

She did as he suggested with another thanks.

A DJ had set up where they'd cleared away the rows of chairs and had begun playing music as the salads arrived. Now, as staff started to clear those plates, his barely touched, Janelle's eaten clean, the DJ introduced Rose's father, who gave a little speech.

Aaron took the opportunity to survey the tables around him. It was a slightly more diverse group than he would have guessed for a tiny town in Colorado. And a pretty good array of ages. Though, he realized, he didn't know which people were locals and which were visitors. He tried to pinpoint the visitors as a plate of chicken was placed before him. He took a little bite and approved of the barbecue sauce.

Naomi got up to say a few words as well, words which had Janelle sniffling into her napkin, but she was smiling.

She'd eaten all of her veggies and two bites of her chicken. He'd eaten all of his chicken and two bites of his veggies. They'd both finished their wine, but she'd also finished her water. The staff came by with champagne, and Jackson led them in a toast to the beaming couple, who transitioned into their first dance.

He offered to go get drinks from the bar, for the table, and Cal volunteered to help him. They took orders and made their way to the little setup.

"How long have you lived here?" Aaron asked.

"We moved here almost four years ago. We were thrilled when we heard you moved in, so we could officially pass on the title of new guys."

"Glad I could be of service. But I've lived in a small town, I'd bet a great deal of money that they still call you new."

The other man sighed. "Yeah, you're right." He elbowed Aaron. "But it doesn't help that no one ever sees you."

Aaron shook his head. "We'll all be new for *at least* ten years. And that's being very conservative."

Cal snorted. "And conservative is not Jin or I."

Laughing, Aaron stepped up to the bartender and gave her their orders, then turned back to Cal. "How did you guys end up here?"

"We were in Pittsburgh. I was the manager of an antique store and Jin worked for an interior designer. We wanted to open our own store and get out of the city. We just started looking around and stumbled across a real estate listing for a retail space here in town. The more we looked into it, the more we liked it. We're hoping to adopt in the next few years, raise a family."

"How about you?" Cal asked as they gathered up the drinks and headed back to the table.

"Basically the same, wanted to get out of the city. I work from home, so I just started looking for some place I could have some privacy and beautiful views."

They arrived at the table and passed out the drinks.

"What work do you do from home?" Cal asked as they took their seats.

"I paint. Mostly oils, some acrylics. Mainly commercial art, for office buildings and such."

"That's fun," Janelle said. "Does that mean you make one painting a bunch of times?"

"No, usually that would be prints. They do the prints right on canvas now, add a little paint on top, and the print looks fairly close to a real painting."

"At least to the average person," Jin pointed out.

"True."

A man approached the table, beelining for Janelle. "Nell, we've hardly had a chance to talk. Let's dance and catch up."

"Sure, Pablo." She smiled at the table, knocked back half her drink and took the man's offered hand.

Aaron missed something Cal asked, and he realized he was

watching Janelle and Pablo make their way to the dance floor, rather than paying attention to what was happening at the table. He turned back. "I'm sorry, what was that?"

Cal grinned.

Janelle was in a fantastic mood. She loved seeing Rose and Ethan so happy and in love. She'd enjoyed meeting new people and spending some time with old friends. She'd danced with Pablo, reconnecting enough to enjoy the conversation, and also put to bed the vague idea that maybe this was the opportunity to take things to another level. Not gonna happen.

She'd danced with Ethan, danced with Rose, danced with Naomi and Rose at the same time. Then the DJ had started picking things up, and she'd worked up a nice sheen of sweat despite the cool air and was thinking about kicking off her shoes.

She'd seen Grandma dancing with Ben at one point, and another man she didn't recognize. She made a mental note to pay herself off for the bet later.

The music transitioned into a slow dance and the little group of friends and locals that she'd been dancing with began to drift away into couples. Good, she could use a little rest. She turned to go to her table and found Aaron approaching her. He held out a glass of ice water, and she nearly swooned.

"Thank you, that's exactly what I needed." They stopped on the edge of the dance floor and she drank greedily. "Are you bored silly with all these strangers?" she asked before drinking more.

"No, the nice thing about strangers is there are plenty of easy questions to ask to get them talking about themselves."

She finished the water and set it down on an empty table. Aaron held out his hand. "Would you like to dance?"

The little jumble of butterflies in her stomach wasn't a surprise. Or unwelcome. "That would be nice." She took his hand and followed him back onto the floor.

He kept her hand and gently turned her into him, his other hand settling at her waist. She closed her eyes for a second to find the beat and relax into his lead. When she opened them, it was to find him watching her. His lips curved up, ever so slightly, and she wanted to trace them with her fingertip.

She tore her gaze away and looked up. "Wow, the stars are amazing out here." They sparkled against a canopy much darker than she ever saw in Los Angeles.

"You're having a good time," he said, his voice low against the music.

"I am. I love Rose, and I really like her husband. I like this town and the people in it. And it's just a good party."

"True." He gave her a slight nudge, and she let him spin her out, reel her back in. The man knew what he was doing on the dance floor.

"I have to thank you," he said, his thumb on her waist, rubbing up and down slightly in a subtle invitation. "I'd known it was time to get out and start meeting people, but somehow I just kept putting it off. You and your grandmother made it very easy."

She stepped slightly closer, and he responded with a squeeze of her hand.

"Glad to be of service," she murmured. Her gaze locked on his lips for just a moment. They looked incredibly soft. When she looked back up to his eyes, she was certain they'd become hotter, more intense.

He spun her again, bringing her flush with his body on the return. She moved her free hand up to his shoulder. The song drew to an end and they stopped, still holding on to each other.

She swallowed. "That was nice, thank you. I should sit down for a minute. Check on Grandma."

"My pleasure." He squeezed her hand again, slowly let it lower, but held on as he led the way back to their table. Except Grandma wasn't at their table, she was a couple of tables over sitting with Rose's parents, so they went there instead.

After introductions, they borrowed the empty chairs and sat

down. Janelle was amused to see that Rose's parents were behaving like proud, married mother and father of the bride, not a divorced couple. Rose really needed to find out what was going on with them. Grandma was telling them about the exhibit they were going to go see in Denver.

"Have you ever been to Hawaii?" Janelle asked Aaron.

"Only once, in college, for spring break. Some friends and I went to Oahu. I'd like to go back and spend a little less of my time inebriated."

"It can hit you especially hard in all that sun."

"You grew up in California?"

"Yes, but we went to Hawaii almost every year. Sometimes more than once if there were weddings or funerals."

"You have a close family."

"I do. Lots of aunts and uncles and cousins. In Canada, too, though. My dad is from Quebec."

"Did you learn French?"

"Fairly decently. A native speaker would know I'm not, but I understand and can be understood. We didn't go visit there nearly as often as we went to Hawaii."

"Hm, I can't imagine why."

She laughed. "My dad's family is more distant. We see his parents once every few years, and he doesn't have any siblings. He has a cousin he's close to, and her kids are nice. What about you? Small family? Large?"

"Very small. Pretty much none. Some distant relatives that I never saw growing up. I have a second cousin on Facebook who sends me stuff now and again."

"Wow. I don't even know what to think about that," she admitted, laying a hand on his arm.

He shook his head. "I'm sure it would be nice to have what you have, but having never experienced it, I don't miss it."

She thought about asking more. What about his parents? But she didn't want to risk the good mood. When the DJ transitioned to another slow song, he leaned in. "If you'll excuse me, I'm going to ask Yuki if she'll risk the dance floor with me."

"Have a good time," she said. Charmed, she watched as Grandma accepted his invitation and they made their way to the dance floor.

"Nell, take this old man out onto the floor and see that he doesn't hurt himself," Francine said, gesturing to her ex-husband. George looked slightly indignant but stood and held out his hand. Janelle took the hand, kissed his cheek, and followed him out.

She chatted easily with her friend's father. He pointed to Ethan. "That's Mrs. Rubinski he's dancing with, she lives in his building. Sweet lady, but I'm glad Jackson's taken over as manager and that Ethan and Rose bought that house over behind the sheriff's station, so they don't have to get interrupted a hundred times a day."

"She said she didn't mind, but I really love the potential of that house. She'll have fun decorating it when they finally move in. And Ethan will have all sorts of new projects he can work on for his YouTube channel as he gets it fixed up.

Naomi and Ian danced by, a bit more energetically than the music called for. Naomi was laughing and Ian looked very pleased with himself.

George spun Janelle into the arms of a man he introduced as Tom, the mayor's husband, and then she ended up with a group doing an energetic chicken dance, much to the DJ's disgust. As the evening wound down, she and Naomi and Rose danced a slow dance, with a few happy tears. They pulled Ethan in, and he made them all smile and promised that they would come to Los Angeles to visit soon once they returned from Spain.

"But," he added, "you should just move here. I think Wildlife Ridge has proven its beauty, its abundance of awesome people and its encouragement of adopting a slower-paced, healthier lifestyle."

"I mean, he's not wrong," Naomi said.

Janelle couldn't disagree.

CHAPTER SEVEN

Aaron had to get up and moving a little earlier than normal, and this after a fun but tiring night out at the wedding, but he wasn't the least bit sorry he'd agreed to take Janelle and her grandmother to Denver.

He hadn't expected to stay long at the wedding reception, but he'd been enjoying himself, and genuinely having a good time meeting some of the locals. Sure, they'd been a little bit nosey, but it had all been in good spirit. Of course, that didn't mean there weren't vicious gossips that he hadn't run into yet. Or even that the nice people he'd spoken to wouldn't turn on a dime the minute they felt threatened by someone or something that was outside their normal.

He'd been there, seen that. Experienced it. He supposed that was why he'd been hesitant to interact. Childhood traumas for the win. But, though he wasn't an extrovert, he didn't want to be a hermit, either. And driving to Denver a couple of times a month for business and errands wasn't the same as having a social life.

It only took a few minutes to get to the B&B where Nell and Yuki were staying. As he pulled into the driveway, they were wheeling out their suitcases. He released the trunk and jumped out to help. Janelle already had one suitcase in by the time he got there, but he managed to pick up the second one before she did. They both thanked him and climbed in, Yuki in front and Janelle behind his seat.

He checked his rearview mirror and met her gaze. Smiling, he checked behind her, then used the backup camera and started on his way.

Once they were on the highway, he glanced to Yuki. "You said it's a special exhibit at the museum that you wanted to see?"

She smiled. "Yes, have you heard of the 442nd?"

Nothing sprang to mind. "I don't think so."

"When the Japanese attacked Pearl Harbor, the Hawaiian National Guard, of course, immediately jumped in to help. But it was mostly made up of Nisei, those born in the United States to Japanese immigrants, so they weren't trusted to stay in Hawaii. Some in the government wanted them reduced to non-soldier status, so that they could do road work and service, but not fight. Instead, they were sent to the mainland and became the 100th Infantry Battalion. The One Puka Puka.

"They trained for a long time, under intense scrutiny, and they won respect. Partly due to that respect, the Army decided to allow Japanese Americans to volunteer for a segregated unit. Many from the internment camps joined, even though they were angry about being imprisoned. They still wanted to fight for our country.

"The One Puka Puka went to Europe and suffered heavy losses, but performed so well that they were one of the most awarded battalions ever, and became known as the Purple Heart Battalion. They became part of the 442nd, which was comprised of those Japanese American volunteers I just mentioned."

"I hadn't thought about the fact that so much of Hawaii's population is Japanese, but that's where the attacks were," Aaron admitted.

"And the percentage was much higher back then. Which was good, because the initial reaction was to put everyone in an internment camp—"

"Concentration camp," Nell interrupted.

"But it would have destroyed the local economy, since the numbers were so large, so that was scrapped," Yuki continued.

"The 442nd became the most decorated unit for its size in US military history," Janelle added. "More than twenty were awarded the Medal of Honor, and I believe nearly ten thousand Purple Hearts."

"Wow," Aaron said.

"My father was one of them," Yuki said. "He survived, though his leg was amputated at the knee. He had two Purple Hearts and a Distinguished Service Cross. He was one who didn't really speak of his experiences at war, and we didn't push him on it. He was part of the original 100th Infantry, very few of whom survived."

"They saved a lot of lives in Europe and some of the towns there put up memorials for them," Janelle said. "My Grandma, mother, her sister and brother went to France a couple of years ago to see a memorial there that was being refurbished and rededicated."

He glanced in the mirror, met her gaze briefly. Her smile was infectious, and he grinned at the road. Traffic was light and they were making excellent time.

"We definitely didn't learn about this in school. I think the only part of this that was taught was the internment centers."

"Concentration camps," Nell said.

He nodded. "Concentration camps. But I went to school in Ohio, so even that was probably one sentence."

"How did you end up in Colorado, Aaron?" Yuki asked.

"Purely by chance. Being a painter means I can work from anywhere, as long as there's space. My real estate agent sent me listings from all over the country. I liked this house, and the location. After several years in the cities, I thought it would be nice to be in a small town again." As an adult, he'd figured he could make small-town living work for him. And if he decided he hated it, he could always leave again. It was being trapped, he'd figured, that had made life hell as a teenager.

"Where were you living before that?"

"I went to college in New York City and stuck around there until

I was established. Then I went to Atlanta for a while, but I missed snow. Which surprised me."

"It can be so pretty," Janelle said. "But I was glad I didn't have to do any driving when we were here in the winter."

"You would get used to it quickly," Yuki assured her. "I spent a winter with your aunt when she had her first baby, in Michigan."

"I didn't know that." Nell propped her hand on the seat next to Aaron's head and leaned in towards her grandmother. "Did you go to California when I was born?"

"For two weeks. But your mother is my firstborn, she's more self-reliant, and while she always wanted me to visit, or to come to Hawaii to spend time, she was eager to establish her family and get her own rhythm set."

"Hm, I guess I can see that."

As they neared Denver, Yuki put the name of the museum into her phone and navigated until they could see the sign. He followed the indicator for parking and Nell sat up.

"You can drop us in front," she suggested.

"And leave you to drag your luggage around? Besides, you've got my curiosity piqued, I'd like to see the exhibit, if you don't mind me tagging along."

"Of course not," Yuki and Nell said simultaneously.

He smiled and found a spot. "Do you need anything out of your suitcases?"

Neither did, so he locked the SUV and they headed to the entrance.

They quickly identified the direction the exhibit was in, but meandered through several rooms on the way. He lingered over the statues. He'd never been able to sculpt, though he'd tried several times. His fingers just did not cooperate in that way.

He felt Nell join him and looked to see her studying him, instead of the sculpture.

"You look kind of lustful," she mused.

The piece was amazing. Two ballet dancers, the male just about to lift the female, the toes of her left shoe still making contact with the floor. His hands were on her waist, her arms up-stretched. Though he wasn't yet holding her aloft, the strength in both of their bodies was clear, the hard work and dedication to their craft shown in every inch of the bronze.

"I've successfully completed one bronze piece. It's technically art, but I keep it in my studio to always remember how awful it is and that I should stay in my lane."

She laughed. "I seriously doubt it's that bad."

He shrugged. "I like painting, so it's not a big deal. But it would be cool to be able to do something like this."

He surveyed the rest of the room. "What's your favorite piece here?"

She looked around, then pointed to an abstract sculpture, very modern, the lines fluid and clean, the color all soft white. It shot off in several different directions, then came back together with elegant grace.

For some reason, he wasn't surprised. He'd chalk it up to his artist sensibilities, if only to himself. He moved closer and she followed.

"You have a good eye," he told her. "This woman's work sells for hundreds of thousands of dollars."

"Wow."

They made their way over to Yuki, who was studying a painting of a building.

"This is awful," she said, her voice low.

"Yes," he agreed. "Yes, it is."

She turned to smile at him, and he offered his arm. The next room was photographs, and then their exhibit. They stopped in front of the information sign, which was titled *Go For Broke.* According to the information, that was the motto of the 100th Infantry Battalion initially, and then later the 442nd Regiment.

They went inside in silence, making their way from photo to photo, reading all of the placards. They were near the end when Yuki raised her hand, almost touching one photograph.

"That's my father." Her voice was quiet, but strong.

It was a black-and-white photo, as the whole series was, depicting five battle-weary men around a lean-to tent. One man was resting against a tree, a rifle slung over his shoulder. Yuki pointed to him.

"He was a good soldier," she said. "And a good father."

Janelle put her hand on her grandmother's shoulder, and they stood for a moment. Eventually she moved on, Janelle and Aaron trailing after her.

"I have something to admit to you," he murmured, leaning down slightly so his mouth was closer to her ear.

She looked up, cocked an eyebrow at him. He was momentarily distracted by the nearness of her lips, and the fact that she possessed such a talented eyebrow.

When he stopped walking, she yanked on his arm to get him moving—and thinking—again.

"I'm falling in love with your grandmother."

"You aren't the first," she told him. "And you won't be the last."

JANELLE WAS glad that Aaron had joined them. She'd enjoyed his company and knew that Grandma had as well. It had been fun to look at art with an actual artist. He was sweet and respectful with Grandma and charming to her. She'd begun to consider when it might be time to come and visit Rose and Ethan again, but they were going to be in Spain for six months. Darn it.

"Did you ladies have a particular place in mind for lunch?"

"We saw several restaurants within walking distance and figured that would do the trick," Janelle said.

"There's one I enjoy a short drive away, and heading towards the airport, if you'd accept my butting in further to your day."

Grandma lightly backhanded his arm at that ridiculousness and headed towards the parking lot. Aaron grinned at Janelle, and she couldn't help but laugh.

They arrived shortly, and Janelle noted that the restaurant was nice without being fancy. They were seated immediately and checked the menus. Since it wasn't quite noon, Nell didn't have to think twice. She quickly scanned the menu and found several options for eggs Benedict. *Mmm*, one was on a crab cake. Sold. It was her main restaurant indulgence, one she didn't give in to often, by virtue of the fact that she didn't go to restaurants often.

She folded her menu and watched as Aaron flirted with Grandma, teasing her about getting the huge steak he claimed was the specialty of the house.

They were all decided by the time the waiter came for drink orders, so they ordered the food as well. She checked her watch. They were doing fine, but they couldn't linger. She was mildly disappointed, and wondered what Aaron was thinking about how his day with them was going. Her lips quirked as he moved his chair just slightly to use his body to block a ray of sunshine that was falling on Grandma's face.

Oh boy.

She cleared her suddenly dry throat. "So, Aaron, what will you do with the rest of your day?"

"I'm tempted to run by the dealership and have a word with the manager about sending me home with a few screws loose, but I've mostly decided that it's not worth my time. Besides, I can't really argue with what their mistake brought me."

She was grinning and rolling her eyes at the loose screws comment, but she had to let out a long "awwww" at the end.

"You're a charmer," Grandma said. "Did your grandmother teach you that?"

His smile slipped, just slightly, just enough for Nell's heart to lurch.

"Nah, my first girlfriend in college did. She's a lesbian now, but she swears it's not my fault."

They laughed and leaned back as the waiter brought their food.

"Do you do much traveling out of the country," she asked Aaron between bites.

He spent the rest of the lunch telling amusing anecdotes about his adventures throughout Europe and Asia. When the check came, there was a minor skirmish, but Grandma pulled the aged dignity card and was declared the victor.

"The mountains really are beautiful," Grandma said, looking out the window as they made their way to the airport.

"So different than the ones you're used to and the ones I'm used to," Nell agreed.

"Do you get out to your mountains often?" Aaron asked, glancing at her in the rearview mirror.

"No, for some reason I never do. I go to the beach a few times a year, and I've driven to the foothills to see the poppy superblooms a couple of times, but I never go up into Big Bear or Wrightwood. My boss does; he's a big skier."

"Maybe that's why you don't," Grandma suggested. "You associate it with Tony the Asshole."

Janelle barked out a laugh. "That's probably true," she admitted.

"You don't like your boss?" Aaron asked.

"Nope," she said. "He's a smart guy, built an amazing business, is often funny, can occasionally be kind, but mostly he's a rude ass who has zero empathy and is the center of his own world."

"Wow, sounds like a winner."

"He most definitely thinks so, and he's successful at most things, as long as you don't count relationships, so yeah, he thinks he's a winner."

"But he's smart enough to give you a raise and promotion every time you even think about quitting," Grandma pointed out.

"True, he seems to have a sixth sense for knowing when I've decided that his next asshole moment will be his last, and he backs off until I'm no longer annoyed."

"One of these days, you'll be ready to quit to start something new for yourself, rather than just to leave something old," Grandma said.

"Yes, that's what I'll do. I've been thinking about how I want to move forward, instead of what I want to get away from."

"What is it that you do?" Aaron asked.

"I've gone through several fancy titles at this point, but basically I run his office and make sure his life goes as smoothly as possible, from the business side. It's a small company, there's only five of us."

"But you keep everything running smoothly so they can make it all happen."

"Basically."

"At least he's given you the titles and raises you obviously deserve, but I've heard rumors that there are actually offices where you can work without being subjected to assholes all day."

"Seems kind of like a myth," she laughed. "But I'm getting close to being ready to do my own thing. I probably won't take another office job. I feel like I've put in my time, worked hard, saved hard, and now I'm ready to be more in charge of my time and effort."

They neared the airport and she glanced into the mirror, met Aaron's gaze. They'd see each other again, the look said.

She agreed.

WHEN THEY WERE SETTLED into the seats, and the flight was taking off, Grandma closed her eyes for a nap. Nell looked out the window and thought about her weekend. She'd loved seeing Rose and Ethan, enjoyed seeing her old friends and meeting new ones. And meeting Aaron.

She hadn't even been on a date with him, and she felt more of an interest, a connection, than she had with the last three guys she'd gone out with. But...long distance? She'd never tried that.

This visit had definitely moved Wildlife Springs up near the top of her list of possible places to settle. She liked everything about the town, including, surprisingly, the snow. As long as she could hire someone to deal with it, she didn't think she'd mind it much.

But adding a possible guy to the mix sort of threw her off. Which was stupid. The fact that she liked Aaron and wouldn't be opposed to getting to know him better had nothing to do with the fact that she liked the town and was considering it for a move.

She fell asleep thinking about handsome men and sweet little towns nestled into the mountains.

Grandma woke her when they were landing. She couldn't believe she'd napped in the afternoon, but there was something about planes that made it easier for her. She texted the valet service for her car, and by the time she and Grandma were at the curb, her car was pulling up. Grandma would be staying with Nell's parents for a week before flying home.

They sat in traffic for an annoyingly long time. She wasn't sure if it was actually worse than normal, or if it just seemed that way after staying in a town with so little traffic there wasn't even a stoplight. A flashing caution light, yes; a stoplight, no. It all seemed so crazy and distant to her now, as she waited through two turns of the light to be able to turn left onto a major street.

She and Grandma entertained her parents with stories from the weekend, and lots and lots of pictures. Her dad barbecued and they sat out on the back porch, enjoying the warm weather. They'd turned on the outdoor lights strung across the patio, but even without them, the stars wouldn't have been very visible. Nothing like the vast expanse that had glittered across the sky in Colorado.

When she got home, she unpacked and climbed into bed with her laptop. She brought up her financial software. There were only a couple of transactions that she needed to process, which took seconds. And then it was just a matter of staring at the life she had built, in numbers.

Though she hadn't quite admitted it out loud, there was enough money to quit her job. Had been for a little while. She had a tendency to keep moving the goal line rather than declare herself the winner. If she had more saved, she could travel more, or spend more on a fancier house, cooler electronics. Stay in a big city with a higher cost of living.

All of that was true, except she didn't want a fancy house, or to keep living in an expensive city. Travel more, sure, that sounded like something to try, but she would probably travel frugally, not lavishly, so she didn't really need much for that. The idea was that she'd have total flexibility in her schedule, so she could take those last-minute fare deals, go off season, that kind of thing.

Hesitantly, she pulled up a real estate site and plugged in the zip code for Wildlife Ridge. She'd considered doing so before, but hadn't quite been ready. She had a basic idea, from Rose, Ethan and Naomi, what sort of prices to expect.

The little guesthouse she lived in, had lived in for ten years, was adorable. It was very cheap, by LA standards, and had everything she needed, except the ability to entertain more than two people at a time. But she was ready to own her own home.

She'd nearly bought a condo more than a decade ago, before she, Naomi and Rose had experienced their revelation about finances. She'd realized that she could buy the condo and hope that it appreciated enough that when she was ready to sell, there would be enough money to buy her dream house. But the housing crash had shown her what a risk that was. Condos lost their appreciation faster than houses, and owners hadn't been able to sell when they needed to, or had been forced to accept deep losses.

She'd decided she wasn't up for that gamble. Instead, she'd stayed in the apartment she shared with a friend, until she'd found this affordable guesthouse. All the money she would have spent on her mortgage, minus what she was paying in rent, went into her savings.

At the same time, she worked hard to avoid lifestyle creep. Every raise, eighty percent of the new money went into her retirement account. Ten percent went into more short-term savings and ten percent into her regular budget. In the early days, that had meant a raise only gave her enough for an extra coffee every month.

Between the raises and the side money she'd begun to make from working on people's cars—a hobby she'd started simply to keep her costs down, but had quickly grown to enjoy—her monthly savings and retirement rates had started small but become much more substantial.

And yet, she didn't feel deprived. She was able to spend what she wanted, as long as she kept those wants reasonable. Sure, sometimes it would have been fun to host a big party for the Super Bowl or have an elegant dinner party for a friend's birthday. But at the end of the day, here she was, thirty-five years old, with enough savings that, while she expected to work at least part time, she could retire if she wanted to and buy a house, in cash. As long as she didn't suddenly expect to live a more lavish lifestyle.

Well, at least if her assumptions were correct about the cost of housing in the towns she was considering. So, now it was time to see what Wildlife Ridge had to offer.

Two listings caught her eye. One was a huge two-story, way bigger than she would want, but it was interesting to see that the price was only eighty thousand above her theoretical top budget. The other was a cabin out in the woods. Cute, but a little rundown. Way under her budget, but in need of a lot of work.

She checked the map. It was out behind the house that Rose and Ethan had just bought, in an area that didn't have many other houses nearby. She wasn't sure she'd be up to quite that level of privacy.

Setting the real estate site to notify her if any new listings appeared, she logged off and put away the computer. She pulled up the book she was reading on her phone and was immediately caught up in the story.

Drowsy, she was just about to switch the phone to Do Not Disturb mode when it buzzed in her hand and a message popped up.

Make it home safe?

It was Aaron's number. She hadn't been quite ready to assign him a contact, but this was the thread she'd used to send him the B&B's address.

Yes, safely tucked into bed. Grandma's at Mom & Dad's for a week before she heads home

Glad to hear it. Sweet dreams

She figured the safest bet was to send an emoji, so she chose the one with a moon and snoring Z's, added him to her contacts, then switched on Do Not Disturb and went to bed, smiling.

CHAPTER EIGHT

With the long, wonderful weekend behind her, Janelle was back at work. Though her boss had been out of the country the entire time, she still had several fires to put out. She'd spent nearly an hour on the phone with one of their vendors, soothing very ruffled feathers. Her boss, known amongst her friends as Tony the Asshole, had started this company from his home twenty-five years ago, and the vendor in question had been one of his first contacts, working to help him realize his vision.

She'd gotten off the phone with a promise that they would have lunch together the next time he was in the area. The other issues had been prioritized, and she was confident she could knock most of them out by the end of the day.

When her cell phone buzzed, she glanced down to find a text from Aaron.

AR: *Would you like to have dinner with me tonight?*

Well. That was interesting, wasn't it? She picked up the phone.

JB: *Aren't you in Colorado?*

AR: *Yes, but I could be in Los Angeles in time for dinner*

She considered it, but it just felt…too soon.

JB: *With Grandma in town this week, will mostly be family stuff*

AR: *Of course, I should have thought of that. Next week?*

She smiled, pleased. She debated her punctuation on her reply. To exclamation point or not…ah hell, might as well be herself.

JB: *Any day!*

AR: *Great, I'll check back with you in a couple of days*

JB: *Perfect*

Returning to her computer, she made a one-dollar bet with herself that her grandmother would tell her she should have invited Aaron to her parents' house for dinner instead of putting him off for a week. She kept the dollar amount low, because the odds of her losing were very low.

She ordered in a steak sandwich for her boss and a turkey wrap for herself. They ate together at the conference table in his office, him nodding approvingly at her bottled water even as he drank a Diet Coke. She'd told him the things were nasty, but back then she'd been drinking regular soda, and he'd made a comment about her weight.

He ranted about a rude hotel employee, then told a hilarious story about a meal he'd had in Prague on a different trip. When she went back to her desk, she rearranged his schedule, since he'd decided to go check out a supplier he'd heard about on the other side of town. She waved goodbye as he headed off, and she returned to her to-do list.

Her phone buzzed, and it was a photo of Rose and Ethan in Spain, in front of the adorable home they'd rented for six months. Janelle gushed about it and was assured the couple was having an amazing time.

When she climbed into bed that night, she opened her laptop, then her financial software. Moving the dollar from her bet hardly felt fair, since she'd been so certain—correctly—that her grandmother would admonish her for not having invited Aaron to a family dinner.

She examined her treats category. Maybe she should see if Naomi wanted to do a spa day. Or a little road trip to a winery. *Hmm.*

Opening the text app on your laptop, she pulled up the message from Aaron and added a new line.

JB: *Grandma said I should have invited you to dinner with my parents.*

There were dots to indicate he was typing. Then nothing. Then more dots. Then nothing. She was grinning when the answer finally arrived.

AR: *I thought she liked me!?!?*

She laughed out loud, for real.

JB: *I thought so too, but maybe we were wrong LMAO*

AR: *Good day?*

JB: *Not bad. Mostly caught up at work. Nice dinner with the fam. You?*

AR: *Since you spurned me, I spent the day doing the things I hate, emails and phone calls. Signed a contract. Tomorrow I'll paint and all will be good again*

JB: *Poor baby. It's all behind you now*

AR: *Until the next time. There's always a next time*

JB: *LOL Maybe you need an assistant*

AR: *They'd just call me or email me to find out what they should be saying when they call and email people*

JB: *I can't find the tiny violin emoji*

AR: *It's all right, I can sense your pity from here*

JB: *It's good we're on the same wavelength. Have a good night*

AR: *You too*

She switched to her internet browser, but an alert popped up, this time indicating a message from Naomi.

NW: *What are we cooking for dinner tomorrow? Something new or an old favorite? Is Grandma coming?*

JB: *Yes, Grandma's coming. I thought we'd get her to show us how to make her shoyu chicken recipe, and actually write it down this time*

NW: *Brilliant*

JB: *Guess who texted this morning to see if I wanted to have dinner tonight?*

NW: *Umm, is it someone who doesn't even live in this state?*

JB: *That is correct*

The phone rang. Laughing, she grabbed it and answered.

"You didn't say yes?"

"I did not say yes. I told him with Grandma in town this week, I would be doing family stuff."

"Grandma and your parents would have been okay with you having dinner with him."

"You liked him," Janelle said.

"I liked the way he looked at you," Naomi said. "The way he listened when you spoke."

"Hmm. How was the triplex you went to see?"

"I'm going to put in an offer. If it gets accepted, I'll send a couple of inspectors through, but I liked what I saw."

"That's awesome. How far was it from Wildlife Ridge?"

"Less than an hour. A bigger town. They have two high schools and even a little college."

"Nice. You're making great progress on your plans, I'm so proud of you, Nay."

"You're right there with me. Even with this purchase, I should be able to pay off the mortgage on my duplex next year, which means my mortgage debt will be down to fifty percent."

"That's fantastic!"

"Yeah. It's funny how it seemed like it took us all forever to make any progress. And then when Rose said she was ready to go full time on her own business, I was thinking it was too soon. But everything just keeps picking up steam and suddenly, I don't just *think* we can do it, I *know* we can…and that we pretty much already have done it."

"You're right, at first it was such a struggle. Like, what the hell difference does it make if I change my IRA contribution from thirty dollars a month to thirty-five? For years, it all felt so incremental like that, but now we are *so far* from where we were, it's amazing."

"I've just about decided on what management company I'm going to go with here, which means I don't need to be here to run my business anymore."

"Are you ready to leave?"

"I'm ready to leave, but I'm not ready to go. By that, I mean I don't need to be here, but there's no particular place I want to go yet."

"Same."

"I'm surprised to hear you say that. I didn't think you were ready to leave your job yet."

"I probably won't unless I find something to do. A part-time job, or even just a relaxed full-time job with no pressure. If such a thing exists. Not that I'm actually looking, mind you, since I haven't even picked a place to live. I feel like I'm waiting for the right thing to trigger it all, either falling in love with an amazing house, or a cool job landing in my lap. Something like that. Then I'll be able to design my life around that and be good to go."

"What about falling in love with a guy?"

"I suppose that's just as possible, but I don't know that I want to design my life around a guy."

"No less silly than designing your life around a part-time job."

"Good point."

"I'm known for them."

"That's true."

HER WEEK with Grandma flew by, as it always did, and before she knew it, Janelle was taking her to the airport.

"You'll let Aaron take you to a nice dinner when he comes out," Grandma said.

"What if he wants to take me to In N Out for burgers?"

"Psh. Not Aaron. He'll take you somewhere nice. And not—" she added when Janelle started to object. "—because he's rich. But because he's a gentleman and he respects you."

"It would be perfectly fine for him to take me to a regular restaurant. Or, even for us to take each other."

Grandma's look was unimpressed. "You're looking forward to seeing him?"

"Yes. I really am." She slanted a look at the passenger seat. "And don't tell me again that I should have invited him to Mom and Dad's for dinner."

"Fine. Does he…how did you put it when we were flying to Denver? Make your loins quiver with excitement at the idea of seeing him?"

Nell busted out laughing, having forgotten about their conversation on the plane. "Oh my god, he totally does!"

She spent the weekend looking at all of the "Best of" lists online that rated places to live. Over the years, she'd gone through the various iterations of these lists, but never with quite this much intent. There were several towns that had a lower cost of living than Wildlife Ridge, and she looked at those first.

One was even more isolated, and she disregarded it quickly. Rose's town was about as isolated as she could handle. Not that this was supposed to be about a comparison to Wildlife Ridge, she reminded herself.

Several were way too touristy. Reject, reject, reject. She'd visited a desert city, spending a long weekend a couple of years ago to see what she thought. She'd been heavily leaning towards a town in New Mexico at that stage. She'd gone in summer, to experience the worst. And had hated it. That kind of heat was nothing like what she was used to in Southern California or Hawaii. Several more towns rejected.

Her phone buzzed, and she saw a message from Aaron. As she picked it up, she also got a message from Rose. She went to Rose's thread first. A beautiful sunset on the beach and a message about their brief trip to Gibraltar.

JB: *Amazing!!!! Are you settled in? Do you feel like locals (no matter how temporary)?*

She switched to Aaron's thread.

AR: *Happy Sunday. How's your week looking?*

She decided she wasn't interested in playing games, she was just going to keep being her. She certainly appreciated that he seemed to be on the same page.

JB: *My evenings are open all week, whatever day works best for you. Are you really going to fly out here? I feel like that's a little bit crazy*

AR: *I'm not saying I don't have a little bit of crazy in me, I am an artist after all. But I have business that I could do there easier than online, and my best friend actually lives in Anaheim*

Her phone buzzed and flashed a message from Rose but she ignored it for now.

JB: *That's good, less pressure for me to be amazingly worth the trip*

AR: *I don't know, business meetings and an eleven-month-old baby aren't much competition for making the trip amazing*

JB: *Pshaw, the baby has it in the bag*

AR: *Tuesday good?*

JB: *Tuesday's great*

Another message from Rose flashed by, which she also ignored.

AR: *Pick you up at your place?*

Normally she would never give a first date her address, but this didn't seem quite the same. She sent the address and switched to Rose's thread.

RC: *Oh yeah, you can hardly tell us apart from the locals! Not! It's great, we go to the little store down the road once a day, and they tell us something new to try. We've also decided to try one restaurant a week*

JB: *Sounds amazing, keep sending pictures*

RC: *You know I will*

They exchanged several heart emoticons and she set her phone down and went back to her online lists. Once again, she found herself comparing the towns to Wildlife Ridge, this time in terms of expense. She'd initially thought she'd find something with a lower cost of living, but it was doable. So all the towns with higher costs were cut.

Down to three towns. She pulled up the local newspapers for the first one, and any online blogs. One town got axed almost immediately. The other two seemed decent. She added them to her master list, bringing it to seven.

She emailed the revised list to Naomi and Rose, then added a little note about dinner on Tuesday with Aaron. She closed her computer and put on a movie she'd wanted to see, but had been waiting for it to hit her streaming service. But she couldn't concentrate, and it wasn't the movie's fault. It was one-hundred-percent Aaron's fault. She'd been thinking about him quite a bit. Somehow, she thought he'd be pleased to know that. Turning off the movie, she gave up, and went to bed. And continued to think about him.

CHAPTER NINE

Aaron was one of the first people off the plane. It was a fairly quick flight, about two-and-a-half hours, but he didn't love being cooped up or stuck in a seat. He had only a carryon so he made it to the shuttle bus to get his rental car in very little time. Without too much annoyance, he was in a car and on his way.

He checked into his hotel and took a shower. His plan for the day had been to do a little commercial work, leaving plenty of time to pack and get to the airport. Instead, he'd hit the studio and decided on the painting of the flowers in a storm, and had gotten caught up. When he'd resurfaced to reality, he'd barely had time to throw what he needed in a bag and get on the road.

Having to rush was slightly annoying, but worth having such a good painting session.

He dried off and scrubbed the towel over his hair, then picked up his phone and opened the message thread with Janelle.

AR: *Do you have any strong feelings about The Lobster restaurant at Santa Monica Pier?*

He got dressed while he waited for an answer. He was brushing his hair when it came through.

JB: *Heard good things but haven't been*

AR: *All right, see you in an hour*

He spent a few minutes calling the other two restaurants he'd made reservations at yesterday, and canceling them. Then he called CC and let her know he was in town, and could come by for dinner tomorrow if they had room for him. The baby babbled into the phone for a minute, which he took as a yes.

There was still time, so he grabbed a bottle of water and sat on the balcony. The view of the ocean was gorgeous, and the people walking along Ocean Avenue were entertaining. Couples strolling, families meandering. Some enjoying the shops along the street, others heading to the beach that was only feet away.

He liked to people watch, although he wasn't one to make up stories about what he thought those people were like. It was more that he wanted to study who they actually were. It was how he'd worked out what kind of person he wanted to be in social settings, what kind of friend he strived to be.

It was how he'd realized that all families weren't the mess that his was and he shouldn't discount the idea of making one for himself.

He wasn't thinking about families, now, though. He was thinking about Janelle. Had been thinking about her a lot, since the wedding. It'd been a long time since a woman had gotten into his head like this. He didn't hate it. He wasn't normally an anxious guy, but there was definitely an uncomfortable—but not unwelcome—buzzing in his body, that felt like it wouldn't go away until he could see her again. Until he had a reasonable certainty that she was feeling what he was feeling.

The address Janelle had given him was less than seven miles away, but according to his phone it would take nearly twenty minutes. Deciding it was time to head out, he called for his car and made his way downstairs. A family in their swim gear shared the elevator down, chattering excitedly. It was the kids first time seeing the ocean, and they thought it was cool that they could swim in the ocean or the pool, depending on their mood. And the weather.

His rental car was waiting at the front. He tipped the valet and headed out. It was slow going until he got to the freeway, then it opened up slightly. He made it to Janelle's house with ten minutes to spare. Her instructions had been to text when he arrived, since it was a guesthouse that could only be reached by walking through the main house's property.

He checked his email and found one from his agent, Kelly. She'd responded to his request for a list of Los Angeles or Orange County art galleries that might be worth his time for a quick visit. Her list had notes with her opinion on each gallery, and why she thought he might like to take a look at them. She was a treasure.

He tapped out a quick reply to thank her for the info and tell her she was amazing, then texted Janelle to let her know he was there. It felt rude sitting in the car, like he'd just driven up and honked or something, so he got out and leaned against the passenger door, facing the main house.

The slight squeak of a gate let him know she was coming, but it didn't really prepare him for seeing her again.

She'd been beautiful at the wedding, her flowing dress and flowered hair lovely compliments to a very pretty woman. And it wasn't as though he'd forgotten. He'd been thinking about her all damn week.

So how come seeing her in a pretty but simple sundress, hair down, plain canvas sneakers on her feet, sweater slung over her arm, felt like a light kick to the solar plexus?

He stood up straight and enjoyed watching her come to him. Hell, he hadn't even kissed this woman—yet—and he felt like he'd been missing his lover for a month.

Taking a step forward as she approached, he bent down and kissed her offered cheek. A vaguely floral scent, the slight brush of her hair, and her hand lightly on his arm, all had his head spinning in a very pleasant way.

"Janelle. I'm glad you said yes to dinner."

"I'm glad you came to Los Angeles." She met his gaze. "Really glad."

The nervous buzz fell away and left him with a much more

pleasant humming excitement. He opened the car door for her and went around to his side. "When I moved to Colorado, deciding to try a small town instead of a big city, I promised myself I wasn't being exiled, and I needed to normalize the idea of driving a couple of hours to Denver, or jumping on a plane to see friends, or go to an event I want to without thinking too much about it."

"That's smart, but…expensive?" Her voice was a little hesitant.

"Well, I suppose it could be if I was super social, but when I say those things, I mean a few times a year. I'm not flying every month. So far I've kept my travel budget to a relatively small percentage of my overall budget. And it's almost always easy to add work to the trip and make it deductible."

He glanced over and saw that she'd relaxed at that.

"Ooh, don't talk so sexy to me this early in a date," she said with a huge grin.

That surprised a bark of laughter out of him. "Let's see… Is it budget percentages or business deductibles that get you going?"

"Both, I suppose, but the budget is my happy place."

"I believe that's the first time I've ever heard those words together in my life."

She sighed. "I know. People are so weird."

He laughed again, charmed when she joined him.

"We can valet at the restaurant or park at the lot down the street and walk over," he told her.

"Oh, let's walk a little bit. Since you mentioned being down at the ocean, I wore walkable shoes."

"Perfect." He pulled into a lot when they arrived. It had occurred to him that they could actually park at the hotel lot, which was also just down the street, but he didn't want her to take that the wrong way.

It had been fairly warm out when he'd gone to get her, but now that the sun was nearly ready to set, it was cooling off a bit. The birds were shrieking overhead and he was glad he was wearing his sunglasses as they were walking directly west. He checked to see that she was as well, and took a deep breath of the sea air.

"I've been to the Bay area, and to downtown Los Angeles, but this is my first time coming to the beach here."

"I grew up here, and I love it, but I have to admit, I only come a few times a year. It's different than when I go to Hawaii and we spend pretty much all of our time at the beach or near it. I guess it just seems like such a pain to deal with the people and the traffic here. But that's not really fair."

"When you're there, you're on vacation. When you're here, you're deciding what to do around your work schedule. It's a different mindset."

They reached the restaurant and he gave them his name. He'd requested a table at the windows, with a good view of the sunset, and they'd come through perfectly.

The view was spectacular and her smiling reaction pleased him. They took their seats and accepted the offer of waters.

"So you haven't been here, either?" she asked.

"No, I asked my best friend what her suggestion for a good ocean-view restaurant was. Her wife is from this area, so they know it pretty well."

"She did a good job. They live down in Orange County?"

"Yes, they met in New York but her wife got a job transfer offer here shortly after, and they decided it would be a good place to raise a family. They had my goddaughter eleven months ago."

"Aww, do you have a picture?"

He pulled out his phone and showed her the latest text from CC, with a picture of Aubrey in the bath, splashing around in a sea of bubbles.

"She's absolutely adorable."

"Yeah, I can't say I had much to do with babies before this, but she's got me thinking that they're not *quite* as terrifying as I'd thought."

"Ha! I have a bunch of cousins and they all started having babies a few years ago. It's pretty cool seeing them become actual little people."

"And these days, with the video calls, they can get used to you even when you're not around a ton."

"That's true. We only started doing that recently, but it's fun to be there to sing happy birthday and watch the candles get blown out, even when you're thousands of miles apart."

The waiter came by and they admitted that they hadn't even opened their menus, so he suggested a bottle of wine and they took him up on that. He quickly returned and poured. They sampled and approved and he disappeared again. Aaron opened his menu but didn't look at it as he asked Janelle if she'd heard from Rose and Ethan.

"They're having an amazing time. They took a month off as a honeymoon, before they start working, and they're traveling around. Then they'll stick closer to home for the rest of the six-month lease. Today they're in Casablanca. There was some mention of Monaco."

"Sounds like a great trip. Are you going to go visit?"

"I thought about it, but I don't know. They swear it's not, but I feel like the whole trip is an extended honeymoon, even if they're going to be working most of it."

"Have you been to Europe?" he asked.

"No, every time I start to look into it, I get overwhelmed because I want to do all the things."

The waiter came by and they were forced to admit, again, that they hadn't opened the menus.

"But I would bet that you have crab cakes?" He glanced at Janelle. "Interested in some of those while we're thinking about the rest?"

"Absolutely."

The waiter left, and this time they opened the menus.

"I have a weakness for lobster," he admitted. "Which I thought might be why CC recommended this place, until I saw the view."

"Win, win," she said. She took a sip of the wine and looked out at the setting sun. He wished he had a camera. But wait—he did. He whipped out his phone and opened the app. "Can I?" he asked, gesturing with the phone.

She started to put her glass down, but he stopped her. "No, just like you were. If you don't mind."

He framed the shot and took a couple of pictures, then showed them to her. As he did, the waiter returned.

"Sorry, still not ready to order," he said.

"Would you like me to take a photo?" the waiter asked.

"That would be nice, thank you so much," Janelle answered.

Aaron handed over the phone and leaned in slightly across the table, matching Janelle. When the waiter left, he checked the photo and sent a copy to her. It wasn't as well shot as the one he'd taken, but he liked it. A lot. He also sent the best one he'd taken of her, drinking her wine.

"Okay, for real though, we need to decide," she said, picking her menu up again.

He scanned the lobster options and made a selection, then closed the menu.

She laughed. "That easy, huh?"

"When we're practically sitting on the ocean and there's lobster, yes."

"Well, you're not wrong about that." She closed her menu as well, took a sip of wine.

"What were you saying about Europe being overwhelming?" he asked.

"Oh, it's that there's too much I want to do. Like, I'll think, hey, how about a trip to Spain while Rose and Ethan are there, that just makes sense. And I'll start looking at what's around, where I'd like to visit, the countryside, the beaches, the historical monuments, that kind of thing. And I'll start to think that's a lot to see, so maybe I should stay ten days instead of a week. And then I'll look at Madrid, all the museums and landmarks and theaters, everything. And I'll think I'd better stay two weeks. But if I'm all the way in Spain, I would be an idiot to not hop over to France while I'm there. And then it all begins again. And pretty soon, I've planned a year-long tour of Europe."

"Well." He considered. "Would that be a bad thing?"

She laughed just as the waiter arrived with their appetizer and took their orders.

The crab cakes looked very nice. She grabbed the two small plates it had been served with and held one close while he used the fork to scoop a cake up and deposit it. They repeated the actions, then each took a plate and dived in.

She made a low moan of appreciation that he felt in his very bones.

He took his own bite. Pretty damned good.

"Anyway," she continued where they'd left off. "I guess not when I retire, although I don't know that I would actually like traveling endlessly. I'm looking forward to buying a house and entertaining more than I've been able to."

"What if you give yourself a two-week time frame and just decide to only plan what works in that amount of time, even if it's just one city or country? Save the rest for later?"

"Valid option. But then, how do I decide where? Spain, because they're there? But then there's that honeymoon thing again. I've always wanted to go to Ireland. But then which city? And New Zealand, that's on my list, but it's so far, so you really have to do it all in one go. I don't know, my mind starts running away from me and I don't end up planning anything."

"Is that how you are with, say, buying a new car?"

"Mm, okay, I get your question, but let's switch it from cars for a minute and say…a new computer. No, that would not be the same. I would order a new computer in about an hour total. Maybe less. I haven't done it yet, but I don't think house hunting will be like that. And I've been researching where I want to move to when I retire, and it's a completely different process. I don't end the research because I get overwhelmed with choices, I just start whittling down my list of possibles."

He nodded. "Okay, interesting. So, where do cars fit in."

NELL DEBATED on how detailed to get with the car conversation. She'd already mentioned her love of budgeting; was it too early to get further into that conversation? Most people found it either boring or off-putting. They didn't want to talk finances, even tangentially.

Ah, well, she might as well be the most real version of herself from the get-go. She ate her last bite of the delicious crab.

"Well, that requires a little backstory." She leaned back as the waiter cleared their dishes. "When Naomi, Rose and I had graduated college, we had a friend who went through a bad breakup, which was made especially bad due to money. She'd moved in with her boyfriend, then couldn't come up with the deposit for a new apartment, no good roommate opportunities in that rush situation of having to get out, that kind of thing. She spent time on all of our couches, and we felt so bad for her, but none of our friend group was really in a position to help out, financially."

The waiter presented their plates, and she immediately went for the lobster tail, dipping it into the clarified butter. Oh, man, it was like heaven in her mouth. She'd considered not ordering the expensive lobster, but after his comments, she hadn't been able to resist. Besides, she was up for paying half, if he'd let her, so she went for it. And she was *so* glad she had.

She looked up to see if he was enjoying his—and found his gaze on her. On her mouth, to be specific. Without conscious thought, she licked her lips clean of any missed butter.

His Adam's apple bobbed.

Smiling, she sampled the corn side dish, which also turned out to be quite good.

"Anyway," she said, waving her fork to focus her brain back on the conversation. "The three of us were appalled at how quickly things could go sideways, and we each examined our own situations and weren't happy with what we found. I mean, the thing was, we all had decent jobs. Even Leslie, the one who'd had the breakup, but she still couldn't get her own place."

He picked up the wine bottle and gestured to her nearly empty glass.

"Yes, please. Nay had worked her butt off to buy her condo, and we were all so impressed by that. But she admitted that if her roommate decided to leave suddenly, she'd be screwed. I still lived with roommates and had been wanting to get my own place, so was trying to save for that. Rose had just gotten an apartment of her own, and was struggling with all the bills being on her shoulders."

He nodded. "The only unusual thing about that story is that you all had decent jobs."

"Yep. Some of our friends weren't so lucky. When jobs were requiring bachelor's degrees, but only paying a pittance. Anyway, Rose had done some looking around online and found this community about financial independence and retiring early. We thought retiring sounded like a million years away, but we learned it wasn't about stopping working, it was about having the freedom to work when, where and how you want. Which takes financial freedom."

He nodded. "Okay, I guess I'm not surprised that's out there."

"So, we made some changes, started being more conscious with our spending and our savings. And that brings me to cars. One of the reasons I hadn't been ready to get my own apartment was that my beater car was taking all of my disposable cash. I'd been trying to save for a down payment on a new car, searching for one that the monthly payment would be doable, but not having any luck."

She paused to eat some more, because he'd almost finished his meal while she was blathering on. But he looked genuinely interested and not at all bored.

"My dad kept trying to buy me a newer car. My parents had given me that one when I was sixteen, which was awesome, but I didn't think they should have to give their college-graduate daughter a second car. We argued a little bit, but finally he made me a deal. He had a friend whose brother was a mechanic looking for a reliable babysitter. He'd had a nightmare experience with someone who'd left the kid in the house while she made out with her boyfriend parked on the street for a couple of hours."

"Jesus. So, even trade, work on the car for babysitting?"

"Not quite. Babysitting for *showing me* how to work on the car."

"Ahh," he said, leaning back in his chair. "Now we get to it."

"Yes. Showing me how he fixed it, how to do oil changes, replace the filters, the preventative maintenance stuff. And then I started to help my friends with their cars. Only, they didn't want to help. They just wanted me to do it, and were happy to pay a little less than the shop down the street charged."

"And a side business is born."

"Pretty much. I really enjoyed it, the more I learned. Didn't mind getting dirty. My dad let me use his garage and driveway when I needed to. Got me some tools for my birthday."

"And was no longer worried that your car was leaving you vulnerable."

She smiled. "Exactly."

Her plate was pretty much empty, and his had been for a few minutes. She finished off her wine. "That was really good."

"Agreed. Are you interested in dessert?"

"Ha, no thanks. I'm completely full, and this will already mean salads for a week," she laughed.

He frowned. "That's ridiculous."

She rolled her eyes. "I'm teasing."

He didn't look convinced but didn't say anything else as the waiter came to ask the same dessert question and take their plates.

"I'm glad your parents were supportive, even when you were arguing about how they should or shouldn't be."

"Me too. My family's pretty great."

The waiter dropped the bill folder on the table, slightly more than halfway closer to Aaron than to Janelle.

"How about we split?" she asked lightly.

He frowned. "I asked you to dinner."

"The dating rules are changing."

"I would rather do this."

"How strongly do you feel about it? Scale of 1 to 10," she asked, when he just looked blank.

He cocked his head and studied her. "Eight."

"All right."

"All right, I can pay?"

"Yes, if it's that important to you."

"How important is it to *you*?" he asked.

She liked, very much, that he'd asked. "Four. Mostly it's important that you know I'm more than happy to pay my share."

"Okay. Thanks."

She laughed again. "You don't have to thank me for letting you buy me dinner."

His lips quirked. "I can say thank you if I want to."

"You're right. I'll say you're welcome for that, and thank you for dinner. It really was delicious and beautiful."

"You're welcome."

She was vaguely aware of the waiter taking the folder with the credit card Aaron had placed inside. But she kept her gaze on his, falling into the whiskey-brown depths. Her breath shortened and she wished they were alone.

"Would you like to walk on the pier?" he asked, after a minute.

She was tempted to ask him where his hotel was. But she resisted. "Yes."

They waited for the waiter to return with the credit card, and when they rose, he offered his hand. She took it without hesitating, enjoying the warm curl of his palm against hers.

"So many people compared to Wildlife Ridge," she said as they hit the sidewalk.

"Do you enjoy it? The crowds, the energy?"

"Not really. I don't mind it but I don't enjoy it."

"What about living in the city? Being able to choose between a hundred restaurants, ten movie theaters and live shows? Living between, what, three amusement parks?"

"Um, four, at minimum, depending on what you consider an amusement park. But no. I like to go to those things once in a while, but not all the time. I'm looking at small towns to move to, where I can eventually retire. I have a list."

He laughed. "I had a list, too. But mine was more from my real estate agent sending interesting listings."

She scoffed. "So backwards."

"I don't know, it worked, didn't it?"

"I don't know, did it? You didn't leave your house for a very long time!"

"Okay, fair point, except that just shows how great my house is. But, I had lunch at the pizza place in town the other day."

"Whew, progress."

"Literally everyone knew who I was," he said with a laugh.

"I guess I'm not surprised. Did you mind?"

"No, it was fine."

They'd made it across the bridge and onto the boardwalk and were passing the aquarium and carousel.

"Will your friends come to visit you?" she asked.

"When CC and Beth are ready to travel with the baby, or ready for a break away from her, I suppose they'll come up."

"And no family to visit?" she asked, a little hesitantly.

He didn't answer as they walked past the arcade. "No. My parents and brother died several years ago."

She swung around, shocked and wanting to give him comfort, but he was shaking his head.

"We weren't close. I mean, I didn't wish them dead, but I had already stopped all contact with them. My brother died in a car accident. My parents were killed, along with nearly a hundred other people, by a tornado. It devastated the town."

He kept them walking, tugging slightly on her hand until she fully faced forward again and resumed their previous pace. The wind was picking up and she wished she had a hair tie. The sound of the waves competed with the noise of the crowd, the kids screaming on the rides, the rides themselves every few minutes. She listened, and breathed in the salty air for a moment before replying, trying to comprehend his loss.

"How long had you been no contact before the tornado?"

He sighed. "Only a few weeks. But we had a bad relationship. For years."

"How old were you?"

"Eighteen. I had just started college."

"Okay. Thank you for telling me."

"I'm not claiming it was easy. But it wasn't as hard as it should have been, and I made peace with it a long time ago."

"You could have been there. A few weeks' difference…"

He squeezed her hand. "But I wasn't."

They'd made it to the end of the pier. He let go of her hand and they both leaned against the railing. A father and son, she assumed, were packing up their fishing gear a few feet away, the boy clearly excited about the day's success.

She wanted to ask Aaron how his relationship with his family could have been so strained that he'd ended contact with them when going to college, but it wasn't the right time. This was a first date, she had to remind herself. It didn't feel that way, mostly. But then she remembered that they hadn't even kissed, and suddenly it did feel that way.

She turned towards him, leaning her side against the railing, brushing her hair from her face as best she could in the wind. He reached up, helped to dislodge an errant strand that was stuck to her forehead, gently swept it behind her ear, where it promptly blew free again.

He moved closer, used both hands to sweep her hair back from her face, his palms warm, his gaze hot on her. She leaned forward… and he was there, mouth on hers, still for just a second, then opening, his head turning just enough, his tongue sweeping in.

She moaned, eager for more, his hands tightening on her, his tongue invading in the best possible way. Her hands found his waist, tucked into his belt, pulled him slightly closer.

The cry of a seagull surprised them, sounding like it was only inches away. They pulled apart, both glancing around to see that the seagull wasn't that close, but people were wandering around, a couple shooting them amused looks.

He smoothed his hands down her hair and stepped back, just slightly, then pulled in a deep breath.

She liked that she'd affected him so visibly. Her legs were feeling a bit shaky, too.

"How do you feel about Skee-Ball?" she asked.

"I have no strong feelings about it."

"Then I'll probably be kicking your butt."

"I did grow up in Ohio. There are a lot of fair days in my past. Don't be too cocky."

She pursed her lips. "Five dollars."

"Five dollars?"

"I'm betting myself five dollars that I beat you."

He laughed. "Aren't you supposed to bet *me*?"

She waved that away. "It's more fun if I bet myself, that way I still have the five dollars either way."

His laughter roared over the ocean, people nearby turning to stare, smiling at his obvious amusement.

She took his hand and started back towards the arcade area.

"How exactly does making a bet with yourself work?" he asked.

"Easy. I make the bet. Five dollars, in this case. I have a discretionary expenses category in my budget. Like, if I wanted to get an ice cream over at that stand, I would apply the charge to my eating out category. But if I decided I really needed that stuffed panda bear, I would use my discretionary category. I suppose I could use my treats category, but that's for more like getting a massage or boosting my eating out category, or if I want to treat Rose to a congratulations dinner on quitting her day job and going full time as self-employed. So, anyway, if I win, I'll take five dollars out of discretionary and move it to treats. If I lose, I'll take it out of treats and put it in something responsible, like my house fund or taxes or whatever."

He'd stopped them at some point in her explanation and now just stared at her.

"I want to kiss you again," he said, his voice a little husky.

She blinked. "That's not the usual reaction when I start talking about budget categories."

He smiled, shook his head and resumed walking.

She beat him at Skee-Ball, and used her phone to move the money while he just laughed.

CHAPTER TEN

After she beat him, handily, at the game, Aaron kissed her again. Well, he waited while she paid herself the bet, a triumphant smirk on her face that made no sense considering she was the winner either way, and then he kissed her.

He backed up until he hit the wall behind him, his arms wrapped around her, pulling her in close to his body. She didn't resist. She melded herself to him and lifted her face. He only had to bend slightly to meet her lips. Her taste exploded over him, once again. Soft lips, warm tongue, tiny little noises that had him going hard. He wanted to take her to his hotel, which was only a couple of blocks away. Hell, he wanted to take her to a back room here in the arcade.

Arcade. Kids. Damn, he needed to remember himself.

He pulled back, opened his eyes, watched hers blink open to stare at him. The glazed look made his arms tighten around her, and he enjoyed watching it slowly fade as a slight bit of color stole into her cheekbones. He wanted to get her somewhere private where he could bring the glazed look back.

First date he reminded himself. Although, didn't the wedding sort of count as a first date? And the museum as a second? Besides, this wasn't a typical one anyway. He'd told her about his family. Hell, he'd dated women for months and never mentioned his family.

But, still.

"I'll take you home."

She sighed and stepped back, glanced around them. "Probably a good idea."

They strolled back to the car, stopping to watch the waves for a while when they found a quiet section along the railing. She leaned in close to his side, and he put his arm around her shoulder.

"Will you miss this?" he asked. "Or are any of your finalists near the ocean?"

"No, I'm trying to keep things to the lower-cost-of-living side, and the beach usually knocks them off the list. I'll miss it some, I think, but I'll still come visit my parents and still go visit Grandma in Hawaii."

"And everywhere has its natural beauty. The trick is to get out and see it."

"I've always loved nature but never taken the time and effort to actually enjoy it. I tell myself that when I'm not chained to a desk, when I can choose to take time off, or only work a few days a week, that I'll get out there and hike. Or even just rent a cabin on a lake for a bit, drive to the Grand Canyon. But I'm not entirely sure I'm not lying to myself."

"I'll admit, I don't really do those things either, and my schedule is really my own." And why *didn't* he do any of those things? Especially now that he lived in a beautiful mountain town. Right next to a state park with hiking and biking trails, a river, wildlife, camp grounds, all sorts of things that appealed to him in theory that he hadn't even given a thought to in actuality. "Maybe I would want to if I had someone to go with," he said, the words skipping past the filters in his brain that should have caught them.

"Maybe," she mused. "Or maybe we're just not really nature people. Enjoy it every now and again but not going to become camping experts who live off the wild."

"True. Or we find somewhere in between."

"Probably."

They resumed walking to the car, his arm slipping down to her waist, hers coming up to do the same. Her hip felt good against his palm. Every part of her felt good against *any* part of him.

"You're going to go see your friends tomorrow?" she asked.

"Yes, but not until dinner. Well, I suppose with traffic, I should head down in late afternoon."

"You said Anaheim, right? If you left around three you'd be there before four."

"That sounds about right. My agent sent me some galleries in Los Angeles that I'll check out before that. I might do some Orange County ones the next day. Then I fly home late on Thursday."

"When you visit, do you say you're an artist looking for places to show your work, or do you play like a tourist, or act like a buyer?"

"I mostly don't say anything. If they ask, I say I'm just looking. If I like the look and feel of a place, I ask questions, which will lead some to think I'm a buyer and some to guess I'm an artist, but I usually leave it at that. If I want to work with them, I leave and let my agent know and she takes it from there."

"Wow, are you in any galleries in Los Angeles now?"

"I did a showing last year, and I have two paintings in a gallery in Laguna Beach."

"Oh, bummer, I want to see your work. Can I Google you?"

"You can."

"I mean, I know I can, but…"

"You can." He squeezed her hip, smiled his reassurance that he didn't mind.

They arrived at the car, and he walked her to the passenger side and opened the door for her before moving around to his side.

The traffic was light now and it was only a few minutes before he was exiting the freeway.

"I'm really glad you came to town," she said.

He liked the way she was twisted in her seat, watching him.

"Best decision I've made in ages," he told her truthfully as he slid to a stop at the curb in front of her landlord's house.

"Will you come in?" she asked when he'd shifted in his seat to face her better.

They were under a streetlight, so he could see the flush on her face, the way her eyes darted to meet his, then away, then back.

"I'd like that."

Her smile was sweet, but then she licked her lips. And whatever she saw on his face made the smile change to inviting. He felt that invitation below his belt.

They both released their seat belts and bolted out of the car. He locked it and took the hand she held out for him as he rounded the front, then led the way to the gate she'd come out of earlier. Had that been only three hours ago? Not even three hours ago, actually.

They went through the gate and into a backyard that had a well-lit path with several lime trees on one side and a strip of very green, healthy lawn on the other. Beyond the grass was a two-story house in white adobe stucco. The walkway went past the corner of the house, where the grass opened up to a full lawn that met with a huge covered patio. A built-in grill and counter space dominated one side, with a large table on the other.

But as they kept going forward, he could see the guesthouse they were aiming for. It wasn't a huge distance from the house, the backyard wasn't quite that large. But it was tucked into the corner in such a way that unless the family in the main house was having an outdoor party, he suspected that most days, Janelle would hardly be aware they were there.

She had a tiny patio of her own, with a bistro-sized table and two chairs. Flowers in pots surrounded the little space, somehow managing to make it feel more open, rather than closed in. The entrance was French doors, which had him questioning the safety a little, but he bit his tongue as she unlocked one side and led him in.

He'd taken her question in the car as more than just an invitation to come and chat. It was pretty clear to him she'd meant for them to take things up several notches. But he wasn't going to assume that she hadn't changed her mind, or wouldn't before they made it to a bed.

That thought was running through his mind as he took in the light green curtains, sage-green sofa, creamy white cabinets in the tiny galley kitchen—but was quickly derailed when she turned and stepped right into his personal space.

His arms came up and around her automatically. She lifted up on her toes, her face two inches from his, her lips right...there...smiling at him. He pulled tighter with his lower arm, giving her support, as well as letting her feel that he was not unaffected by her actions.

Her smile widened. "I like you," she whispered.

He felt the grin stretch across his face, almost laughed at the pleasure of the feeling that shot through him, completely different than the kind of pleasurable sensations he'd been expecting.

"I'm glad. I like you, too. Want to dance?"

"Ooh, that's a nice idea. But maybe some other time? Right now, I think what I would like most is for you to kiss me until my legs can't quite hold me up, and then we could lay down on my bed. For safety."

"Safety is critical."

"It is."

They were still smiling when their lips met, but that was okay. He clicked his teeth against hers, and that was okay, too. Her fingers dug into his shoulders and that was *more* than okay, except he wanted to feel them without his shirt in the way. Time to stop playing and get more serious.

A low growl came out of his own throat, which shocked him for a moment, but was quickly forgotten as she pressed impossibly closer. He moved one hand to her neck, slid his fingers into the welcoming warmth of her hair, slid his thumb over her jawline. His other hand went to her thigh, and he began to slowly gather up her dress, until he got to the bottom edge. He held on to the fabric with his fingers, used his knuckles to caress her slowly, in a completely different rhythm than the reckless abandon of their kiss.

She sighed and dropped to her heels. Not standing on her tiptoes wasn't quite the same as her legs giving out, but he wasn't in the mood to be completely literal. He moved the arm from her lower back to under her butt and lifted.

She squealed a little, which had his mouth pulling free and his grin returning.

Going with it, she locked her legs around his waist. The hand that had been teasing her thigh was now under the dress, palming her butt through what felt like silk panties. Maybe satin.

"Smooth," she said.

"You ain't seen nothing yet," he countered. He had no idea what he meant by that, but she pursed her lips in mock seriousness and tilted her head.

"Bring it," she said.

He growled, this time totally intentionally and over the top, and buried his face in her cleavage. He motorboated her shamelessly as she gripped his shoulders and threw her head back in laughter.

Making a lover laugh during the prelude had never actually been a goal of his, but he felt like a hero. He lifted his head and grinned. She lowered hers and bit his bottom lip.

Oh hell.

He stepped forward until he found the hallway, but instead of continuing down it to find a room, he used the wall. He didn't *quite* slam her against it, but it was close. She gasped and released his lip. He claimed her mouth, and just like that, they were back to reckless and breathless.

Losing himself in the kiss, his hand kneading her butt, her fingers grasping his hair, tugging him closer though there was no space between them. Then her hands disappeared and she was scrabbling at his shirt, trying to pull it up from behind him. He tore his mouth free and gasped for breath.

She returned her fingers to his hair, gripped tight, and growled, "Bedroom."

"Yes, ma'am."

Aaron stepped back from the wall, allowing her legs to find the ground again. He held on to her until she was steady, then she grabbed his hand and stalked to her bedroom. She'd truly had no intention of bringing him back with her, so there was a discarded dress that she'd considered wearing, as well as her work clothes, left across the foot of her bed. She wasn't, in theory, opposed to sex on a first date, it was just that in fourteen years of having sex, she'd never actually been intrigued by someone enough to try it.

She shoved the pillows at the top of the bed aside, then whipped the comforter, along with the dress and clothes, right to the end of the bed. There, mess handled. She'd changed her sheets on Sunday and that was good enough for her. Aaron didn't seem to be too concerned as he'd come right up behind her and palmed her breasts over her sundress.

Which was nice. Really, really nice. But she wanted to touch, too. She reached behind her but that was stupid and accomplished nothing, so she grabbed his arms and pulled them away, then spun around. She lifted his shirt before he could get in her way, and tried to tug it up, free from his pants.

He took over that job, so she moved to the first button that was done up and began working on it. He slid his belt free and tossed it behind him, then started on his slacks. She got all the buttons undone and pushed the sides of his shirt away. He pushed his pants down and took over with the shirt, working on the cuffs. Damn, she'd forgotten about the cuffs.

She toed off her shoes while he managed the cuffs and shrugged out of the shirt. Both went for the hem of his undershirt at the same time, but she gave it up as soon as he demonstrated he was on the job, and just went for his skin.

He sucked in a breath as she danced her fingers along his stomach, up to his chest and back down again. She leaned in and nibbled around one flat nipple, then pulled back to see his response.

"No, no, don't stop," he protested.

Oh, she wasn't planning on stopping. She kissed the valley

between his pecs, but he put his hands on her upper arms and pulled her back.

"Your clothes need to come off, too, Nell. I want to touch you all over."

Oh, well, that seemed reasonable. She grabbed two fistfuls of the dress and yanked it over her head. Handled. She went back to exploring his chest, deciding on the point of his collarbone as her next area of consideration. She felt him working behind her, felt her bra release. Moved her arms as needed so that he could pull the bra down and off.

Then she was moving, his hands around her hips as he lifted her up and settled her onto her back on the bed. Again, reasonable. She could work with this. Reaching up, she tried to pull him down to her but he backed off, hooked her panties with his fingers and yanked. She lifted her hips and dropped them as the fabric cleared her knees.

He tossed the underwear aside, and she reached for him again.

He didn't move. He stared.

She would have been embarrassed, maybe even covered herself, but the hungry look on his face was more than enough to assure her that he liked what he saw. Still, enough with the staring.

She sat up…and madness overtook her. Instead of grabbing him, as she'd planned, she cupped her breasts and offered them to him.

"Fuck," he groaned, and moved. His hands were soft and gentle, nothing like the fierceness of his word. He cupped her hands in his, touching mostly her fingers, not her breasts, using her to squeeze herself carefully. Except his thumbs. Those he used to brush over her nipples until they were dark and stiff and begging for more.

She freed her hands, and he replaced them easily with his own, his mouth moving in to take over with her nipples. Clearly he'd shaved before their date; his face was smooth and soft against her skin, and she wanted to know what it would feel like in the morning.

He pulled her nipple between his lips and her thoughts stopped being so coherent.

"So beautiful," he murmured after several long minutes, bringing her back to herself. Sort of. She took the opportunity to push him so he landed on his back. Then she straddled him and looked down.

"My turn," she said, trying to sound wicked.

"Have at it," he responded, putting his hands behind his head, feigning relaxation. She knew it was fake because his muscles flexed and bunched between her thighs.

"You're so good to me."

"I'm a giver."

She laughed and smoothed her hands all over his chest, then moved lower, scooting until she sat on his thighs. He was so sexy, she had to stare at him for a minute. His short, dark hair was mussed and his hazel eyes were watching her. His arms were strong enough to hold her, but didn't look overly muscled. She wondered what he looked like when he was painting.

"I just want to eat you all up," she admitted.

Taking his cock into her hand, she studied this length and girth. He clearly wasn't self-conscious, and certainly had no reason to be. She swiped a thumb over the tip, then used both hands to grip him, squeezing lightly.

He bit his lip, which she found extremely sexy.

She bent over and took him into her mouth. First the head, then kissing and licking all around, before taking in as much of him as she could manage. When he was nice and wet, she put her hands around him, squeezed tighter this time while sucking at the tip.

"Oh, fuck," he groaned.

She moved one hand and took him down again, losing herself in the taste and feel of him.

"Nell, no more. Come up here," he rasped.

She kept her head where it was, but looked up at him. He reached for her, and as much fun as she was having, she knew it was time.

Letting go, she took his hands, let him help to pull her up, didn't resist as he turned them over. He somehow had a condom in his hand, and she watched as he rolled it on.

He gripped her hips in his hands as she wrapped her legs around his butt, whining when he scooted back and lowered his face to her center. He went straight for her clit, his tongue a tool of the gods as he worked her until she was wriggling and crying out.

"Aaron, please, inside me, now."

"Yes, yes, yes," he muttered as he moved up until they were face to face. He reached down and guided himself to her, until he was lodged at her entrance. She lifted her hips and he drove in, both of them gasping.

She'd been ready for him, so wet and ready, and now they danced, in sync with each other in a way that had her ready to climax but also wanting to go on forever. He was straining above her, one elbow braced at her shoulder, the other hand twining through her hair. Her ankles were crossed at his back but she moved, drawing one higher up.

It changed her position just so, and holding on for longer wasn't possible. Feeling like it was bursting through her whole body, starting with her curled toes, the climax overtook her and she let out a shout.

She moved her foot back down to cross with the other and held on as Aaron increased his thrusts, lowered his forehead to hers and froze, groaning as he finished.

They remained still for a couple of minutes, catching their breath, before Aaron shifted off of her and to her side. He propped himself up on his elbow and studied her.

"I think if we give it a few dozen more tries, we can probably get that right." The lazy smile of satisfaction on his face was at odds with the words.

"Practice makes perfect," she agreed.

He smiled wider and leaned down for a kiss before rolling away to deal with the condom.

She propped herself up and enjoyed the view, both going and coming.

"You probably have a very nice hotel room to get back to, but you're welcome to stay."

He stalked towards the bed. "This is LA, traffic is a bitch. I'm not going out into it unless I have to do something important, like pick up a lady for a date."

"That's a good philosophy to adopt here." She got up and headed towards the bathroom. "Help yourself to water or whatever from the kitchen. I'll grab an extra toothbrush."

Before long, they were back in bed, this time with Aaron stretched out on his back, head pillowed on his hands, as she propped up on her side next to him.

"Would you like some company while you visit the galleries tomorrow?" she asked.

"That would be great, if you can get away from work."

His quick, easy agreement made her smile. "I've taken off exactly one sick day in about twelve months, so I think it will be okay. If you want, I can disparage all of the artwork and say, 'if only there was an original Aaron Romero available, I would be ready with all the money.'" She said it in the breathiest airhead accent she could manage.

He snorted. "You haven't even seen my work yet."

"True. I should have looked you up." She wasn't sure why she hadn't, actually. "I'm afraid I'm not very educated on art."

"It's nicer to see in person, anyway. You'll have to come view my studio. And you don't need to be educated in art to know what you like. You don't even need to like my stuff. Art's personal, and that's fine. And you have good taste, unless you had someone else come in to decorate here?"

"My dad helped me paint, but I picked out the colors and furniture and everything, with the girls' help." She was ridiculously pleased that an artist thought she'd done a good job. When she'd decided to stay in the guesthouse long term, rather than go get a big apartment or buy a house or condo, she'd made a concerted effort to make it look nice and to personalize it.

"You did a great job. It's very warm and welcoming." He yawned.

She reached behind her and turned off the lamp. His hands came up to frame her face and he kissed her, long and slow and sweet.

"Goodnight, Nell."

"Mm, night, Aaron."

She snuggled into his side and closed her eyes. That had been an *excellent* date.

A light sound came from him. Not a snore, for sure, but the deep, even breathing of someone who was asleep. Literally seconds after he'd said goodnight. No way.

She moved back and grabbed her phone from the bedside table, using the slight light from the screen to check. He was completely out. Wow, impressive.

Sighing, she turned the phone on and jotted out a quick email to her boss, then another to a coworker Jonie, who would need to cover a couple of things. Then she remembered to turn off her alarm. Finally, she texted Rose and Naomi.

JB: *Shhh. I have to be quite or I'll wake Aaron up*
NW: *!!!!!!!!!!!!!!!!*

Rose, who was nine hours ahead, responded seconds later.

RC: *Woooooooohooooooo*

She sent a kissy-face emoji and then a sleepy one and set the phone to Do Not Disturb, put it back on the table, and closed her eyes with a smile.

CHAPTER ELEVEN

Aaron woke to the smell of coffee and the low sound of a television in another room. He stretched out across the bed, finding the sheets beside him relatively cool. He cracked open one eye to look at the clock on Nell's side of the bed. Eight-thirty. Pretty much his normal unless he pulled an all-night painting frenzy, which was rare.

He'd sort of hoped to wake her up with another round of mind-blowing sex, but he supposed being a nine-to-fiver had her used to a pretty regular schedule that didn't include waking up at eight-thirty. But she'd left coffee. He touched the mug. Still hot. Hopefully she hadn't been up since six and gotten annoyed with his lazy ass.

Squishing the pillows behind him, he sat up and grabbed the coffee. There was a bowl with creamer and sugar packets. Damn, she was good. He grabbed one of each, dumped them in and leaned back. It was a small thing, sure, but it had been a long time since someone had taken care of him like this, and he savored the feeling along with the warm brew. The quiet sound of bare feet on wood floor preceded Janelle's head peeking around the doorframe.

When she saw he was awake, she smiled and moved fully into the doorway, leaning against the jam.

"Good morning," she said.

"Good morning. Thank you for the coffee. Have you been up for ages?"

"No, not too long. I slept in a bit."

"Sorry—" he started before she interrupted him.

"I promise, it's not a big deal at all. I'm kind of a zombie as I start my routine, so it's completely fine. Coherent conversation before I've even peed isn't really possible."

He laughed and patted the bed next to him. She sauntered over.

"And now that you're properly awake?" he asked, setting his half-empty mug back on the table.

"Well, I'll admit, I was starting to feel a little…itchy."

He pulled her down to the bed. "Let's see what we can do to fix that."

An hour later, they were satisfied, showered and headed out. The only thing he could find lacking in Nell's house was her breakfast options. And since he was a guy who bought all of his meals pre-made, he couldn't fault her for that. But, seriously, whole-grain cereal and soy milk? He'd offered to take them to breakfast, and she'd laughed but agreed.

"And I'm paying. You would have been perfectly happy to eat your cardboard and milk water, so I appreciate you doing this favor for me, so that I don't waste away to nothing," he said as he unlocked the passenger-side door.

She slugged him, but got into the car without another word. He rubbed the spot on his arm as he passed in front of the windshield and she was laughing when he got in.

He made a quick run to the hotel to change, then they had breakfast at a little diner next to a car repair place that Nell told him was where she sent anyone who needed work done that she couldn't do without a shop available to her. And, once in a while, the owner let her use his lift on Sundays when she needed to do work on her own car.

When she asked where they were going, and he showed her the names and addresses of the shops, she offered to drive. He'd happily agreed. She brought them to a parking garage in Beverly Hills and pointed to the gallery they were heading to.

She'd worn green jeans, a black top and black boots, and looked fantastic. He'd gone for regular jeans and an untucked white button-down shirt with the sleeves rolled up a bit, and she'd said he looked fine. Then she'd laughed and fanned herself, so he figured he was doing okay.

They walked into the gallery arm in arm, and his immediate perception was class without pretension. Which was impressive. A sales associate looked up and offered a good morning, waiting to see if they appeared to want interaction or not. When he smiled and indicated that they were going to look around, she just told them to let her know if they had any questions.

"So, tell me what it is that you do, what kind of art? I thought you said something about art for office buildings. This is not that."

He gestured towards a particular painting he wanted to look at, and they moved to it. "I do that, but I also do this. I paint a dozen commercial-style paintings a year and a few gallery-style paintings a year. My agent sells the commercial paintings to a broker, who gets the prints into stores or online catalogs for hotels and office buildings. She also works with galleries to place my other work or to arrange a showing."

"Okay, I see now. Sort of like painting for a job and painting for a fun side gig, but your fun side gig possibly makes more money at the end of the day."

"I appreciate your assuming so, and yes, that's about right."

"Why do you still do both? What if you produced a dozen gallery-style paintings a year, instead?"

"I enjoy it," he said simply. "I've found a nice balance, it brings me more money than I need, so why not?"

"I think that's great. As long as you have a retirement plan, you're pretty much set."

He laughed and nudged her to another piece he wanted to see. "Do you like this one?"

She hesitated, bit her lip. "I don't dislike it, but I don't love it."

"I agree."

Apparently deciding they'd been there long enough to prove they weren't just doing a random walk-by, the sales associate made her way to them. "Can I get you a drink? Water, tea, coffee? Mimosa, wine, champagne?" Her smile was genuine and not at all predatory, which he appreciated.

"I'm fine, thank you," Nell replied.

"Me too. We're just getting a feel for each other's tastes," he said, to see how she would respond.

"Oh, I love that. Please let me know if I can help."

He had the impression that she would have been ready to extend the conversation if they'd shown an inclination, but instead she read the room and walked back to the other side of the gallery. He was definitely giving this one his approval.

"What's your favorite piece here?" he asked.

She looked around, moving towards one area, then another, before she stood in front of a small painting. A woman lay on the grass, her arm over her eyes. Next to her was a tray, on which a pitcher of lemonade stood next to a glass that was mostly empty. Beyond the pitcher and glass was a book, set upside down to keep the reader's place.

The painting was beautifully executed, the grass looked touchable, the book—seen partially through the lemonade, partially through the glass and partially in the clear—looked like he could pluck it out and start reading. The woman, her body stretched mostly off-scene, was wearing a tank top, the purple strap bright against her sun-kissed skin. Her honey-colored hair against the grass, the definition of her shoulders, the arm over her face, all of it was very well done and came together in a lovely painting that he wouldn't be opposed to hanging in his house. And the color scheme worked really well with what Nell had done in her own home.

"It's an excellent piece. Actually, everything in the gallery is very well done," he said. "But I would say this is one of my favorites, as well."

"Whew, I feel like I passed a test."

She said it with a grin, but he turned to face her fully. "Don't think like that. I promise, I have my opinions, but I'm not a pretentious snob. I love the ranges of art, both the artists and the viewers. I want everyone to find something that speaks to them, and I'm not about to criticize what that is for anyone."

She didn't laugh it off, but studied his face and then nodded. "Good. I like that. I like *you*."

He kissed her. Lightly and quickly, so as not to scandalize her or the sales woman, but he couldn't not.

Although he would remember the store, he asked the woman for her card and asked her to write down the information for the painting of the woman on the grass, before they left.

Nell drove them to the next gallery and, although it was fine, he didn't think it was nearly as nice as the first. But nothing too annoying or objectionable. Janelle pointed to a flower figurine as her favorite, and asked for his. He chose a still life of a bowl of fruit, which was very nice, but he wouldn't actually buy it.

There were two sales associates, a man and a woman, and both were annoyingly eager to do their part to separate him from his money. And clearly assumed that *he* was the one with money and pretty much ignored Nell. Definitely not going to be on his list, though he couldn't fault his agent for including them.

The best thing about the second gallery was the coffee shop next door. It had a nice outdoor seating area and an excellent selection. Janelle got a flavored water, which he did his best not to sneer at, and he got a dark roast, and they took a seat outside.

California was doing its best to charm him, offering a crystal-clear day, seventy-seven lovely degrees with a slight breeze, excellent coffee and the longest date he'd ever been on.

"Tell me about your friends. How are they taking to being new parents?"

"They've had some freak-outs, for sure, but they're doing pretty well. Beth, CC's wife, has supportive family, so her mom stayed with them for a week, and is close by for when they think the baby is dying because she cried even though her diaper was changed and she'd eaten."

"That's great."

"Let's see…CC is an accountant, but she's staying home with the baby for the next couple of years. She says once she gets her feet under her, she might do some part-time work from home. Beth is some kind of corporate admin for an advertising firm. CC was my first girlfriend in college. We dated for six months before calling it quits, but by then our friend group was pretty established, and neither of us wanted to give that up, so we decided to stay friends. Now, most of that group has gone their separate ways, but she and I are still close."

"How do you like being a godfather?"

He'd had girlfriends who simply could not deal with his friendship with CC, even though Beth came with her, and he was glad to see that Janelle didn't seem to be worried about it.

"Once they explained that it didn't necessarily mean I would be taking custody of an infant if they were both suddenly killed in a freak accident, I think I've taken to it pretty well. If, by that, you read I know when to send presents and when to book plane tickets, and how to wave at her on video calls."

She laughed. "Yeah, I guess that's about all it takes at this point. And really, just being there for her if she needs you."

"That part might be a little more stressful as she gets older, but she has aunts and uncles that are local, too, so it's not all on me."

"Good." She checked her watch. "The other place you want to see is sort of on your way south, so it's probably better if you drop me off before you go to that one."

"All right." He picked up her hand, which was resting on the table. "I'd like to see you again."

She smiled. "It's a good thing we've both been getting used to those video-chat options."

"Yes. And look…I know this is kind of early, so if it's not what you want, tell me, but...I'd like to know if you plan on seeing anyone else."

She cocked her head. "I'm not seeing anyone else, have no plans to, and will absolutely bring it up if that changes. You?"

"Same. On all points." He leaned in, and she met him halfway for the kiss.

CHAPTER TWELVE

Janelle set her lunch out on the table and arranged her tablet. She was doing a video call with Rose and Naomi in a couple of minutes. Naomi had originally planned to come to Janelle's, but she'd gone into escrow on the building near Wildlife Springs and decided to go with the contractor she'd selected on an inspection of the property, and had flown out to Colorado the day before.

Janelle had baked a batch of six chicken thighs a few days before, eaten one, saved one for today, and frozen the rest for later. She had rice and a side salad to go with it. The sauce from the chicken soaked into the rice for a delicious meal. It was kind of a lot for lunch, but this way it would feel like they were having dinner with Rose.

The tablet rang, and she answered the call as she was pouring dressing on her salad. They called out their hellos but Naomi cut them off quickly.

"Janelle! What is that you're putting on your salad?" she asked.

Janelle frowned, looked at the bottle. "Dressing? It's one my dad gave me when I had lunch with them this weekend. He knows I like cilantro and thought I would love it like he does. He's right, it's delicious." The creamy dressing had quickly become her favorite, though she probably shouldn't use it every day, as it wasn't as healthy as her usual vinaigrette.

"Hmm. Okay."

"What?"

"Nothing, nothing. Hey, Rose, the vacation's over and you're back at work, right?"

"Yep, and it's barely made a change in our lives, I love it! I mean, sure, we're not heading out to see different cities every other day like we were, but that's okay, we were getting tired of never being home. It's so awesome being in the house with him in one room, doing his thing, and me in the other doing mine, and knowing that our schedules are our own and we can make them whatever we like."

"I love it," Janelle said. "I'm so happy you found your dream, and that Ethan's is able to slide right in there with you."

"It's pretty amazing. Naomi, how did the inspection go? Any worries or do you think escrow will close okay?"

"Nothing beyond what we planned for, I think it will be fine. So far, I like working with this guy, he has good suggestions but doesn't treat me like an idiot without a clue, and respects when I make a final decision."

"That's huge," Rose said. "I'm so glad he's working out."

Naomi was eating a pasta salad, sitting at Rose and Ethan's dining room table in Wildlife Ridge. "So far, so good, and I think this will be the perfect project to test out our relationship. It doesn't need a ton of work, so it can't go too terribly wrong, but if it goes great, I'll know I can trust him with a bigger project, if one becomes available in the area."

"You're going to look for more in Colorado?" Nell asked.

"Eventually. I'd like to get something that needs more work, and is therefore cheaper to buy."

"Ooh, sounds like you would need to travel back and forth more, which means you'd visit us more, so I say that's a great thing," Rose said happily.

"Well, the point of having a good relationship with the

contractor would be so that I *don't* have to travel back and forth, but sure, let's go with that."

"Great, I will," Rose said. "Now, Nell, time to fess up. What's going on with Aaron?"

"Why do you say that as if I didn't give you a full update three days ago, and what do you think has changed since then?" she asked before taking a sip of her water.

"Well, how can I know what's changed until you tell us?" The indignation is Rose's voice was masterful.

Janelle nearly spit out her water. "Ha, okay, fair enough. Well, you know we did the video chat a couple of times and talked on the phone a few times, and lots of texts. But," she said dramatically—and then took a bite of her chicken.

"You are such a bitch," Rose said as Naomi laughed.

"But that chicken and rice looks delicious," Naomi added. "Is that the recipe I sent you?"

Janelle nodded as she chewed, then cleared her throat. "Anyway, last night, we did our first dinner video date. And you guys, the man can't cook, which, fine, whatever. But, to compensate, he boils his food."

"Excuse me?" Naomi asked.

"Say what?" Rose nearly shouted.

"Right. I'd suggested we cook our dinners at the same time and eat together, and he'd been skeptical, but agreed. So, there's apparently this meal delivery service. It's like those ones we've been hearing about for ages, where you get all the ingredients and just have to cook the stuff up? You get the recipe and everything? Except, in this case, the food is already cooked, so you're just reheating it. And while you can microwave it, that apparently doesn't feel like cooking, and the results aren't as predictable, since everyone's microwaves are different, so they recommend that you put the food, which is sealed in plastic, into boiling water to reheat."

She had to raise her voice over the uncontrolled laughter coming through the tablet. "So there we are, with him reading his recipe cards to see how long he needs to boil the different components, while I'm making my quinoa chicken bowl, since I figured I've made it often enough I wouldn't have to pay too much attention to what I'm doing."

"Holy crap, that's awesome. What did he make?" Naomi asked.

"Hanger steak with a red pepper sauce, seasoned fries and roasted Brussels sprouts. I have to admit, it looked amazing when it was ready to eat, and he said it was delicious."

"And they all go in the same pot, together," Rose said, trying to contain her laughter.

"Yep, but in their plastic pouches. He set a timer and added the Brussels sprouts near the end, and then the fries and sauce a minute later, and then pulled it all out and plated it."

"Wow," Naomi said.

"Was he embarrassed?" Rose asked.

"A little bit," Janelle admitted. "So don't tease him if you talk to him."

They both promised, and Ethan stuck his head behind Rose's to say hi, so they chatted with him for a while.

"So," Naomi said when Ethan had gone out of the room again. "Janelle, isn't this the week Aaron's coming back to California for his goddaughter's birthday party?"

"Yes, he's coming in on Wednesday. Would you like to have dinner with us on Thursday? The party is Saturday, and he's invited me to go with him."

"Of course I'll do dinner on Thursday, and did you say yes to the one-year-old's birthday party?"

"I did."

Rose and Naomi pretended to high-five each other.

Nell frowned. "You guys don't think this is all super-fast?"

Naomi shook her head. "Listen, too fast in relationships is for high school kids, even college kids, whose brains are still growing and learning and becoming who they'll be, and they fall for the insta-love feelings. Or for those who never quite got over that and do it perpetually on repeat. That's not you. You date. You experience guys, you know who you like and who you don't like. This feels different to you because it *is* different. Doesn't mean it's forever, I'm not saying that, but it's different, so it's okay if you move forward in a different way than you're used to."

"Well said," Rose added. "I completely agree. If you were the girl who calls us up every other month to say she was in love, that would be one thing. But you're not, and you should just keep doing what feels comfortable to you, not what you think would make sense to the rest of the world."

"Hm. Okay. I can't really argue with any of that."

"Because we've got your back and always will…and we're almost always right," Naomi insisted.

They cheered each other with their glasses to the screen. Nell had the best friends ever, and she wasn't about to forget it.

AARON'S FLIGHT WAS ROCKY, which was annoying on its own, but it also made him spill his drink on himself, which was super annoying. Fun to meet up with the woman you're trying to impress when you smell like beer.

She'd offered to pick him up from the airport, which had made him feel pretty good, but he'd need a car to get to a meeting while she was at work and had said he'd grab a rental. He *had* taken her up on her very nice offer to stay with her, rather than get a hotel. It had given him pause for a minute, before he reminded himself that it wasn't really any different than staying at a woman's house for a long weekend while dating, even when you lived in the same city.

He'd mentioned it to CC, and she'd told him to bring flowers or chocolate or something. It felt a little childish needing to be told something like that, but at least he wouldn't be showing up empty-handed. Thank god for best friends who had your back.

He picked up the car and changed his shirt in the parking garage, leaving the other one out of the suitcase so it didn't stink up everything. Then he ran his errands and got stuck in traffic. A lot of traffic. The kind where you watch the light change three times before you make it through on your turn. The kind where the GPS on his phone said his destination was two point three miles away but it would take eighteen minutes to get there.

It wasn't as though he needed to be somewhere by a specific time, though he'd been shooting to get to Nell's around the time she would be home from work. They had four nights together before his Sunday-morning flight. Losing an hour to traffic should be no big deal. But it was somehow soul-destroying to be sitting in bumper-to-bumper traffic, inching forward, listening to the inane chatter on the radio for the brief moments he attempted local stations.

How was this a thing people did every day?

He checked the time. Nell had left work and would be almost home. He'd connected his phone to the car's hand-free system, so he used the voice prompt to call her. It rang twice and then was answered with a cheery, "You're here!"

Suddenly his shoulders dropped from where they'd crawled up to his ears and his jaw unclenched enough for him to smile.

"I'm here. But I had an errand to run and I'm stuck in traffic. How the hell do people do this every single day?" he asked.

"Got me. I made a very concerted effort to make sure that my commute isn't too bad. It's about twenty minutes but usually moves fairly well. I take it you're not moving so much?"

"I could tell you the life story of the guy in front of me, based on having memorized the thirty-three bumper stickers he uses to explain how life works."

She laughed, and he felt the last of his frustrations drift away. Well, except the part where he should be kissing her now, but wasn't. He'd been waiting three weeks to kiss her again.

"I'm just pulling up to my place. Where are you?"

"On La Cienega, trying to turn left onto Olympic."

"Okay, once you turn you'll be able to move a bit, it won't be so bad. Probably."

"I could probably walk to you in the same amount of time."

"In Wildlife Ridge, you probably would."

"Its charms have been growing on me for the last forty minutes." She laughed again.

"How was work?" he asked.

"It was okay. My boss is contemplating a slightly new direction, work with a new shop, that I'm not loving. He's probably right that it will make some good money, but it will mean most likely stopping work with a couple of smaller shops, which might lead to their closing, and I don't like that."

"Isn't it bad that they put themselves in a situation where that's a possibility?"

She was quiet for a moment, and her voice was a little tight when she answered. "It is, but that's in large part his fault. He made demands when he began working with them that limited them to *mainly* working with him. Arguably, they would have been better off not working with him, but then they may not have been as successful at the beginning. A hard choice to make, and they trusted him to stay true to their agreement and not do something like this."

"That makes sense. I'm sorry they're in the position now. How serious is he, and will he listen to you if you make a recommendation?"

She sighed. "Sorry, I didn't realize how annoyed I was by this. I think it's looking pretty likely, and at this point, I don't think he wants to hear any more from me on the subject."

"No need to apologize. I know this kind of thing must suck, it's one of the reasons I'm glad I went into art. Of course, that has its own level of bullshit. You can't really escape it altogether, I don't think."

"Ain't that the truth. Did you turn?"

"Yes, and I'm actually going fifteen miles an hour now. Rejoice!"

"Woohoo!"

"My phone says I'll be there in twelve minutes. Is dinner ready?"

Her burst of laughter was better than any music. "I could put on a pot of water to boil."

He grinned. "Or I could make a reservation."

"How do you feel about Mexican food?"

"I'm a fan."

"Then we'll go to a place not too far. I'll call for a reservation now."

"All right. I'll see you in a few minutes."

The rest of the drive was pretty painless, and he was soon parking about halfway down the street from Nell's house. By the time he'd gotten his suitcase out and had reached her place, she was at the gate, holding it open for him. Damn, she was beautiful. Her hair was in a ponytail that brushed past her neck, her slacks and blouse clung to her in all the best ways, the almost-hot-pink of the blouse highlighting the gorgeous tones of her skin.

He wanted to paint her, he realized.

She darted a quick kiss at him, then ushered him into the backyard and through her French doors. Once she'd closed them, she turned to him and stepped into his waiting arms.

"Mmm," he said. "I was waiting for this."

He pulled her in tight, hands locked at her lower back. Hers wrapped around his back and clamped onto his shoulders, holding him just as tightly. They kissed.

And kissed. And kissed.

Finally, they pulled back and looked at each other.

"Video calls are nice and all," she said, "but this is better."

"One hundred percent."

She dropped her hands and he let her go, following her to the bedroom to deposit his suitcase.

"What time did you get for dinner?" he asked.

"Six-thirty."

"Perfect, I just want to check my schedule for tomorrow and Friday and make sure nothing is planned that will have me driving in that kind of mess again, if it can be avoided."

"Want some help?"

"That would be great."

They sat on the bed as he showed her the appointments. There were only a few, but they were scattered around the city.

"Actually, this looks really good."

"My agent made them, I guess she took commuter times into consideration."

He checked the time. Not quite enough to ravish her before dinner. Damn it.

She saw him looking, guessed what he'd been thinking, and punched his shoulder, but he liked to think that was regret in her expression.

"I'm going to change into jeans," she said, and walked away. But not far.

He pulled his clothes out and hung them up. "Any chance we can do a load of laundry while I'm here? Someone spilled beer on my shirt on the plane. And by someone, I mean me with a little help from extreme turbulence."

"We can do that. Do you want to start it now to run while we're gone?"

"Nah, I left the shirt in my car, I'll grab it when we come back in."

They headed out, Nell taking his hand in hers after she locked the door, like it was the most natural thing in the world.

The restaurant wasn't far. It was small and dark and crowded, and he heard a lot of Spanish being spoken, so he guessed it was fairly authentic. A woman was making tortillas at a station in the corner, with the competence of someone who'd performed the same action hundreds of times. They were seated immediately and a waiter brought them waters.

"Can we get guacamole while we decide?" she asked.

The waiter assured them that they could and moved on.

When it came, the guacamole was delicious. As were the fresh-made chips, from both flour and corn tortillas, and also the meal they ate while drinking margaritas. When they wandered out an hour and a half later, he was pleasantly full.

"No nice beach or pier to walk along over here," she said.

"Oh, no. I guess we'll just have to go back to your place and find something else to do."

She snorted, then slapped a hand over her mouth and nose. "You did not hear that."

"What?"

She laughed and wrapped her hand around his arm, leaning her head against his shoulder as they walked back to her car.

"So, yesterday I decided to walk to the coffee shop."

"Gasp!"

He bumped her shoulder then stepped aside as she unlocked the car doors and headed for the driver's side. "Shut up."

"Did people greet you by name?"

"Two people did. And I saw a car drive past that was painted to look like a lion."

She started the car. "Oh, wait! Grandma and I saw a car that looked like a snake while we were there. Just before we first met you, actually."

"So that was fun. The coffee wasn't as good as we had the other week, but it was fairly good and the pastry selection looked pretty great. I had just eaten, so I didn't try anything."

"Did you sit and drink it there or walk home with it?"

"I sat."

"And how many conversations did you have with complete strangers."

"Three."

"It's so not LA!"

"Or New York."

"But you didn't hate it."

"No, I didn't hate it. One guy spent about five minutes telling me about the weather and how it looked for the next couple of days. I didn't ask about the weather."

"But now you know." She laughed.

The space she'd parked in was taken now, so she had to go around the block. He frowned. "We should have taken my car. What time do you leave in the morning?"

"It's fine, this neighborhood isn't bad. And I leave at eight-fifteen, most people will have already left by then."

He looked at his watch, then waggled his eyebrows at her.

They stopped at his car and got the smelly shirt as well as the packages he'd picked up while running around town. Or, crawling around town, really.

———

"THIS GIANT BOX is Aubrey's birthday present. Maybe you can help me put it together tomorrow. I think we're going to need to take the rental car to the party, it probably won't fit in your hatchback."

The picture on the box showed a giant game of Connect Four. "Isn't that a little advanced for a one-year-old?" she asked.

"That's what I asked, but I was assured that she has plenty of toys, will be getting plenty more, and this will last for years and she can play it as she gets older. But basically, they want to set it up before the party so that all the little guests who are older, Beth's nieces and nephews, mostly, can play and be distracted."

"Ah, I see. I guess that makes sense."

"And, I should warn you, I've promised to be there before the start of the party to help with setup. The subtext I got was that Beth's family, while generally great, are a bit insane when it comes to these children's parties and CC needs some support on her side. If you want to opt out or take your own car and come down when it starts, I completely understand."

"Don't be silly. It sounds like she can use more people who are there strictly to be on her side. And I have lots of experience with nieces and nephews and these kinds of parties, so I might be able to help."

He stared at her for a beat, and she wondered if he'd hoped she'd opt out.

"You're automatically on their side?" he asked as he picked up the box that wasn't decorated with the game labels.

"Of course, they're your family. I mean, unless they turn out to be crazy tyrants whose idea of a one-year-old's birthday party is no fun and no sugar, but considering they talked you into this gift, I'm not too worried about that."

"Okay. So I'm going to need to you keep that sweet, accepting vibe going when I tell you that I brought you something. Part thanks for putting me up during my visit, part I missed you a lot, even though I've enjoyed getting to know you better over video calls, and part I'm an artist who really, really enjoys seeing people love art. So, don't say no."

He used a little pocket knife to slit open the tape on the box and pulled out a rectangular package wrapped in paper.

Not sure what to think about all that, she accepted the offering and started to pull off the paper. It became clear fairly quickly that it was a frame. She turned it over and caught a glimpse of paint. Her breath caught.

Oh no. This was too much, wasn't it? She couldn't take this.

She finished getting the paper off and stared at the painting they'd seen at the art gallery in Beverly Hills. There hadn't been a price, at least that she'd seen, but come on! It had been hanging on a wall in an art gallery in Beverly Hills! It couldn't be cheap, that much was for sure.

"Oh, Aaron. I can't…you know I can't take something like this."

"How strongly do you feel about it?" he asked.

She tore her gaze from the painting to look at him. His expression was carefully blank. She had the distinct impression that she could hurt him right now. She didn't want to hurt him, but this… this was too much. *Right?* So how much did it matter to her? He'd not done anything to make her think that he liked to use his money as a tool of power.

Was this that? Or was it just what he'd said it was?

Nothing he'd done so far had been about playing games. So why would he start now? If it was as simple as what he'd said, then how strongly did she feel about not accepting such an expensive gift?

"Have you ever dated someone who took advantage of you because of your money?" she asked.

"Yes. Well, they tried to. They didn't succeed."

Hmm. "Okay. But if things go badly with us, I'm either giving it back or burning it."

His smile lit up his face. "Maybe you could donate it to Good-will, instead?" He moved in close, but didn't touch her.

"Maybe," she conceded.

"I'd rather we just make sure that you want to keep it."

"That would be preferable. Thank you. You know I love it."

"Can I hang it for you tomorrow while you're at work? I have experience in that."

"That would be great. Should we put the game together, see how it all works before dragging it down south?"

"Tomorrow. Or Friday, since Naomi will be here tomorrow."

"You have other plans for tonight?" she asked.

"One or two. Maybe you could help me out with them."

She sighed, heavily. "I suppose." She lifted her face and let him kiss her. And kiss her. And then she kissed him back.

CHAPTER THIRTEEN

Work was almost done for the day and Janelle couldn't stand it any longer. She texted Rose and Naomi.

JB: *Last night I checked airline fares to Denver against my travel and fun budgets. There's a flight in three weeks that's totally affordable. And one next week that's technically affordable. I was going to book the next-week flight tonight...*

Naomi answered first.

NW: *Do it!!!*

Rose's response was only seconds later.

RC: *Yes!*

JB: *Then today, Tony was saying he and his friend are going to New York City on his buddy's private jet tonight. So I said, well, then you can drop me off in Denver, as a joke. He said sure, no problem*

RC: *Yay!!!*

NW: *Do you need a ride to the airport?*

JB: *LOL no, thanks*

She wouldn't have put it past her boss to think he could just show up and tell the pilot there'd been a change at the last second, so she checked with Tony's friend's assistant to make sure he'd gotten the word and would update the pilot. Then she'd run home on her lunch break to pack a bag. It was only going to be until Sunday night, so she just had a little bag. She chatted with the girls for a minute, securing Rose's approval to use her apartment if needed, though they expressed severe doubt that such a thing would be necessary.

They had heartily approved of her decision to keep the painting Aaron had gifted her and were definitely fans of her continuing to get to know him better. Naomi had only grilled him lightly at dinner, and they'd all had a good time making pizzas with their individual toppings.

Aubrey's party had gone well, and she'd enjoyed meeting CC and Beth very much. Nell had been able to distract Beth's cousin Sharon from her determination to turn a kids' game into an Olympic-level competition, and Beth and CC had both noticed and appreciated it. She was pretty sure she had the ladies' approval.

On the way home, she'd said something about enjoying his family, and he'd done that quiet thing again, but he'd done it holding her hand, so she wasn't worried. Family wasn't a simple issue for him.

They'd talked on the phone, or video, every day since he'd returned to Colorado three weeks ago. And she just wanted more. A couple of times she'd had the sense that he was going to offer to buy her a ticket, but he'd bitten his tongue. Rightfully so. Or maybe she was imagining things. But she didn't think so.

She was certain he'd be onboard with her coming out there, but she liked to have backup options, just in case, and that was Rose's apartment. He hadn't mentioned needing to be anywhere this weekend when they talked, but she wasn't going to assume she knew his full schedule.

It was time. She called his number, and he answered right away. She'd wanted to wait as long as possible, in case he was in the studio painting.

"Hey," he answered.

"Hey. I'm wondering if you're going to be super busy this week-end, because my boss is flying across the country tonight, and he said he could drop me off in Denver. In about four hours."

"Suddenly my schedule is looking pretty clear. Or, rather, booked. Wait—"

She laughed, and he joined in.

"You're coming here. Tonight. So all is right with my world. How long can you stay?"

"He's picking me up on Sunday evening, at six."

"Not long enough, but I'll take it."

"Rose said I can use her apartment if you don't want to play hotelier."

He snorted and otherwise ignored that. "I'll pick you up."

"I'm happy to rent a car so you don't have to drive back and forth twice."

"If you think you'll need a car, we'll figure it out. But if that's the only reason, I'd rather pick you up."

"That's the only reason. You can pick me up. I have to run, but I should be able to get texts while we're in the air, so send a message if you need to."

"All right, be safe, I'll see you soon."

"You too. When I get off the private jet, I'll expect my personal chauffeur to be waiting." She hung up to his bark of laughter. She'd been surprised with how much she'd missed him and was feeling all kinds of fluttery at being able to see him again, sooner than expected.

Her boss and his friend one-upped themselves in showing off and entertaining her on the flight, so it didn't seem like long at all before they were landing and she was finding her way to the front of the terminal. Aaron pulled up smoothly just as she reached the curb, and she had to laugh. But even as she did, her stomach gave that funny little flutter when she saw him coming around the front of the car.

"Well done, Mr. Romero."

"We aim to please."

She dropped her bag on the ground and jumped on him. He caught her easily and held her tight as they fused mouths. Only the honking of a horn and the worry that she was too heavy for him to hold for long had her pulling back.

"Oh, you please quite well."

His lips quirked. "Ma'am."

He picked up her bag and put it into the backseat then opened her door for her. Soon they were on their way, and she turned slightly in her seat to look at him as they talked. Much better than video.

"So, what's new with you in the last twenty-four hours?" she asked.

"Question first. Did you eat?"

"Yes, did you?"

"I did. So, twenty-four hours. Hmm, the only thing I can think of is that big ol' contract I signed with the gallery we liked in Beverly Hills. Other than that, nothing much."

"Ahhh! I can't believe we're driving and I can't jump you! I'm so happy for you, that's amazing!"

"My agent and I are pretty pleased. How about you?"

"Psh. Nothing much. I had to try and reassure my favorite vendor that things were probably going to be okay, without lying to him. He's aware that I'm more hoping than promising, and we're both eyeing the exit door."

"I'm sorry, I know that's not what you want."

"No, but maybe it's the thing I need to get me to make an actual decision instead of just keeping on with how things have been for a long time. I love my coworkers and my boss does things like drop me off in Denver just often enough to make me not want to murder him when he's an ass, so I've just been coasting, instead of moving on."

"If things have been good and making you happy, there's no shame in not having changed." He reached over and took her hand, resting both on his thigh. "You'll do what's right for you, I have no doubt."

They made good time and it didn't seem like long at all until he saw the steam from the sawmill and took the exit to Wildlife Ridge. All of the businesses were closed and the streets were empty of foot and car traffic as they slowly made their way through town.

"I'm trying to remember ever driving anywhere in California where I couldn't see a single person walking or a car driving," Janelle said.

"I was just thinking the same thing. If this was a movie, we would need the music to tell us if it was charming or creepy."

"You're right," she said, laughing. "You're so right."

He pushed the button to open the gates at the end of his drive and slid through. Moments later they were pulling into his garage. She took her bag from the back, even though he gave her a look, and followed him into the house. As soon as the door closed behind her, she moved into him. He was ready, pulling her into his arms and meeting her kiss with as much desperation as she felt.

He stumbled back until he met a wall, then lifted her up so she could wrap her legs around his hips. When he knocked his elbow against something with an audible thud, he tore his mouth free to curse.

She laughed. "Aren't we supposed to be adults now?"

"I should be showing you the house. There are a lot of rooms. Several of them have beds."

"I missed you. I missed *this*."

"Me too. Better to show you the house in the daylight, anyway."

She laughed, then clutched his shoulders when he started to move, carrying her away from the wall until her butt landed on a counter. She glanced around. Kitchen, large, modern. The marble was going to be cold as hell under her ass.

"Let's go to your bedroom."

He groaned, but pulled her back off the counter. She let her feet drop to the floor and looked around for her bag. He spotted it and grabbed it, then took her hand and led her to some stairs. He wasn't running, but his long legs were stretching to their full stride. She smiled at his back and, once they'd reached the top of the stairs, pinched his butt.

His growl was hella sexy. He pointed at her. "You. On the bed." He pointed at the bed.

She had to bite her lip to keep from laughing as she considered the best way to make him crazy. One option was to tell him about her exercise system of always going up and down a flight of stairs twice, and asking if he wanted to wait for her or join her. Instead, she decided she'd be getting plenty of exercise this weekend and moved to lean against the wall beside the door. She crossed her legs, casually…but she also reached up and started to unbutton her blouse.

His arm was still pointing towards the bed but his eyes were focused on her fingers as she opened the buttons. She made swift work of them and left the shirt hanging open as she moved on to the button and zipper of her slacks.

He dropped his arm and yanked his shirt over his head and shucked his pants so that they dropped to the floor at the same time as hers. She kicked off her flats as he bent to remove his shoes. While he worked on that, she sauntered to the bed, her shirt flapping open.

She'd invested in new underclothes. This matching set was purple lace with black satin, and she felt sexier than she ever had in her life. A glance over her shoulder showed that he was removing his shoes while watching only her.

She put one knee on the bed, and his hands stalled. She crawled up to all fours then rose to her knees. She fluffed her hair a bit, just for fun, then slowly took off the blouse.

Was that the sound of him gulping, or was she imaging things?

"Fucking hell, you're amazing."

The whisper was quiet, but she for sure heard that. She grinned, dropped down to her hands, and looked at him over her shoulder again. He was frozen in place, one shoe in hand, expression so hot she felt herself get wet.

She arched her back and gave her butt a little wiggle.

His frozen state shattered, and he tossed the shoe and was on the bed before she could blink. His hands were soft and gentle as they reverently cupped her rear. He kissed the small of her back and squeezed her cheeks.

"So pretty. I like the purple."

"I thought you might."

He teased his thumbs under the edges of the fabric. "I've been thinking about touching you. Remembering touching you. Imagining touching you." He slid his hands down the sides of her thighs, then back up the fronts, fingers curling in to tease along the gusset of her panties.

"I've been thinking about your hands touching me. And your mouth." She smiled as those hands clenched at her words.

"You didn't tell me that. We've talked on the phone all these times and you never mentioned that," he admonished as he continued to explore her skin and pepper her back with kisses.

"Neither did you," she pointed out, her breath catching as he moved both hands to her front, one to cup her breast and the other between her legs.

"Yeah, but you're the one who's supposed to be better at communication."

"Oh, am I? I think I missed that memo."

He sighed. "I'm the recluse, remember? You're the one who makes friends with anyone, including isolated hermits." He nudged her with one hand on her chest, urging her to rise up to her knees. She did, leaning back against his supportive body, turning her face into his nuzzling lips, her knees spread wide.

"I see. So it's my job to start the phone sex?" she asked.

His fingers were pressing and teasing her center, pushing the panties into her wetness, circling her clit, at the same time his other hand toyed with her breasts, teased her nipples to hard points.

She reached behind her and grasped his thighs, gasped when he bit her earlobe.

"That's right," he said before suckling the injured lobe.

She no longer had any idea what the conversation was about and her head dropped back to rest against his shoulder as he increased his tempo, his fingers dancing madly below, pinching and pulling above until she felt the spasms starting deep in her core, overtaking her with a release that left her knees week.

He banded his arm around her waist while she caught her breath.

"Mmm," she managed, enjoying the sound and sensation of him chuckling against her ear, his whole body moving against hers.

She reached between them and unhooked her bra, slid it free and tossed it onto the pillows. Reaching below the arm that was still supporting her, she pushed her underwear down to her knees. When she straightened up, his hands moved to cup her breasts again, this time without the thin barrier of lace between them.

She reached over her head and behind her, latching on to his hair and clenching tight when he lightly nibbled along the curve of her neck and shoulder. It made her want to bite him. She took one of his hands and brought his finger to her lips, kissed it gently, then bit.

His hips jerked against her, then again when she sucked the digit into her mouth.

He cursed, and she tightened the hand still holding his hair harder, using him to hold on.

"Are you ready—" he started to ask.

"Fuck, yes," she interrupted.

He made a noise that was part groan, part laughter. She went back down onto her hands and somehow he had a condom and was sheathing himself. She wiggled her butt to encourage him, and he made that sound again.

She faced forward and closed her eyes so she could just feel, his hands on her hips, his cock at her entrance, stretching her, filling her, joining with her. He waited while she adjusted around him, clenching and unclenching her muscles. She took a deep breath, then pressed back against him. He slid out, then pushed in, harder and harder with each thrust, both of them gasping for breath.

His hand slipped around to her front, teasing her clit, and she came with a short cry. She dropped to her elbows and he slowed his thrusts, long, slow glides through her swollen channel until he froze, deep inside her, and came.

They dropped to the bed, her flat on her front, him partially on her but mostly to her side, as they caught their breaths.

"Maybe it's best that we don't live near each other," she suggested.

He snorted. "Worried we might not make it out of the bedroom?"

"Or that we'd give each other heart attacks inside of a month."

"Hmm." He ran his palm over her ass. "I think I'd be willing to risk it."

She smiled into the comforter. "Yeah. Me too."

Eventually he rose to deal with the condom and she rolled off the bed and retrieved her clothes, putting them on a chair. She pulled her tops out of the bag she'd brought and appropriated a couple of hangers from his massive closet.

The room was very nice, large but not enormous. Clean and picked up, even though she hadn't given him much warning. The walls were soft gray with white trim. The bed cover was a darker gray, and the pillows and sheets were creamy blue. A slat oak bench with a dark gray cushion sat at the foot of the bed, where she piled the extra pillows.

The closet was perfectly organized, with built-in shelves and drawers. Button-down shirts in an astonishing array of colors, slacks that were all neutral, and soft sweaters that made her want to touch, hung in neat precision. But it wasn't too perfect. The hamper lid was open and a shirt he'd tossed in had hung up on the edge. A jacket was slung over an ottoman and one pair of shoes was next to it, instead of on the shelves designed for them.

She heard the toilet flush and left her bag on the ottoman but took the bathroom kit to join him. When they climbed into bed, he snuggled in and they talked in low voices for a while. As was his habit, when he closed his eyes to go to sleep, he was out within one minute. She resisted rubbing her fingers along his smooth cheeks, which then made her realize that he'd shaved before driving out to get her.

Her heart melted a bit, and she closed her eyes to resist temptation.

CHAPTER FOURTEEN

Waking up to Janelle sleeping in his arms was definitely something that Aaron wouldn't mind getting used to. Even though he kind of had to pee and didn't want to disturb her. He gently moved a strand of hair away from her face so he could see her. Was it creepy to stare at her when she was asleep? Her nose twitched, and it was unbearably adorable.

Her eyes blinked open. Apparently his staring was palpable.

He kissed her lightly on the lips. "Good morning."

"Morning. Been awake long?" she asked.

"Only a minute."

"I don't want to mess up your work schedule," she said, stretching a bit. She'd put on underwear before they'd gone to bed, but nothing else. He'd done the same. He watched carefully, but the sheet stayed up over her breasts despite that palpable stare. Apparently its effect on cotton wasn't as strong as it was on Nell.

"I'm not worried. What about you, are you on vacation?"

"I'm going to do half days today and tomorrow, full day on Friday because there's a meeting I need to attend by video, and relax the rest of the time while you're working. Then we have the weekend."

"Sounds great. How about going out for breakfast?"

"I could cook us a couple of eggs," she offered.

"If you don't want to leave, we can do that. But I've been wanting to check out some of the restaurants." He grabbed his phone. "I did a little research. There're two bars, one with basically peanuts, but the other has a kitchen. Not so much for breakfast, but just to give you the overall picture. There's a fancy restaurant, Monarch."

"I ate there with Rose, Naomi and Ethan. It was very good."

"Okay. There's a more casual restaurant, Quail's Nest, a diner, a barbecue place, a cafe, and the coffee shop with bakery. Besides the fast food and Starbucks, I mean."

"Let's see the menu for Quail's Nest and the diner."

He pulled them up on his phone and they scrolled through.

"I have a weakness for eggs Benedict," she said. "It looks like Quail's Nest serves a classic version. Want to try there?"

"Sounds like a plan."

They took their time getting ready, much of it spent playing in the shower together. They decided to drive, since he did need to get to work before too long, and she suggested they could take a walk around town when he was finished working.

Since it was a Wednesday morning, he was a little surprised at how many people were in the restaurant. He tried to guess who were tourists and who were locals. He recognized Francine Chapman, the mother-of-the-bride from the wedding, who was clearly surprised to see Nell there, and gave a little wave. There were a couple of others he'd seen but not yet met.

A waitress arrived and offered them water and coffee. They both accepted the coffee and Janelle asked for orange juice. She'd introduced herself as Lucy, and she had an accent that was just sort of… odd. But she was pleasant and returned quickly with Nell's juice.

He ordered waffles, and Nell her eggs, and when they were alone again, he leaned in close. "What do you think the deal with the waitresses accent is? It sounds so…" he stalled, unable to come up with an explanation for the sounds they'd been hearing.

"Fake? Like, high school drama student trying to speak with a Russian accent?"

"I was thinking more like Jamaican—"

He paused while Nell snorted.

"Or French."

She recoiled at that. "No. It couldn't be. Wow." She wrinkled her nose. "You think?"

"You're the one who speaks French, I'll defer to your opinion."

"I don't know. It's just…weird."

He shrugged, and studied her. His…date? His girlfriend? His woman?

She cocked her head and studied him in return. "Did I forget to brush my hair?" she asked.

"You're beautiful."

She flushed but didn't look away. "You're sweet. And handsome. My grandmother told me so."

He snickered. "How is she? Did she try that knitting class you told me about last week?"

"Yes, but she hated it. She says it's because it was boring, but I've seen her try to do crafts before, and I can pretty much guarantee it's really that she hates having to follow the rules to get the result she wants. I told her to try a pottery class, the kind where they teach her the basics but she could just sort of free-form whatever she wants."

"I can see that for her."

Their food arrived, and they were quiet as they tucked in. He found himself watching a family that was in the booth to their right. They appeared to be a mother, father and two sons, though his assumptions could be completely wrong. He watched the way they interacted. The kids appeared in the eight- to twelve-ish range and were old enough to behave and young enough to be bored just sitting there with their parents.

"Do you know them?" Nell asked.

He realized he'd been watching them—discreetly—more than he'd been eating. He returned his attention to his food and Nell.

"No, I just tend to people watch. How are the eggs?"

"Fairly good. What do you see when you look at them?"

She sounded genuinely curious, not annoyed that he hadn't been paying attention to her.

"I see a family that appears to like each other. And love each other. And respect each other, even when one brother doesn't want the other brother to play with his game. They don't all look like clones of each other, but that doesn't seem to matter."

She cocked her head. "Clones of each other?"

"Mom looks trendy, Dad looks like a baseball player, oldest looks like a skateboarder and youngest looks like a gamer."

She blinked, slid her gaze to the side again, then pursed her lips and nodded. "Seems about right."

"Isn't there some sort of saying about us learning how to be the people we're going to be by watching our parents? But I decided that wasn't going work for me, given who my parents were, so I watched other people in action. Then I could decide which ones I wanted to be like, and which ones were idiots or assholes."

Understanding washed over her face, and she reached out for his hand.

"I don't really want to talk about it. Not right now." He knew he had to. Almost wanted to, only because it meant that he was feeling serious things about her, and he liked that. He didn't like that it meant he'd have to fill her in on his past, but it was worth it to be with someone who he wanted to consider a future with.

"Of course not." She touched his hand for a second, then picked up her fork for another bite. "I bet you have a new picture of Aubrey, and her mothers would be ashamed of you for going this long without showing her off to me."

Something that he hadn't even been aware of loosened inside him. Not only had she dropped the subject, she'd reminded him that he *did* have a family. One he'd chosen.

"Beth's mom sent me this one, when she was babysitting." He picked up his phone and showed her the texts, relating the story he'd been told about Aubrey's latest antics.

When they left, Lucy sent them off with a cheery "au revoir," that confirmed what the accent *should* have been but left him amused at the shock and confusion on Janelle's face.

They were home within minutes, and he made sure Nell had a comfortable spot at the kitchen table to work, a good Wi-Fi connection and a bottle of water. Then she trailed him up to see the studio.

Nervous would be a strong word for what he was feeling, but he was maybe a little on edge, wondering how she would view his art. He was pretty sure she'd looked him up online. She'd basically told him she would. But she'd never brought up his work and he hadn't asked.

He pushed the door all the way open and stepped back to let her inside. She stopped and surveyed the whole room, then headed for the wall where he'd hung his latest piece. He'd finished it two days before and hung it up so that he could photograph it for his agent.

It was the one he'd started the day after they'd met. He was pleased with how the stormy sky had turned out, how the flowers looked both battered and beautiful, full of life, like they'd sucked in all that rain, danced in the wind and shouted out their victory to the world.

Well, that's how he saw it, anyway. He glanced to Nell.

She had her hand at her throat, her gaze intent on the painting.

A little breath escaped him. That was not a look of disdain.

"Aaron. Wow, Aaron, this is amazing. I love it so much."

He would have preferred criticism to platitudes, but he would have dealt with either one. The pure truth behind her statement humbled him in a way he hadn't expected. It forced him to clear his throat before he could respond.

"I'm glad you like it."

"I don't like it. I love it. I think you should either keep it or charge a fuck-ton of money for it."

He laughed and pulled her into his arms. "You're amazing."

She sighed. "I know, but now I have to deal with the fact that you are, too."

He smacked her butt and she giggled into his shoulder, then pulled free to look at the rest of his studio. She told him which of the commercial works she liked best and which she thought would be most appropriate in a corporate office, a dentist's office or a home office. He agreed with most of her guesses.

Eventually he sent her on her way and got to work prepping a stack of canvases for later use. He liked to do these when he wasn't yet ready to start on a new work, and right now his head was too full of Nell to give a fishing boat on a sunny lake the proper attention.

When they were done, he checked with Nell, then made them both sandwiches and grabbed the grapes from the fridge and a bag of chips. They ate an easy lunch, and Nell showed him a text from Rose with her and Ethan sitting on a porch, feet up on the rail, sun setting off to their side.

"Did you bring your swimsuit," he asked her.

"I did. Did you want to go swimming?"

"We can, but I'm thinking you need to answer that with a picture of us in the hot tub under the stars."

"Ooh, I like the way you think."

He moved to his office to do the emails and phone calls part of his work. He should have done them first so he'd be in a cheerier mood when he joined her at the end of the day, but he hadn't thought of it.

She was stretched out on the couch, a tablet in front of her. He came up behind her and could see that she was reading a book. He picked up her legs, sat, and started to massage her feet.

"You don't look like you enjoyed the second half of your day as much as the first half," she commented.

"I don't love the office stuff so much. It's okay, it's not horrible, it's just…annoying. Emails and contracts and phone calls and, well, people."

She smiled. "It's so nice when someone has a job they love, even if there are aspects that are annoying. Were you always an artist?"

AARON'S HANDS paused on her feet when she asked her question. His face sort of froze, but then he shrugged and met her gaze.

"It goes back to that family thing."

"Okay." If he wasn't ready to talk about it, she was fine with that.

"I should explain about my family."

"If you want to. Or it can wait. Up to you."

He looked down at her feet. Began massaging them again.

"My brother was two years younger than me. From my earliest memories, my parents preferred him to me. And he was quite happy with that. My dad was a jock and so was my brother. My mom was a cheerleader in high school, and proud to have snagged my foot-ball-hero father. My brother was doing his best to walk in those same shoes. He wasn't the cliched quarterback, but he was the favored receiver who was in the running to smash the record for most touchdowns at our school, and maybe even the district.

"He was also an asshole, which, really, wasn't much of a surprise because they were, too. I used to joke to my friend that it was a good thing I didn't have a sister, because my mother would have gone full-on Texas cheerleader murdering mom with little provocation."

"Yikes."

"Yeah. Meanwhile, I'm over there preferring to play video games to football, reading books that're not only *not* assigned by the teach-ers, but banned by the schools, and taking the only art elective the school offered."

"They weren't appreciative of your differences."

"They were not. At first I tried to fit in to a degree, but I realized pretty quickly, mostly because they were assholes, that there was no point in that, so I just did my own thing. I tried an emo phase for like a minute, but that wasn't really me, either."

He glanced to her, finally, and she gave him the grin he needed. His thumbs dug into her arches with the perfect amount of force, and she gave him a deep sigh of appreciation.

"By the time I was thirteen, I had very little to do with them. I worked as soon as I could, any odd job, including painting barns, and when I was sixteen, I got my license and had enough for a beater car, insurance and gas. My friend's dad helped me buy it. Of course, my dad was apoplectic that it was a Hyundai, not a Ford or Chevy."

"Of course."

"My parents insisted I leave the spare key with them, and once in a while, once he was in high school, my brother had the charming habit of 'borrowing' it for dates or to take his friends out to beat up mailboxes or whatever. When he was sixteen, they bought him a used Ford, also a bit of a beater because they didn't have a lot of money. He and my dad worked on it together to keep it running."

"And I suppose it never occurred to them to give you any money towards yours, help with maintenance, or apologize or something like that."

"You suppose correctly." He ran a hand up and down her leg for a minute, then maneuvered out from under her. "Want a drink?"

"I'm good, thanks."

He went into the kitchen and came back with a glass of water, which he set on the coffee table. She'd sat up, so he sat next to her and she snuggled in.

"Derek's car broke down and they hadn't had a chance to fix it, so he decided to take mine. I was studying for my finals. Senior year, extremely ready to get out and never look back. I'd already been accepted to the state school with a good art scholarship, and I knew I could afford it."

He made a soundless laugh that brought an ache to her heart. "I hadn't even told my parents. And they hadn't asked. I'd also been accepted to a college in New York City, with some scholarships, but I was hoping to hear back from more scholarships so that I could make it work. It was going to be a stretch, though. My parents didn't make enough—or at least, weren't responsible enough with it —to buy a better car for Derek, but they made enough that the financial aid was tricky."

"Our higher-education system sucks."

"Yeah, well. I was figuring it out, and making sure my grades were top level was part of that. I didn't even know he'd taken the car until we heard the sirens."

She swallowed hard but didn't say anything to interrupt.

"I don't know how we knew, guessed, that it was him. Small-town nosey, maybe they would have run out there anyway; maybe I would have stopped studying and stood at the window, staring at the space where my car was supposed to be. But we knew. It was a long dirt road a little ways back behind our house. My parents ran over there. I heard my mom scream."

He picked up the water and took a long drink, put the glass back down. "Anyway. His buddy was dead, because of course they weren't wearing their seat belts. He went through the windshield and was dead before the ambulance got there. Derek was unconscious, barely alive. They took him to the hospital."

"Was there another car involved?"

"No. Thankfully. It was a sharp turn, he took it too fast, lost control. The town immediately rallied behind them, all the parents. Kids out letting off steam, racing their car, lost control. A total accident, an all-American accident. Boys will be boys."

"Your car."

"Yeah, well, that wasn't mentioned. Derek was in the hospital, my mom was there twenty-four seven. There were vigils in front of the hospital, acres of flowers at the site. For about two days. And then the girl came forward."

"Uh-oh."

"Turns out they'd been out to her place. Her parents were away for the weekend, and so the boys decided it was the perfect time to party. She objected. They took turns raping her."

"Fucking hell!"

"The cops had found my brother's phone, and by now they had the test results from when he was admitted. Drunk. And on the phone…they found video. He'd recorded them holding her down, ignoring her crying and begging. Them raping her. It was *all* on his own phone."

"The town turned."

"Yep. To their credit, they rallied around the girl. I was a little surprised, to be honest. I think it was the video that did it. The money they'd been raising for Derek's hospital bills went to the girl. Derek died without ever waking up. My dad lost his job and started drinking heavily."

"Hmm… I'm trying to find some sympathy."

"Yeah. I took my finals. Went to New York. About a month later, the tornado hit. They were two of the eighty-three who died. The town was devastated."

"The girl?"

"She and her parents had already moved. Even though the town was mostly being supportive, they took the money and moved to the city. It was good, she was able to get a therapist and she went to college the next year."

"You kept track."

He shrugged.

"You were done with them before you even left town."

"I wanted to be. Instead, I had to go back, deal with the house, the insurance. The house had been my grandparents', passed on to my dad, so it was free and clear. I got some insurance money. Not a lot, but enough to make college in New York a little easier."

"Which you hated."

He shrugged again. "I didn't do anything to deserve it."

"Just as much as your father did to inherit the house. What about your friend? The one whose dad helped you out."

"They were okay, but their house was damaged. They ended up moving away, closer to the city where he went to college. We stayed in touch for a while, but it sort of dwindled away as we moved on with our lives."

"Wow. I'm sorry your parents sucked. Your brother might not have turned into an asshole if they hadn't."

"Maybe, maybe not. Either way, a lot of people have much worse. Lots have better. It was all a long time ago."

"You went from a small farm town in Ohio, to putting yourself through college in New York City and becoming a successful painter who has showings and hangs in galleries and actually makes money. It's impressive."

"It doesn't suck to make money doing what you love," he agreed, bringing them back to the start of the conversation.

"I bet not."

"You don't love your work?"

"No. I don't hate it, and I like most of the people I work with. I like doing admin work, getting things accomplished. But it's not something I would ever use the word love to describe. Plus, I've worked there my whole adult life. I started when I was still in college."

"What do you see for your future?" he asked.

"I've been working on being able to leave. Well, first I worked on my F-You Fund. I wanted enough money to feel like I could quit my job at any time without freaking out, knowing I should be able to find a new job within a reasonable timeframe. Once I got that, I wanted to be able to quit and not worry about getting a new job right away at all, take a year if necessary."

"And you achieved that…"

"Yes, and the funny thing was that once I'd earned the first, it wasn't much longer to save for the second. I was more relaxed at work, more confident. My boss gave me better raises."

"And where are you now?"

"Now I can enjoy the perks of the job while I decide on my future. The longer I work there, the more padding I have. I could leave today, but I would still need a full-time job to live in Los Angeles, unless I stay in that guesthouse forever. Or I could leave today and go somewhere with a lower cost of living and either live frugally without working, or work part time and have a bit more fun."

He nodded. "You haven't decided."

"Not quite. I thought it would be more obvious what I wanted once I reached this point, but…" It was her turn to shrug. "I've done a lot of reading on early retirement, or financial independence. One of the problems people have is that they retire away from what they've been doing, rather than into what they *want* to do. Depression can be an issue, and it surprises people, because they ascribe all of their unhappiness to working a job they don't like."

"Really? Wow. It makes sense when you say it like that, but it's hard to think of people quitting their jobs and being able to do what they want, but ending up depressed."

"Yep. So, I just want to take my time and figure out how I see my days going. I'm very young to have this level of independence, I know that."

"You made a lot of sacrifices to reach this point."

"It didn't hurt that my parents are comfortable, so they pay for me to go on vacation with them to Hawaii, to see the family. I did make sacrifices, but not like some people have to do just to make it through the year, let alone put a huge amount into savings."

"Some people have it better, some people have it worse. But you took your situation and did way more with it than most would, and now you can reap the rewards."

"Yes. I've been lucky but I've worked my butt off. And now I deserve dinner and a hot tub."

He laughed. "Yes, you do."

CHAPTER FIFTEEN

They decided to walk to Wolfhound Tavern for dinner and beer. Since his was the only house at the end of Toad Lane, part of the walk was just them until they neared the sports field at the corner of Dragonfly Road. A soccer game was in full swing, though it looked to be a pickup game, not anything official.

They stopped to watch for a minute and chatted with a dog walker who was also taking in the game. The mostly high school kids were going at it hard, and there were a fair number of people on the sidelines egging them on, but it appeared to be all in good fun.

They turned the corner and crossed the street, and walked past the elementary school.

"Oh! The shops have put out their window boxes and planters. It looks so pretty and charming. It's funny, I don't know if I would have even noticed, back home."

"Well, back home the shops have flowers nearly year round. Here, the colors are especially bright and eye-catching because last time you came through, it was all snow."

"That's true." Nell checked her watch. "We should pop into the hardware store and say hi to Rose's mom or dad, whichever of them is working today."

He hadn't known the Chapmans worked at Hammerhead Hardware. "Do they own it?" he asked.

"Yes. They divorced when Rose was in college, before I met her. They both still own the store, though."

"They didn't look very divorced at the wedding," he pointed out.

"Yeah, they were really good, weren't they? Rose had always said they didn't speak to each other, and they never came to visit at the same time. When she came home she found out they'd started sharing duties at the store, and her mom mentioned going to Denver with him for a date. Rose is curious, but can't bring herself to ask them what's going on."

A man wearing a Broncos hat was coming out of the hardware store as they arrived. He tipped his hat at them. "Going to be a nice evening. Pretty sunset, I'll bet."

"Oh. Great. Thanks!" Nell said.

They entered the store, a little bell announcing their arrival. George gave them a wave from the counter.

"Good timing," George said. "Did Walter give you the weather?"

Aaron laughed. "He did. Is he the weatherman?"

"It's just his passion, I guess you could say. Or one of them, anyway. If you want recommendations on excellent wines, he's your man for that, too."

"Good to know."

Francine stuck her head around a doorway behind the counter. "Nell! Aaron! I'm so glad you came in. I was going to call you after seeing you at breakfast, but I didn't want to intrude. Did you need anything, before I forget and spend all our time chatting?"

"No, nothing, we just stopped in to say hi. We're going to Wolfhound Tavern to have dinner."

"Excellent. Are you in town for long?" Francine asked.

"For the rest of the week. I'll head back on Sunday."

"We're pleased to see you out and about in town," George said to Aaron.

"It was a terrific wedding, and I'm glad I went. It was nice to start to meet people and remind myself that there's a whole town here to get to know."

Francine beamed. "It really went off so beautifully, I know Rose was very happy."

"I just wish she hadn't run off to Spain," George grumbled. "I like having her back in town."

"She'll be home before you know it," Nell assured him. "It's already been two months."

"Be grateful she's going to settle here, instead of Los Angeles," Francine added. "Especially when they have babies."

"I am, believe me."

The bell rang again, and their waitress from that morning, Lucy, walked in. George went to help her pick out some light bulbs.

"That girl," Francine said quietly, giving a little shake of her head.

"We met her this morning," Nell said. "She was nice, a good wait-ress, though a little…standoffish."

Aaron blinked. He hadn't noticed that.

"She studied abroad in France when she was in high school, and she's never been the same since. Let me see…that would have been about ten years ago. She's a good girl, she just sometimes acts like she's too good to be living here in Wildlife Ridge."

Lucy and George were already returning to the counter. Next to him, Nell began speaking to her in French. Lucy's face lit up in such pleasure that Aaron felt guilty for having thought she was weird. She and Nell spoke animatedly for several minutes before exchanging a brief hug. Then Nell took his hand and led him out of the store. He turned to wave at the three before the door closed.

"Wow," he said as they continued on towards Main Street. "What did you say?"

"I said I'd heard she'd been to France, and to pardon my terrible skills and accent, but did she still speak the language? As you saw, she did, and about as well as me, actually. She was excited and said we should have drinks sometime."

"Well, okay then."

He pointed to The Wolfhound Tavern across the street as they headed towards it. "I was driving around and went to the street behind the restaurant. The sheriff's station is back there. I wonder if that makes this bar the more family-friendly one and Cougars, down the way, a little more exciting?" he asked.

"Ooh, maybe. Although I've never heard Rose mention anything truly exciting happening."

They walked in and took a look around. The lighting was cozy-dim, there were tables for eating on one side and a couple of pool tables and cocktail tables on the other. Straight ahead was a large U-shaped bar. There were a couple dozen people inside, and the noise level was low with a country song playing fairly loudly. Of course, it was only six o'clock.

Nell took his hand and moved to the tables with menus standing tall in little wire baskets, which also held napkins, ketchup, mustard, salt and pepper. She shuffled through the menus and handed him one food menu and one beer menu.

A kid who didn't look old enough to serve alcohol, and therefore immediately made Aaron feel ancient, took their orders. He decided to try something different and went for Aunt Leslie's Pear Cider, while Nell chose the Bugger Off Bitter Red, which was listed as an Irish ale.

They'd started checking the food menu when a man came up to their table and took a seat. It took a second for Aaron to remember him as Ian, who they'd met at the wedding.

"There you are. And you've brought back our Nell...well done. First round's on me."

"Thanks, Ian, that's very nice. Do I remember right that you're the manager here?" Aaron asked.

"I am. My uncle owns it, and he's here now and then, but he prefers to do the business end in the back. I'll introduce you if he shows his face." He said to Nell, "I heard from Ethan; he sent a picture of he and Rose at some beach, just to make me cry, I think."

"Aww. Is it time for you to take a vacation, Ian?" Nell asked.

"Well, I suppose it is, but it's just not the same without a beautiful woman by my side. You busy next week?" He returned with a huge grin.

"Hey now," Aaron said, with no heat in his voice.

Ian put his hands up in surrender. "How about Naomi? I heard she was buying a building out near here, surely she'll come to Wildlife Ridge."

"Surely she will," Nell agreed coyly without saying more.

Ian moved his hands to his heart in a gesture of being deeply wounded. "Gah."

Nell laughed and moved back as their waiter brought drinks for them, as well as one for Ian. They took their drinks and clinked glasses.

"You tease me, but I'm glad to have you here."

He made recommendations on their food selections, then headed off after encouraging them to grab him for a game of pool when they were done eating. Aaron went for the fish and chips, and Nell for a burger that was dripping with sauce and had her using up most of the napkins in the holder on the table.

Nell grabbed the bill when it came, surprising Aaron. He'd thought they'd settled this issue.

"I thought you were okay with me paying," he reminded her.

"Sometimes, yes. Sometimes it's my turn. This seems like a good time."

He frowned.

"Wasn't part of our conversation this afternoon about how I'm doing pretty well? I don't need you to buy me dinner."

He managed to keep his sigh internal. "How strongly do you feel about this?" he asked.

She cocked her head and considered. "Seven."

He considered throwing out an eight, but realized that would be just to win, not because he actually felt that strongly. He just…liked paying. Which was outdated, he knew it. "I could pay for my half," he suggested, but she knew she'd won and just rolled her eyes at him.

Putting her credit card in the folder, she angled it out so their waiter could see. "Besides, I like the points," she said. "And my treat category is bursting at the seams."

"So this is a treat, not…what was it? Your dining out category?"

She winked at him. "Being with you is a treat."

Outwardly he snorted. Inwardly he kind of melted.

They waved to Ian when they stood up, and he came to join them at the pool table. A foursome were playing, but their game was almost over and they indicated that they would be happy to turn the table over when they'd finished. A fresh round of drinks appeared, and they stood around one of the cocktail tables. Ian introduced them to Sandy and Ron Bakshi, and Jake Steele, who were standing at the next table watching the game.

"Oh, Mr. Romero, I'd hoped to meet you," Sandy said, turning to face him.

"Please, call me Aaron."

"I'm Sandy. We moved here about eighteen years ago, but I remember what it's like, the culture shock of a small town like this. So I hope you don't think I'm a crazy lady when I say I looked you up and was hoping to talk to you about your art."

He smiled. "I'm from another small town, so I know how it goes. Are you an artist?"

"Unfortunately not. I'm a tutor. Online. Which is the best commute ever."

He laughed. "It is. I set up a studio three rooms from my bedroom, so I can't complain." Glancing over, he saw that Janelle was laughing at whatever Ian had said, and talking with Ron and Jake. He heard something about carburetors and returned his attention to Sandy. "What subject do you tutor?"

"Math, most levels. But my best friend is a teacher at the elementary school here. I met her when my daughter was in her class, and we became friends. They had an art teacher, but she retired a couple years ago, and they haven't replaced her. Mandy tries to do an art day once a month with her kids to make up for it, but she has no training or—she'll admit this herself—skill."

"Okay." He tried not to frown, but he wasn't really sure where this was heading. Elementary school kids?

"We thought you might have some ideas. The kids are too old just to play finger painting. They want some guidance on how to actually do something."

"I have no training in teaching, and, I'll admit, no particular affinity for it. But sure, if she'd like to talk, I'm happy to bounce ideas with her."

Sandy smiled. "That's great! I'll talk to her and text you to see when you have time. We'll buy you lunch or something."

"Not necessary. Why don't you guys come out to the house sometime?"

Her eyes lit up and they exchanged numbers.

The game at the table finished, and Ron and Ian decided to team up against Nell and Aaron, with Sandy and Jake cheering them on from the sides. If by "cheering on" you meant the occasional whoop from Sandy and high-five from Jake. Both seemed perfectly content to offer those congratulations to whoever had done well, regardless of which team they were on.

Aaron called for another round, managing to pay for it while Ian and Nell were bent over the table, teasing each other about a difficult shot Ian was going to attempt. He and Nell barely squeaked out a win, mostly because they all sucked equally.

"Man, you manage a bar with a pool table," Aaron teased Ian.

"Well, I'd like to say I'm usually too busy working to play, but really it's my terrible hand-eye coordination."

Aaron sat out the next game, so Sandy and Nell could take on Ron and Ian. The game ended when Sandy shot the eight ball into a pocket by mistake. They said their goodbyes, promising to return.

As they walked home, Aaron's arm around the slightly tipsy Nell's waist, he realized that tomorrow would be eight weeks since the day they'd met. They'd only spent a fraction of the hours since then together, but he felt more comfortable with her, with her in his life, and with his life in general, than he had the previous eight years.

NELL RACED up the stairs to Aaron's bedroom, with him close behind. Then, more slowly and carefully, she went back down the stairs while Aaron watched her from the top. When she'd made it back up, he shook his head and led the way to the bedroom.

They changed into their bathing suits and ignored the temptation of each other's naked bodies, because the sun was getting close to setting and she was determined to follow through with Aaron's brilliant idea of sending a retaliatory photo to Rose and Ethan.

Besides, there was plenty of time for other kinds of fun.

Aaron got towels and led the way to the back porch. The large round hot tub was in the corner, with steam already rising from it when she lifted the cover, since her brilliant man had remembered to turn it on before they'd left for dinner.

She wrapped her hair into a bun and secured it while Aaron went back to the house to get them waters. She dipped her toe into the heat. *Ooooh.* She slowly lowered herself down and got comfortable as he returned, three candles in jars tucked under his arms, along with the two bottles of water, his phone, and a lighter.

"Is the water okay?" he asked. "I can change the temp."

"Feels perfect."

He put the candles down and lit them, set his phone up on a nearby table, angled to catch them and the western sky, then slipped into the water. He wore loose dark blue trunks that floated up as he stepped into the water, then, when he stood on the step and fiddled with something above the hot tub, the material clung to him in very loving ways.

Apparently what he was fiddling with was music, and Adele began to croon to them. Nell managed to keep her hands to herself as he sat down next to her, his arm coming up behind her shoulders.

She leaned into him, and they listened and watched as the sun dipped below the mountain. There were still dots of snow though it was now the end of June. He used his watch to activate the camera shutter on his phone a couple of times as the pink and orange slowly appeared, the sporadic clouds catching fire over the next few minutes.

"Wow," she murmured.

"Right?"

"Do you ever paint sunsets?"

"Once in a while."

The sky continued to light up, with Aaron taking pictures every so often, the music washing over them quietly, the heat enveloping them. Finally, the lights faded away and darkness settled around them. She wasn't sure if she squirmed or sighed, but Aaron laughed and rose to grab the phone. He'd already assured her that his case was waterproof, so she wasn't worried when he handed it over.

She gasped over several of them, even though she'd just seen the beauty firsthand. She might need to upgrade her phone, as it was several years old and wouldn't have come close to the quality of these pictures.

Picking one out, she forwarded it to her phone, which did *not* have a waterproof case and so was safely in the house. Then she went ahead and forwarded a bunch more to her phone. She put it on the ledge and turned to him, fitting herself onto his lap with her legs wrapped around his back, his hands around hers, supporting her.

"I'm really glad you came," he said.

"Me, too."

"You should do it again."

"You can count on it. Any trips to California in your near future?"

"Count on it."

She wore a bandeau-style top with wide straps, and he slipped a finger under one, followed its lead down to her breast. She wasn't used to a house that was so private that she didn't have to worry about the neighbors looking over a fence. Out here, the only lights were from the house and the candles behind him.

But she didn't think he was starting anything, more like lazily exploring her body. For whatever reason, she'd never been self-conscious about her body with him. He'd shown an appreciation for her from the beginning and not said anything to make her doubt the truth of that. She wouldn't mind losing another couple of pounds, but wasn't really giving it a lot of thought these days. If she lived here, she thought she'd like to go for regular hikes in the state park. Which was kind of weird. She never went for hikes in Los Angeles, though there were plenty of options.

She held on to his arms and leaned back so that her shoulders were in the water again. The stars were bright now, the sky so much darker than she could see in LA without driving for a couple of hours. It was so beautiful here, so peaceful.

His fingers were still tracing their way around her suit, but with no urgency. She picked out a couple of constellations, and he pointed out another.

She wondered what it would be like to be sitting like this, with him, in different parts of the country, or the world. Spain, Ireland, New Zealand. All the places she'd mentioned wanting to travel. But with him by her side. Was she finally ready to actually see the world? All of her vacations in the last decade had either been to family, or research trips to check out potential towns to live in. Maybe it was time to just have fun. She could finally see herself doing that, with Aaron. Except, could they really travel together?

"What are your plans for the morning?" she asked, trying to pull her brain in a different direction.

"Well. I do need to work. So, we can either sleep in and have bagels for breakfast. Or not sleep in and go out. And then I'm painting."

"Let's sleep in and have bagels. I'm going to work in the morning and then walk over to Jake's garage in the afternoon."

"Jake, the guy we met tonight who looks a bit like Grizzly Adams?"

She sat up so she could unwind her legs and sit next to him, her arms along the back, her legs floating up in front of them, toes sticking out of the water. "Yes. I'd like to see his shop, ask him some questions about volume of customers, full-time and part-time employees, that kind of thing. We got into it a little bit at the bar, but it wasn't the right place to go into details like that."

He snorted. "You thinking of opening a garage?"

She smacked his shoulder. "Don't laugh, it could happen. But I don't think I want to own one. Maybe work there part time. But I don't know enough about it, which is why I want to ask questions."

"I have a hard time imagining you in coveralls with grease all over your face."

His tone was almost joking, but a little too close to mocking for her taste. She moved over so she could see his face.

"You're a snob," she accused.

"I'm not a snob, that's a ridiculous thing to say."

"Of course you are. You drive a brand-new fancy SUV. How old was your last car."

"Two years, but that's just for convenience, so I don't have to worry about the warranty and have car issues."

She let that one slide, not even bringing up how they'd met.

"And your clothes."

Looking baffled, he glanced down, as if he could see what he'd been wearing before changing into the suit. "What about them? They're not snobbish."

"Oh, please, they're very nice quality."

"Liking quality makes me a snob?"

"What store are they from?"

"I have no idea, you would have to ask my personal shopper."

She raised her eyebrows at him.

"Again, that's convenience, which is an entirely different thing.

"Well, I can tell you he didn't get them at Target."

"I am quite certain that *she* did not. She buys quality items that will last a long time."

"Oh, really, how long have you had the shirt you were wearing today?"

He just looked at her peevishly.

"Okay, what's the oldest item in your closet?"

"I don't know, and I don't care, as long as what I pull out to wear is in good shape. She comes in every six months and cleans things out and brings in new stuff. I have no interest in spending any more time and effort on it than that. That hardly makes me a snob."

She growled at him. He was refusing to see the point. "You pay a woman to cycle your closet every six months, I bet there's not one thing in there that's more than a year old, it's all designer brands—"

"High quality," he muttered.

"Whatever. You have this huge house for one person."

"For privacy and security. If there'd been a smaller house with those attributes, I would have been happy to buy it instead. It sounds like you're saying I'm frivolous, not snobbish."

She honestly had no idea what she was saying anymore. He'd never behaved badly, so what was she complaining about?

"This is a ridiculous thing to fight about."

"We're not fighting," he argued.

She resisted the urge to splash him. Drawing in a deep breath, she tried again. "I'm not saying your frivolous, I'm saying you're a snob who thinks he's too good to date a mechanic."

He sat up straight, his mouth hanging open for two long seconds before he snapped it shut. "That's insane."

"Yeah, it sucks, that's for sure."

"That's not what I meant, and you know it."

"You didn't even talk to Jake tonight, only Sandy and Ron."

"What am I going to talk to him about? Spark plugs and lug nuts? You think he wants to talk about oil paints and stretching canvases?"

"I don't know, he might. You act like it's impossible he'd care about art, or have a reasonable conversation with a stranger about something other than cars. That's ridiculous. And snobbish."

CHAPTER SIXTEEN

Luckily for Aaron, the hot tub cycle came to an end before he responded to Janelle. He picked up his phone. "You want more jets?"

She checked her fingers. "No, I'm getting kind of pruney, let's go in."

He climbed out and offered her a hand, which she took. They dried off, and he tried not to stare too hard at the way the pink suit skimmed along her fantastic butt. She walked ahead of him, draping her towel around her hips, unfortunately.

They walked into his closet, and he braced himself for more shit about his clothes. "Look, I don't want to fight about some guy I've said two words to."

Her lips quirked. "I thought we weren't fighting."

Then she sighed at the same time she stripped off her bathing suit and dropped it on the towel she'd draped across the ottoman. "Look, is it possible you have some hang-up about mechanics? Who remind you of your father and brother?"

He froze. "Huh? That guy didn't look anything like my father or brother."

She gave him a very patient look. "I don't mean appearance."

Taking a robe he'd offered her that morning, she wrapped it around herself and picked up her wet things, moving into the bathroom while speaking to him over her shoulder. "But you were a bit stand-offish to him tonight, and you were rude when I mentioned going over there. If you've never met him, the only reason I can think of is his job."

He was standing there in wet swim trunks, staring at where she'd been. He hadn't been standoffish. Or rude. Had he? Just because he didn't want anything to do with the stupid mechanic, he was rude?

"You laughed at me," she added.

Shocked, he tried to remember. "I would never laugh at something you wanted to do. I was just surprised."

She came up behind him and teased her fingers between his skin and the wet fabric, then drew the shorts down. He used the towel he was still holding to finish drying off. Had he been an ass?

She came around to his front and smoothed her fingers over his face, which had apparently scrunched up.

"Okay. You didn't laugh. You sort of snorted."

"I'm sorry."

"I guess I'm still sensitive to people making fun of me for being a woman who likes to work on cars. And, maybe I'm worried about being good enough for you."

He gaped at her.

She laughed. "Because you're rich."

"Oh. That's ridiculous."

"Yeah. I know. I was thinking about what it would be like if we traveled together. And how you would want first class and nice hotels and I would want to pay for coach and AirBnB."

He sighed. "I would pay for all of that."

"That's part of the problem."

He wrapped his arms around her. "You've shown, quite conclusively, that you are not irresponsible with money. There is not one single doubt in my head that you would take advantage of my wealth. None. I'm sorry I made you feel weird about the mechanic thing. I didn't mean to, and I would be thrilled if you found something that made you happy."

She sighed. "Thank you. I'm sorry, too."

"You'll get over the money thing. I'll talk dirty to you about budgets and categories until you give in to my every desire."

She laughed. "Okay, give that a shot. In the meantime, if we're done fighting, can we have make-up sex now?"

"Yes. But we aren't fighting."

"Then no make-up sex."

He felt everything inside him loosen, only then realizing he'd tightened up. "Well, I guess it could be considered a fight." He sighed and ran his hand over his hair. "I didn't intend to be rude to Jake. Or you."

"I don't think he noticed. Or worried about it if he did. If I didn't know you, I wouldn't have thought you were rude to him."

"I haven't thought about them in a long time," he admitted. "My family. Maybe I shouldn't admit that."

She wrapped her arms around him but leaned back so she could watch his face. "There's nothing wrong with that."

"I don't think I have a problem with mechanics. Maybe it was just too soon after our conversation."

Her thumbs moved up and down his spine. "Well, consider this. If my choices were to become a part-time mechanic so that I could quit my job and move to Wildlife Springs, or keep doing what I'm doing and stay in Los Angeles, which would you choose."

His arms had come up around her, as well, and now they tightened. "Is that a possibility? Will you move here?"

She sighed. "I don't know. But it's one of the reasons I want to talk to him, find out more about it. I've never actually looked into it before. But he had mentioned being super busy and his son going off to college, so he'll be turning away more business, and it made me curious."

"I know we're not really there yet…but I would be very happy if you decided to move to Wildlife Ridge, and I could not care less about what you chose to do for work once you were here."

She leaned up on her tiptoes and kissed him. "Good answer." Her knee sneaked out from behind her robe and rubbed along the inside of his thigh. "Hmm."

"I don't think I'm mad enough for make-up sex," he murmured into her ear, nuzzling her hair.

"Darn, we'll have to try that again some time."

"After-hot-tub sex, though. With you all warm and pliant in my arms. That seems pretty doable."

"I'm feeling quite pliant."

He smiled, bent, and put his hands behind her legs, picked her up into his arms, and carried her to the bed. She stretched out on top of the comforter, her come-hither smile the sexiest thing he'd seen in his life. She lifted one knee and let it fall open, but only slightly.

Plucking a pillow from the mound at the top of the bed, the one his interior designer had made him promise to faithfully reproduce every morning, he slid it under her hips. He gently pressed her other leg up, then out, so she was splayed open before him.

"Stop staring at me," she teased.

"Yes, ma'am." He moved in, tasting her, enjoying her, until she was crying out for him to enter her. He rose up and turned her to her side, kicking away the pillow, rolling on a condom, and sliding one arm under her head so she was supported. His other hand went between her legs, guiding himself into her as she pressed back for more.

She was so welcoming, so warm and wet, and he imagined being able to do this every single day for the rest of his life. His cock twitched inside of her at the idea, and she moaned. He wrapped his arm around her and together they found their rhythm, moving until he felt his balls draw up.

He fingered her clit, needing only a little pressure from his fingers before she shattered in his arms. Her release put him over the edge, and he filled the condom, his arm tight around her, hers coming back to claw him closer, until they were both spent.

When they'd cleaned up and climbed back into bed, he used

some of the pillows to prop himself up and drew her between his legs to rest against his chest.

"Are we there yet?" he asked quietly.

She drew in a deep breath, and he knew he didn't have to remind her that he'd said they really weren't less than an hour before.

"I don't know. My brain says we can't be. But here I am. And I don't want to leave."

"I don't want you to leave, either."

"That's scary."

"I know." He tightened his arms around her, and she sighed.

"It's been two months. And we weren't even together for most of them."

"I know."

"You just told me about your family. We barely know each other."

"We know each other."

"Yeah."

Her fingers plucked at his, twisted around them, tweaked them. He let her play.

"I don't know if we're there yet," she finally continued. "But I know you're important to me, and that I *want* to be there."

He nodded against her temple. "That's a pretty good place to be for right now. Can I plan on coming out there for the Fourth of July?"

"Definitely. We can go see the fireworks off the ocean."

He yawned, and she turned to look up at him. "Did you know that when you go to sleep, you do so immediately?"

Well, that was confusing. "What do you mean? What else would I do."

She laughed. "Try to go to sleep for a while. Maybe succeed, maybe fail."

"If I tried to go to sleep and didn't, I'd probably get up and do something else. Why would I continue to not sleep?"

She smiled and sat up so they could rearrange the pillows and lay down. "No reason at all."

PERHAPS IT WAS because she'd teased Aaron about not being able to fall asleep, but after he was out for the count, Nell realized she was not going to be following any minute soon.

She pulled her phone off the nightstand and arranged herself on her stomach with the pillow shielding Aaron from the light of the screen, though she didn't really think it would matter. Opening the text thread with Naomi and Rose, she sent the picture of them in the hot tub, with the mountains and the sunset as background.

The phone showed Rose typing an answer almost immediately. It was a row of hearts. She smiled.

JB: *Remember last year when I said I figured I was probably getting too old to end up with a family of my own, and I was going to be the best aunt of anyone who aunted, instead? And you guys said there was still time to meet someone and have a family of my own, and I said what were the chances of that?*

Three little dots showed Rose typing a response for nearly a minute.

RC: *There's always a chance. Especially for someone as awesome as you. You deserve everything you want, and that includes an awesome guy and a family. Do you think it could be Aaron?*

JB: *I'm beginning to wonder. I mean, even when he's an idiot, he's awesome.*

RC: *Was he an idiot?*

JB: *Kind of, but only for a minute and when I pointed it out and he realized it, he apologized. And I was kind of one, too*

RC: *That's a good sign*

Little dots appeared showing Naomi was typing.

NW: *That picture is amazing. You look happy. And that makes me very happy*

Nell sent a few hearts of her own.

Naomi typed some more.

NW: *He seemed very confident in himself. Which can be a good thing or can hide an asshole. Especially towards women*

Janelle smiled. Naomi was good at driving to the heart of things. She thought about how she wanted to respond.

JB: *He's attractive and wealthy, but he didn't grow up either of those things (I mean, he was probably attractive but he didn't think so due to how he was raised). So he settled into himself before either of those things became a reality for him. He's confident, but he's not a player because for the most part he prefers his own company.*

She hit enter and waited for a response. Aaron rolled over onto his stomach and moved his hand to her back. She waited to see if he was awake, but his breathing evened out again. Smiling, she read Naomi's response.

NW: *Fair enough*

JB: *So, tonight I met the guy who owns the garage in town. We got to talking, and I'm going over there tomorrow. I want to ask some questions about volume of business in a small town, that kind of thing*

Dots appeared for both of them, then disappeared. Then reappeared.

RC: *Let's video call*

Janelle sighed. She was awfully comfortable but she knew Rose was right.

NW: *yes*

JB: *Ok but give me a minute to get out of bed and downstairs*

Rose sent her an emoji of a tongue sticking out.

She eased out from under Aaron's hand, then slid off the bed. Grabbing the robe that he'd loaned her, she headed down to the couch and initiated the video call.

"Okay," Rose said as soon as all of their faces were on the screen. "Were you in fact implying that you were thinking of moving to Wildlife Ridge and opening your own shop?"

"More like, if I moved to a small town with a garage, would there be enough business for me to do some work on the side without pissing off the owner? Or if there were no shop, would I maybe want to start one, but I don't think I want to own my own business. Basically just doing more research."

"Tell me this," Naomi said. "How many small towns are on your list now, including Wildlife Ridge?"

"Five."

"And how many of them have mechanic shops?"

"I'm not sure, I hadn't been researching that up until now."

"Right." Rose was becoming excited, and it was infectious. "Because you didn't actually see a future for yourself in any of them, like you do in Wildlife Ridge!"

"Exactly," Naomi agreed.

Janelle considered that. It was true, she supposed. But other things had been moving her closer and closer to a decision.

"It would be pretty stupid of me to move to a town because of a guy. Right?" She sounded ridiculously unsure, even to herself.

"If you compare two towns side by side, and you can't decide between them, you might as well take the one with the guy you really, really like," Rose pointed out.

"It would be pretty stupid of you *not* to move to a town because of a guy, too," Naomi added.

Hmm. Well. Hmm.

"Those are two very interesting points. I don't know if I'm ready to leave LA and my job, and it's weirding me out that I didn't start giving it super-serious consideration until I met him."

Naomi scoffed. "And until you spent more time in a town that feels right. And until you got comfortable with the idea that the money you have in savings is enough, and you could see a future for yourself, outside of the rat race, if you moved to that kind of area. Oh, and your boss deciding to move in a direction that makes you uncomfortable."

Rose jumped in. "And it's okay if part of your thought process is that you finally met a guy you can see yourself having a future with, too. And that maybe it will or won't work out, but it will be a hell of a lot easier to give it a chance if you're living in the same state. And it's not like you have to move in with him, you can stay in Salmon Springs for as long as you'd like."

"Okay. Maybe. I'll see what I find out tomorrow."

Naomi frowned at that. "If he tells you there's no room for someone to do side business and he'd make it his mission in life to run you out of town if you tried, would you not move there?"

"I mean, that's not the impression I was getting, but no. That's not really his say."

"Right," Naomi said. "Then anything he has to say will only push you forward, so what's holding you back?"

"I—I don't know. I love it here. But I've been doing all this thinking about what I want in the future. How do I know when the future is actually the present?"

"I've been thinking the same thing," Naomi said. "The exact same thing. Tell me this. What would you say to me if I pointed out that if I rented out the condo I live in, the rental income would cover both my mortgage and the rent on an apartment in Salmon Springs?"

"I would say when are you moving to Colorado?" Nell said without a second's thought.

"How about if my answer is, when you agree to go halfsies with me on the moving truck?"

Janelle sat back, her mouth literally falling open.

Rose was squealing and Naomi was laughing.

"See, it's so much easier to visualize for someone else. I was sitting here wondering why you're even thinking about waiting, and I realized you would say the same thing to me. So...why are we waiting?"

"Damn. Why *are* we waiting?"

"You're not," Rose chimed in. "Let's get you both to Wildlife Ridge!"

"You need time to find a tenant," Nell said to Naomi.

"And you need to give notice to your boss and your landlord. July first is only a couple of days away. Do we give thirty days' notice, or sixty?"

"Thirty," Rose said immediately.

"Sixty," Nell said. But she was smiling as she said it, and she couldn't believe how right this felt. Now that she'd said the words, her questions and doubts were disappearing.

"Sixty," Naomi agreed. "Whew!"

They chatted for a few minutes more before hanging up.

Janelle felt energized. Well, it wasn't *that* late...and Aaron *had* said he wanted to sleep in, so maybe he wouldn't mind getting woken up to share her enthusiasm. Not her news; that could wait until tomorrow. Just her mood.

She found that he'd rolled over again, his arm flung out to where she'd been lying. As she watched, he moved again, a bit restless. She climbed into bed, and he immediately moved towards her. She kissed his bare shoulder, with a bit of tongue. Then she kissed his pecs the same way.

Pretty soon it was obvious that he did not, in fact, mind being woken up to share her mood.

CHAPTER SEVENTEEN

While they ate their bagels, hers toasted with butter and his just with cream cheese, she broached the subject.

"So, you know Naomi and I have both been planning to leave Los Angeles sometime in the near-ish future. We've decided to go ahead and move to Wildlife Ridge. In September. *This* September."

He'd stopped chewing towards the end of her sentence, and now he sped up so he could speak, which nearly had him choking. She waited while he drank some coffee.

"When did you decide this?" he finally managed.

"Last night. After you went to sleep, I was still awake, and so was Naomi, and Rose was just getting her day going, so I came downstairs and we had a little video chat."

"And you decided to move here?"

"Yes. I'll stay in Ethan's apartment building while I look around. I'll keep an eye on the real estate site for something that I want to buy."

"You're *moving* here?" he asked again.

"In September."

He shoved aside his half-eaten bagel, pulled her off her chair and dragged her upstairs.

It seemed he approved of the plan.

NELL LOOKED DOWN at herself as she approached Aaron's house that evening. She'd had fun with Jake at his shop, and it was obvious. Though she'd borrowed a pair of coveralls, there was still some dirt smeared across one shoulder of her top, and she should definitely not wear these shoes into Aaron's house. She'd scrubbed up, so her hands were clean, but there was an itch on her cheek telling her she may have missed a spot.

She hadn't intended to get dirty at Bighorn Automotive, but she'd told Jake about the Porsche she'd restored, so he told her about an old Mazda he was working on, and one thing led to another until they'd spent an hour under the car together. She'd thoroughly enjoyed herself.

Using the garage-door opener Aaron had given her, she went inside. The garage opened up into the laundry room, and she left her shoes there. She could hear Aaron on the phone nearby, so she was quiet as she entered the kitchen.

He sat at the bar counter, the phone in front of him on video, telling Aubrey her singing was amazing. He looked up at her entrance, his gaze running over her. His lips quirked, and he waved her to him. When she approached, he swung the seat around and pulled her onto his lap.

She watched the screen as Aubrey babbled in Beth's arms. CC looked over Beth's shoulder and saw Nell, and spoke over the baby.

"Nell! We just heard that you're moving to Colorado. I want to be happy for you but it was nice having you in our state, giving this one another reason to come visit."

"True, but I'll just drag him with me when I go visit my parents. Also, have you been to Hawaii? Because my grandma's house is large, and she always wants me to bring people when I come visit."

"Oh, you're *good*. You're very good, and we like that," CC said with an appreciative grin. "And no, I've never been to Hawaii, so let's make that happen."

When they hung up, she turned around and looked at Aaron. "Did I overstep?"

He frowned. "What do you mean?"

"Asking your friends if they wanted to go to Hawaii?"

"Family is super important to you, if I've read you correctly. You're offering to treat my friends like family."

"Well, yeah, I guess that's about right. Except I don't think Beth, CC and Aubrey are your friends. I think they're *your* family."

"Then, no. I don't think you overstepped. I think you were being you. And you may recall, I like you."

She wasn't sure there was really anything to say to that.

"I got good gossip from Jake," she told him.

"Yay?"

She bumped his shoulder. "Word is that George was seen mowing Francine's lawn early on Sunday morning."

He frowned. "I know they're divorced, but they run the store together. We've seen them together ourselves, several times. Why is it weird that he's doing that for her?"

"Because his car wasn't parked on the street, it was in the garage. Which was open, of course, since he'd pulled the lawn mower out."

"Okay?"

She sighed. "So, speculation is that he got there the night before, parked in the garage, and was still there the next morning."

"Ah. Will you tell Rose?"

Janelle laughed. "I'm pretty sure Jake already told Ethan."

"Do you think it's a good thing or a bad thing? If they get together."

"I think it's great, if they're happy. If they have issues, it will suck for Rose."

"Then I'm happy for them. So, do you want to stay dressed as you are and we can walk to get pizza, or do you want to change and go to the fancy restaurant? Or the barbecue place?"

"I'll change tops, and check my face, but let's do pizza."

"Sounds good. And since you're going to be getting at least partly naked, tell me—how hungry are you?"

She pursed her lips. Then gave him an eyebrow waggle and turned to race up the stairs, pulling her shirt over her head as she went. She'd decided that all the sex and walking around town meant she could forget about her stairs rule while in Wildlife Ridge, so she let him catch her at the top of the landing.

AARON WAS glad Nell had gone out of the house after lunch. When she'd told him that morning she was moving to Wildlife Ridge, he'd been happy. When she'd left, he'd wondered if the happiness would change to worry or concern.

Instead, he was annoyed that she was waiting two months to make it happen.

He felt like he knew her well enough to trust that if things went south, they could still coexist in the same town. Maybe he was wrong, but if the worst that happened was that he'd decide to pack up and move to Europe, so be it.

After working on a painting meant for the home decor section of a large department store, then having lunch with Nell, he'd sent her on her way and started a new painting. One that centered around her gorgeous face. And amazing hair. Those bright eyes. Kissable lips. The little freckles above her top lip. He would have felt weird painting it while she was downstairs reading a book.

He'd never painted a lover before. And he rarely painted portraits. But her face was always in his brain, and he wanted to see it on his canvas. Wanted *her* on his canvas. It wouldn't be for sale, he was sure of that. Maybe, if she did suddenly turn into a crazy person, he'd burn the finished painting and feel better. Or maybe not.

In the meantime, he needed to keep her out of his studio. This was one painting he didn't want seen until it was finished.

When she'd re-dressed and came down the stairs, he considered going right back up again. Her jeans were skin-tight, her top a sort of wrap thing that crisscrossed between her breasts. Silver dangled from her ears, almost to her shoulders, and made him want to tease her neck. Again.

"Should we walk or drive?" she asked. "I was thinking after pizza we can stop at Cougars, check out Wolfhound Tavern's competition. I passed by there when I walked to the garage this afternoon, and it looked nice and dive bar-ish."

"And that's a good thing?"

She grinned. "Could be fun. Could be awful. Don't you want to know, either way?"

"I guess I do. Let's drive."

"Okay, my turn?"

He tossed her the keys, and she was so surprised she almost missed them. Then she gave a little happy dance and marched out to the garage, her little purse bumping against her side.

She got in and spent a couple of minutes adjusting the seat and mirrors before turning on the car. The sound of the engine seemed to please her as she ran her hands lovingly over the leather steering wheel.

When she put it in reverse and studied the display screen that showed the rearview camera, he decided he might as well get comfortable, as the three-minute drive he'd been envisioning was looking like a much different reality.

She tested his turn signals. Then the emergency break. Then the navigation.

Finally, she turned to him, said "nice" and started to back out of the garage.

He chuckled, and she flashed him a grin before turning onto the road and heading into town. When they reached the intersection for Main Street, a car painted to look like a ladybug drove past.

"Oh, hey!" Nell pointed. "It's the same car I saw as a snake."

"I think it's the same one I saw as a lion last month."

"We are definitely going to have to ask about that. I have questions."

She turned onto Main and paused to let a family of four dart across the street to the Starbucks. Only a moment later, she was turning into the parking lot behind the strip mall that held the pizza joint.

When they got out, she waited for him to come around and handed back his key fob. "Thanks, that was fun."

"No problem."

There were ten shops in the two-story building, with City Pizza below Wildlife Ridge Florist and next to Sammie's Liquor. When they walked in, it was bustling. All the tables were taken and there was a short line of folks waiting to order.

"Okay, so maybe we take it home, or to the park, and then we can walk over to Cougars after," he suggested.

The woman in front of them turned around before Nell could answer.

"Janelle, Aaron, how nice to see you again. You remember me from the wedding? Shirley Romano?"

"Sure, Mayor Shirley," Nell said.

The older woman laughed. "Just Shirley is fine. My husband grabbed a four-top table over there, would you like to join us?" She gestured to the dining room and Tom, who was chatting with a man at the table next to him.

He looked to Nell, who nodded. "That would be great, thanks."

"Have you eaten here yet? The pizza is great, but I'm a hot wings fan myself."

They discussed the menu and favorite pizzas to be had around the country, then took their order numbers to the table and joined Tom.

"Maybe you guys can answer a question we had," Aaron said when they'd settled in. "Nell and I have seen this car around town a couple of times. Painted like different animals?"

"Ah," Tom said. "That would be David Zieglar. He's a real estate agent here in town, though he covers a much wider area, of course. His office is next to the hardware store."

"Okay, yeah, we walked past that office," Nell said.

"Right, well, David's hobby is that car. He paints it up every month, then strips it and does it again. He's gotten quite good at it, I'd say."

"Yes, it was a little more questionable in the early years," Shirley added. "He has another car he uses if he's driving with clients who are from out of town, but that car's his baby."

"It's fun," Nell said. "I thought the snake was well done."

"I can't even imagine trying to do the artwork on a car like that," Aaron agreed.

"Do you think you'd want to do a show here in town?" Shirley asked abruptly.

Aaron blinked at her. He'd honestly never considered such a thing. Did they get enough people who'd want to spend that kind of money? He knew there were tourists in town, but he had no idea if they were the kind who'd spend big art money.

She must have seen his confusion, because she laughed. "I don't know if it's doable, I'm just throwing out ideas. I have to admit to a complete lack of knowledge about the art world. But I bet we could figure something out."

"Well," he said slowly. "Normally there would be a gallery first, but I know some small towns have worked out alternatives. We could talk about it, if you'd like."

"Let me do some research," she said. "Nell, when are you moving out here to keep Rose in line?" she teased just as the food arrived.

Aaron had the distinct impression that just because she'd changed the subject and recognized the lack of a gallery, didn't mean the possibility of some sort of showing was gone from her mind.

When the food was plated, a mix of pizza and wings for all of them to share, Nell turned to Shirley. "As a matter of fact, Naomi and I have both decided to move here. Sometime in September. We haven't told anyone yet."

"That's wonderful news!" Shirley exclaimed as Tom high-fived Aaron. "Well done, Aaron, bringing in more fresh young people."

"I'm afraid I can't take much credit," he admitted. "I think you've got to give this one to Rose, Ethan and Wildlife Ridge's charms."

"Well, maybe a tiny bit of credit," Nell said, bumping him with her shoulder.

He made sure his hand was free of pizza grease before running it along her thigh, giving it a little squeeze. The food really was delicious, but maybe that was just because he was in an excellent mood.

Which reminded him...

He excused himself to use the restroom, went out the back door and jogged up the stairs to the florist. There were no other customers inside, so it only took him a couple of minutes to get a pretty little vase of flowers and deposit them in the back of the SUV.

When he returned to the table, the couple was telling Nell about the beautiful trails in Beddow State Park that she should try out.

"Did I hear you guys mention going to Cougars?" Shirley asked as they polished off the last of the pizza.

"That's what we were thinking," Nell told her. "We went to Wolfhound Tavern last night, and that was fun. We thought we'd give the competition a try."

"It's less country, more rock," Tom said. "They don't really have a kitchen, and they're not so big on the microbrews like Taphouse is. They have more pool tables than Wolfhound."

"Just don't tell Ian you went," Shirley said with a wink.

"We'll keep it to ourselves," Nell promised.

"Won't do any good," Tom pointed out. "He'll have heard before you finish your first beer."

Aaron had to laugh at that.

After saying their goodbyes, they drove back down Main Street and parked behind Cougars. The difference between this bar and last night's was apparent as soon as they opened the door. For one thing, he had to wait a good twenty seconds before his eyes adjusted to the dim lighting. It was smaller, but managed to pack in four pool tables and about a dozen tables to sit, in addition to the L-shaped bar. Maybe Nell's eyes adapted better than his, because she took his hand and pulled him to the bar just as he was ready to start moving.

The music was loud, with a rock song he recognized, though he couldn't identify it. As Tom had said, there were no fancy microbrews but plenty of choices. He asked for a Sam Adams and Nell ordered a Modelo. They took the bottles and moved past the jukebox, where two young women were enthusiastically pushing buttons, and found an empty table.

There was a small stage that he hadn't noticed early, in the far corner. A sign above it proclaimed karaoke was on Thursday nights at eight. He gestured at it. "Have you ever?"

She dropped her head into her hands. "Don't make me relive the horror," she begged. "I'll just say college and drunk and leave it at that. And we're going to need to leave by seven forty-five."

He managed not to laugh. "Clearly you were traumatized."

"Definitely. Maybe someday I can work past it, but today is not that day. How about you?"

"I've never done it, and the world should be thankful for that."

She laughed and waved at someone across the room. "Trisha works at the bakery," she told him. "She lives in Ethan's apartment building."

"I think you might already know more people in town than I do," he admitted.

"Is that a good thing or a bad thing?"

"Neither, just an observation." He'd met more people since knowing her than he had in…well, he couldn't even say. He supposed he would have started coming into town, eventually, but he doubted he would have been as open to embracing the residents, without her influence. "You must have a lot of friends in Los Angeles. Are you going to have a hard time leaving?"

"A lot of my college friends have already gone back to their hometowns, or married and moved on, or got jobs in other cities, that kind of thing. There are still people in the city I get together with, but I've been making peace with the idea of leaving for several years now."

"And you'll have Rose and Naomi here."

"Yes! I'm super excited about that. We had already vowed to visit each other often, but we honestly never considered moving to the same place, which seems kind of silly, in retrospect. I mean, we were pretty much looking for the same thing. Small town, close-ish to a big city."

"I'm surprised," he agreed.

"I guess sometimes you get wrapped up in your plans and don't pull back for the big-picture view."

"I can see that." Hadn't he done the same?

All of the pool tables were occupied and it was getting closer to eight, so when they finished their drinks, he paid the tab and they headed home.

When he pulled into the garage, he surprised her by going around to the back of the car and opening the hatch. He pulled out the vase of flowers and handed it to her.

"Happy two months since we met," he said.

Her astonishment was evident. She took the vase but wrapped her arms around him and lay her cheek on his shoulder. "I really like you," she whispered.

"I'm glad."

"Let's go swimming," she said, and led the way into the house. She put water into the vase and set it on the kitchen counter, fussing with the flowers for a bit with a goofy smile. Then she took a picture and looked around for him, held out her hand, and led him upstairs to change.

CHAPTER EIGHTEEN

Janelle woke up in a very good mood on Friday. The flowers on the counter during breakfast made her smile. The goodbye kiss to Aaron as he went upstairs to paint made her smile. The beautiful day made her smile. She decided she'd make one of her favorite soups for dinner, since she had a bit of time before she needed to be on the laptop for her meeting.

She walked to the grocery store, waving hello to several people she recognized and a few she didn't. Her wait in line was short, but she had a lovely conversation with a mom and her little girl about the girl's stuffed bunny.

A van was pulling away as she walked back up the driveway, and when she went into the kitchen, Aaron was moving plastic packets of food from a box into the freezer. She put her bags on the counter and looked over his shoulder at the recipe cards he was holding.

"They look pretty good," she admitted.

"They are. We can have a couple tomorrow so you can see I'm not force-feeding myself boiled cardboard."

Laughing, she unpacked her groceries. She moved around the kitchen, pulling out what she needed.

"For someone who doesn't cook, you do have a pretty good selection of the basics," she said.

"Before I moved in, CC, Beth and I went to the store and they filled my cart with stuff."

"That would explain why some of it is put away in places that make zero sense."

"Feel free to move anything around. I probably won't even notice. Does it bother you?"

The change in his tone had her popping up from the cupboard where she'd been examining a selection of plastic cutting boards. "Does it bother me that your silverware is next to the refrigerator instead of the dishwasher? Not really, though I might eventually take you up on the offer to move things around, if you really wouldn't care."

"I really wouldn't care, but no. I meant that I don't cook. I didn't exactly spend much time with my mom in the kitchen. I'm pretty sure that if I'd tried, she would have accused me of being gay in very unflattering terms. Not that I wanted to try, anyway."

She walked around the counter and he turned to meet her. Walking straight in, she wrapped her arms tight around him. "Baby, I don't care that you don't even toast your bagel. I'm just glad you have a toaster. If you want to cook with me sometime, great. If you want to watch TV or sit at the counter and drink wine while I cook, great. I'm just glad you're enough of an adult to have figured out a way to feed yourself good, healthy meals without having to eat out every single day."

He squeezed her tight, then leaned back so she looked up at his face. "How long does it take to do what you're doing?"

"Less than an hour."

"Okay. Maybe I'll sit here and watch you."

"But no wine," she teased.

"It's not my fault you decided to cook dinner at nine in the morning."

"You'll thank me for it, later. When all the goodness has simmered together to create greatness."

"I'll thank you for it now," he said, bending down to kiss her. "Thank you."

"My pleasure. You want some orange juice instead of wine?"

"I'll get it."

She went back to selecting two cutting boards and pushed away the sadness she felt for the little boy who'd grown into a strong man who knew how to take care of himself.

"Wow," he said when she'd finished chopping the first onion.

She looked up. "What?"

"You're good at that."

"Eh. Okay, I guess, but I wouldn't say I'm above average. Do you ever watch cooking shows?"

"No."

"Ah, well then. Trust me on this one."

"Did you learn to cook from your parents?"

"Yes, and grandparents. My dad cooks a lot, my mom has a few signature dishes. Grandma Yuki is a great baker. I picked up some from all of them. I wouldn't say I'm passionate about cooking, but it was a great way to cut down on expenses when the three of us started playing with our budgets."

"Groceries versus eating out."

"Right, but also eating in together instead of always going out to socialize."

She finished with the onions and poured a glug of olive oil into the Dutch oven she'd set on the stove. She fussed with the heat until she had it where she wanted and turned to the meat.

Opening the package of boneless porkchops, she dumped them out onto the second cutting board and threw the package away. She picked up the board with the onions and swept them into the hot oil, gave them a little stir, then went back to the pork.

"But you three never lived together?" Aaron asked as she diced the meat.

"Nope. It never worked out that way. Naomi and I are considering sharing an apartment in September, since she'll probably move into one of her units once the building is ready. She'll only need the apartment for a short time."

He cleared his throat. "You know, you could move in here."

She glanced up at him, cocked her head. "You don't think it's too early for that?"

"It's earlier than I would have expected, but…it's you."

Her heart melted. "I don't disagree, but I don't want to move in because it's convenient. And it's easy enough to stay at Salmon Springs. It's so close, anyway. But I'm glad that we're on the same page. I feel good about what we have going here."

He raised his orange juice glass to her. "Good. Me too."

The gleam in his eye made her wonder if they were actually on the same page, or if he was waiting until the right time to give her a nudge to move in.

"Have you ever moved in with a partner?" he asked.

She turned and stirred the onions a bit. "No. And I always figured that I would insist on moving into a new place together, rather than one person moving into another's space. But I guess that's pretty dependent on circumstances."

"Yeah, I would think so."

She peeked up at him without lifting her head. Looking a little less cocky now, she mused. "How about you?" she asked.

"Once. About ten years ago. She was a little younger, so just finishing college, where she'd had three roommates. She moved into my apartment."

"Did she pay rent?"

"We decided she should concentrate on paying off her student loans, instead. So she paid what she would have paid in rent as additional payments to the loans."

"Nice. How long did you live together?" She switched back to the other cutting board and started on the garlic.

"A little over two years."

"And when it ended, how did that go?"

"Eh. We weren't exactly friends at the end, but we weren't

assholes. She found a place pretty quickly, I helped her cart her stuff over."

"She had savings for a deposit?"

"No. She'd really put all her extra cash towards the loans. Which is what we had decided on, together."

"So…"

"So I gave her the deposit money and two months' rent."

She smiled at him then turned to check the onions. Looking good. She spooned them out onto a plate and added some more oil to the pot. "How had she done with her loans at that point?"

"Almost had them knocked out. I gave her the rest to bring it to zero."

"Hm. More than ten thousand, or less?" She slid the diced-up pork into the pan and turned back around.

"A little less." He shrugged.

"You're a good guy, Aaron."

"It's not so hard. Helps when you have money. By then, I'd started selling the commercial stuff regularly enough that I was comfortable. And I'd sold my first big piece not too long before we broke up."

"Yes, it does help."

She opened the cans of tomatoes and chilies, then pulled out a bottle of beer and popped the top. She lined them all up for when she needed them.

"Wow, really? Beer?" Aaron asked.

She laughed. "Yes, sometimes we put beer or wine or even liquor into food as we're cooking."

"Hm, maybe I should look into this some more."

She opened the hamburger and slid it into the pot, threw away the package, and stirred it all together. The smells were definitely making her happy.

"I should probably at least offer to help clean up," he said. "But I'd be worried I'd toss something you're still using."

"You're totally fine, I'm enjoying the company."

"Have you ever had a cooking disaster?"

"Oh, boy. The worst. I had roasted a chicken for dinner and decided I was going to be super awesome and make stock from the carcass."

"Sounds good so far."

"Right, so to make stock, you put the bones, some veggies and spices into a pot, add water, and let it simmer for a long time. You skim some stuff off the top, but just let it do its thing for hours. Then you strain the liquid, throw the rest away, and you have nice, flavorful chicken broth."

She stirred the meat and added in the garlic, chili powder and cumin, gave it another stir then started to clean up. She put the cutting boards in the dishwasher and opened the beef broth.

"So…I put the colander in the sink and dumped the whole pot into it."

He frowned.

"Yeah. I dumped the broth right down the sink drain and caught all the garbage."

"Oops."

"I was not happy."

"I guess not."

She stirred some more, then added the tomatoes, broth, beer, chilies, coriander, oregano, salt and the plate of cooked onions. She nudged the heat up.

"I guess it's not too tragic. Luckily, I was the only witness to the incident and my dramatic sorrow."

He laughed as she rinsed out the cans and threw them into the recycle bin.

"Do you have any favorite dishes you'd like me to try out?" she asked as she gave the soup another stir.

He didn't answer, so she looked at him over her shoulder.

"I'll think about it."

"Good." She moved to him. "There, that wasn't too bad, was it?"

"Relatively painless. That's it?"

"Yep. That'll come to a boil in a minute. I'll drop the heat and let it simmer for three hours, then add the beans. We can have some for lunch or save it for dinner. It will only get more flavorful the longer we wait."

"Let's save it for dinner then."

She kissed him. "It's a plan."

"I love you."

Janelle froze, her lips an inch from his. She dropped down to her heels and studied his face. He was watching hers intently. She could see a bit of nerves, but a lot of certainty.

"It's kind of crazy, isn't it?" she asked. "I feel like it's way too soon. But…I love you, too."

"I don't care if it's crazy. I just know it feels very right."

"It does." And it did. She didn't feel anxiety over saying the words—only that the feeling wouldn't last. She'd never felt this way before, and she didn't want it to end. She wanted it to simmer and just keep getting better and better.

CHAPTER NINETEEN

Janelle wasn't surprised that the move went smoothly. She and Naomi both happened to be people who loved to organize and plan. It was simply a matter of doing some research, making lists, making plans, more lists, and adapting when things invariably went screwy.

Aaron flew out the week before and helped them both with packing and carting boxes around. The truck arrived on Friday and the movers loaded the furniture they were keeping, which wasn't much, and the boxes, which were plenty.

They'd slapped orange duct tape on Nell's boxes and blue on Naomi's, so they could easily separate them at the apartment. Naomi decided to sell her old car and pick up a truck or SUV when she got to Colorado. Aaron had offered to drive back Nell's car to Wildlife Springs with her, as had Naomi, but her dad had been the clear choice.

Her parents had long known her plans to leave eventually, and they fully supported her, but they were sad to see her leaving the state.

"Who knows," she'd told her mom. "You could always move to Wildlife Springs, too. Wait until you come visit."

Her mom, a die-hard sun worshiper, had shuddered. "How about we plan to go to Hawaii at the same time?" she'd suggested.

"Okay, Mom, but you do have to come visit occasionally. You can come in the summer."

Aaron had met her parents when he'd come out for Fourth of July, and it had gone well. He was a charmer, after all. And her parents had long moved past the grilling-of-her-partners-as-adversaries stage, and were well into the hoping-to-become-grandparents stage. Though they appropriately made no mention of such things in his presence.

Quitting her job hadn't gone exactly as she'd expected. Instead of being annoyed that he'd have to deal with someone else, even if that someone was her coworker, who she'd been training for years to take over for her, he accused her of going to the competition.

When she told him that wasn't the case, he'd accused her of starting her own business to compete with him.

When she'd told him that was not the case, either, he'd accused her of lying, tried to get her to sign a nondisclosure and noncompete agreement, and told her she shouldn't bother coming in the next day.

Even for Tony the Asshole, the paranoia and shittiness had been unexpected. But, hey, it gave her plenty of time to pack up at her leisure. She even took a weeklong trip to Hawaii to hang out with Grandma. Aaron had flown out to join them for a long weekend and been drafted into helping make saimin, Grandma's specialty Hawaiian soup.

He'd been uncomfortable and uncertain, but Grandma had put him at ease fairly quickly, and he'd proudly shown off the results at dinner. The visit had been a huge success.

Now she'd made it to Wildlife Ridge, and though she'd wanted to spend the night at Aaron's, she'd shared Naomi's bed and given hers to her dad. Today, they were having a barbecue at Aaron's and she would, again, go back to the apartment. Then she'd drive her dad to the airport and her life in Colorado would truly begin.

She was excited on a lot of levels, but as she watched Aaron handing towels to Naomi to take outside, she had to admit that he was a huge part of it. She loved him and being able to see him every day was making her a bit giddy.

Her dad, loaded down with a tray of meat destined for the grill, winked at her as he walked by. Janelle had grabbed the fruit salad she'd bought premade, feeling no guilt considering how hard they'd worked to unpack everything, when the doorbell rang.

Aaron just shrugged when she looked his way, so she continued to the backyard to put the salad on the table.

She and her dad were lighting the barbecue when Aaron reappeared with Jake Steele. The mechanic had trimmed his beard slightly, but was otherwise unchanged from June. She shook his hand and introduced him to her dad.

"I'm sorry to interrupt," he began, as her dad moved off and Aaron stayed by her side. "I heard you were in town and having yourselves a bit of a barbecue here, so I hoped you wouldn't mind a quick chat."

Aaron glanced at her, then back to Jake. "Did we screw up? Should we have invited people? Are we pissing the neighbors off already?"

Jake laughed in a way that transformed him from grizzly old man to everyone's favorite grandfather. "No, that's not what I meant. But I was at the grocery store and it was mentioned, so I figured I wasn't breaking in on a quiet family meal or something like that."

"Oh, okay. Good."

"But if you wanted to have a little welcome home barbecue for Ethan and Rose in October, and invite some folks, that would go over pretty well."

Aaron nodded. "We'll run that past them."

The fact that her ex-hermit didn't even hesitate with that made Janelle incredibly happy. He really seemed to have embraced life in Wildlife Ridge, as well as her friends and family.

"Janelle, you'd asked me about how much mechanic work folks

here needed, and if I'd be upset if you did some stuff on the side, helping out friends for a bit of money and all that."

"Right." She hadn't been too worried about finding more work, knowing she could do a little bit of that. She'd futzed around online a bit looking for some remote work options, but hadn't seen anything that appealed. They'd mostly been for full time, and it was amazing how quickly she'd gotten past any desire to do that.

"I've been thinking on things since we had that talk. My boy, Jasper, he just graduated high school and he's off to Denver next week for college."

The pride in his voice was unmistakable, and Nell gave him a big grin. "That's awesome, congratulations to him."

"Thanks, Nell. He's been working with me at the shop these last three years, I've gotten to the point where he's doing most of the oil changes, tune-ups, the basics. He's going to take some courses, business and mechanic, and he'll get the shop one day."

Aaron gestured to the table where she'd set the fruit salad and they'd put out a pitcher of water and a pitcher of margaritas. "Why don't we sit down? Would you like something to drink, Jake?"

"A seat would be nice, but no drink, thank you. I promise not to take more than a few more minutes."

"No problem," Nell assured him as they took seats.

"My wife was strict, wouldn't let Jasper put in more than ten hours a week, so that he didn't have that distracting him from school or socializing."

"I think I like her," Nell said.

"She's a good mama, that's for sure." More pride in his scratchy voice. "Anyhow, what I'd gotten to thinking about was that it was already a bit difficult, as I'd mentioned, turning townspeople away for work, even with Jasper's help. I'd surely hate to start turning away more. Any chance you'd like to put in those ten hours for a few years, maybe even a few more than ten, if you feel like it? I'd also let you store a project car there, if you wanted to work on another Porsche, or the like."

"Oh," she managed, thinking hard. "That's a thought, isn't it? A very interesting thought. Let's run some numbers and I'll mull it over a bit, and let you know right away."

They did just that and then she waved him off, after he once again turned down the offer of food or drink. She returned to the kitchen to find Aaron grabbing the chips and dip they'd bought.

"Hey," she said.

He looked over. "Hey. That was pretty convenient, wasn't it? See, I told you everything would work out if you moved here."

She laughed. "Did you? Huh, I don't really remember that conversation." She wrapped her arms around him, leaned back to watch his face. "You don't mind?"

The genuine confusion on his face went a long way toward relieving her bit of worry.

"Mind if you work?"

"Mind if I work as a mechanic."

He frowned. "Is this back to thinking I'm a snob? Do you really think I have a problem with it?"

"I guess I wasn't sure, so that's why I asked."

He put his hands on her shoulder. "I have zero problem with it. None. I promise."

She blew out a breath. "Okay. Sorry."

Naomi walked in carrying Janelle's phone.

"This has rung three times. We checked the screen the last time, and it was Tony the Asshole."

"You're kidding me." She reached out for the phone and opened recent calls. Yep, three from Tony in five minutes. It rang as she stared at the screen, but this time it was Annette, who'd worked in the office with her.

She shrugged her shoulders at Naomi and Aaron and answered the phone as she headed back outside. "Hey, Annette."

"Oh my god, he's losing his mind, are you ignoring his calls? And hey, how are you? I want to hear all about it. Later. But first—"

"I wasn't avoiding his calls, I was actually in a different room from the phone until just now."

"Wow, really?"

She laughed and wandered over to the barbecue, where her dad had started the meat. "Really. I don't need to be reachable at all times anymore. And besides, isn't it Saturday? I may have lost track, but I thought it was Saturday."

"It is. But he really, really wants to talk to you. Did you hear about Jonie?"

She turned away from the grill and went to sit on a lounger. "What about Jonie? Is she okay?" Her friend had been the one she'd trained to take over for her.

"She quit. Last week. With no notice."

"Holy crap!"

"Yeah, it's been bad here. We didn't want to bug you while you were in the middle of your move."

"I'm so sorry."

"Don't be, it's not your fault. I told him I'd call and see if you'd answer for him, but my advice is to not bother."

"Eh, I don't mind listening to him. Maybe I can figure out something to say to make it better for you guys."

"I wouldn't spend too much time trying to think of those magical words," Annette said with a laugh.

"I'll give him a call. If he annoys me, I'll hang up and block his number."

"Okay, sounds like a plan. When you have some time, give me a call and we'll catch up."

"I will. I miss you guys."

"We miss you!"

She hung up and saw that Naomi was floating on a raft, but holding on to the edge of the pool nearby so she could listen. Aaron had poured her a margarita, and he held it out to her now.

"Jonie quit without notice."

Naomi snorted. "Color me surprised."

"I *am* surprised. She's worked there for six years, she knows what he's like, she knows what I did, and she agreed to do it."

"She knew what she could see, but you handled so much, handled *him* so they wouldn't have to deal with him."

"I guess. I mean, I wasn't secretive about it, I would tell them things. I had to, so they could cover for me and be backup."

"Apparently it wasn't enough. Or he's stepped up the Asshole bit."

"Maybe. I'm going to call him."

"You don't have to," her dad reminded her.

"Oh, I'm way too curious not to."

AARON WATCHED as Janelle took a healthy swallow of her margarita, put the glass down then picked her phone back up and called her old boss. He wasn't worried she would suddenly change her mind and move back to Los Angeles, but he *was* worried that the man she'd dubbed Tony the Asshole would say something to upset her.

"Hey, Aaron, can you bring me a clean plate to put this meat on?" Andrew called to him.

Aaron did so, and tried to ignore the conversation happening twenty feet away.

"She'll be fine, she never did take any of his shit," her dad explained. "Which is probably why he respected her more than the others. The more she was willing to tell him to fuck off, the more he respected her. Especially because she wouldn't have actually disrespected him, she would have done it professionally."

"She mentioned that the closer she got to her financial freedom, the more he gave her raises."

"Yeah, the guy's an asshole, but he's not an idiot."

"The meat smells great," Aaron said, as the plate he was holding was piled high. "Thanks for handling the barbecue."

They moved to the table and took seats.

"One of my pleasures in life. I have to admit, I've known my girl would be leaving California for a while now, but I kept hoping it would be later and later, even while knowing she shouldn't put up with that dumbass for too long. I'm sad to see her go, but this is a beautiful town here, and she already seems one hundred times more relaxed." He gestured at the mountains around them. "Beautiful."

"It is. She wants to try hiking, go explore the state park that's nearby. Would you want to try and do that before you leave?"

"No, I'll let her get settled in, and her mother and I'll come out for a visit then. When it's warmer. My wife is not a fan of snow. Maybe we'll invest in some hiking boots back home and break them in before we come."

"Good plan."

"Are you interested in hiking?"

"Well, I'll tell you…its charms are a lot more appealing to me now than they were a year ago."

"My girl has a way."

"That she does. Do you think she'll take this job with Jake?"

"Probably. I know she loves to tinker with the cars and doesn't want to sit home on her butt all day, so why not?"

"That's what I'm guessing, too. Though I'd hoped she'd take some time off for herself, first."

"Well, she's had two months without working, that's pretty huge."

"True. I didn't really think of it that way, since moving was a job on its own."

"Bah, hardly a chore for her and Naomi. They had it all figured out in the first week."

Aaron was about to agree when he saw Nell put her phone down and go to Naomi, who took her hand and allowed her raft to be pulled to the steps. They were laughing when they reached the table and immediately started in on the food.

"Starving!" Janelle said and began to fill her plate, Naomi right there with her.

"So, what did he say?" Andrew asked.

"He offered me a job, working remotely. When I told him no, he said it could be part time. I couldn't hold back my laugh at that one."

"And how did he react to that?" Aaron asked, pouring fresh drinks for everyone.

"Oh, it pissed him off. He tried to blame me for Jonie being, and I quote, 'useless.' I hung up."

"Bravo!" Naomi said, lifting her glass. They all toasted to that.

They'd almost finished eating when her phone rang again. She glanced over and nodded to confirm it was Tony, since she was in the middle of chewing her burger.

Naomi jumped up, grabbed her phone, and motioned Nell over to the side of the pool. "Grab your margarita."

Nell finished her bite and grabbed her glass. She posed, drink raised to the camera, background of sparkling pool and majestic mountains, until Naomi was satisfied, then they returned to the table.

"I shouldn't," Nell murmured as they scrolled through the shots. "It will piss him off, but also encourage him."

"This is the one," Naomi declared.

"Let me send it to Rose while I think about it."

Aaron left them to it and started carting the leftovers back to the house. Andrew followed his lead. "If you can't be the cook or the mechanic, be excellent support staff, right?"

Aaron had no answer to that, and he glanced back at Nell to find her watching him. She rolled her eyes and turned back to her phone.

"Of course, you don't have to be super handy when you've managed this level of success," Andrew continued as they reached the kitchen. "It's a great house, and Nell tells us your art is really doing well."

He took a deep breath and pushed his annoyance aside. The man was trying to be friendly and get to know his daughter's lover. The one she'd moved one thousand miles away, in part, to be with. "I've been lucky. Both sides of my career have done well, and it's pretty great to do something I love and make good money from it."

"When Nell first told us her plan to retire early, we thought she was crazy. But the fact that she never loved her job, never had anything she wanted to pursue with passion…that decided it for me.

Truthfully, if she'd come to me early on and said she wanted to be a mechanic, I probably would have resisted that, too."

"Do you think she's passionate about that?"

"No, I think she just enjoys it, but maybe she'll become passionate, now that she has time to do it more. And if not, that's okay, because she's found her way to success without it. But I'm glad she doesn't have to put up with a job she just tolerates any longer."

"Yes, me too."

When they made it back outside, Naomi looked disappointed and Nell looked amused. "How about this," Nell said. "I would guess there's a decent chance he'll check my social media. I'll post the pic to Instagram."

Naomi pursed her lips while she considered. "Okay. I can live with that."

Nell clicked around on the phone and then sat back with a grin. "Much less petty this way, but still satisfying."

The ladies swam and floated in the pool while Andrew called home to his wife, and Aaron sat and watched while checking his emails. Apparently he wasn't watching well enough, because the light spray of water that splashed him was a complete surprise.

He looked up to find Nell smiling at him. When her smile slid away, he wasn't sure why.

"Hey," he said, looking past her to see that Naomi was back to floating on the raft. He looked around. Andrew was still inside. Nell made a move to join him, and he spread his legs to give her space.

"Hey. I'm sorry my dad said something stupid. He didn't mean it like that."

"I know, don't worry about it."

She put her wet hand to his cheek. "No, don't pretend it didn't hurt. He's trying to bond with you and only knows a few things about you so far. He cooks, but he's useless with cars and very much not handy around the house, so he figured that was something you guys had in common. He doesn't know that you're a master with a drill and can put together IKEA furniture without even reading the directions."

He barked a laugh at that, but she wasn't finished.

"Not that it would matter if you were useless with a drill, like he is, or whatever. I'm just pointing out what he was saying had more to do with being proud about what I can do, and pretty much nothing about what *you* can or can't do. *And*, I'll point out one more thing," she added, poking him in the chest. "I have zero doubts that if you wanted to do either of those things, you could. But since you couldn't give two shits about them, there's no reason to. Unless you're at Grandma's house."

The rock that had taken up residence in his chest melted away. He hadn't even realized he'd gotten so…glum over Andrew's words, but Nell had known. Had seen. Had understood. And had fixed it.

"Sorry, I didn't mean to be a downer."

"Psh. It only makes sense that a father figure's offhand remarks would have much more impact on you than logic would have you think."

"I hadn't even thought of it like that," he admitted.

"It's easier to see in someone else," she pointed out.

"I love you. Are you sure you can't stay the night?"

She smiled and kissed him. "I love you, too. Not tonight. But maybe I can cook you dinner on Sunday and breakfast on Monday?"

"While I enjoy your cooking, that's not why I want you here."

"I know. You've got your admittedly pretty-good frozen meals for that."

"Then it's a plan. I'll assume that from now into the future, I don't need to say out loud that you can invite Naomi—or whoever you want, really—at any time."

She smiled and kissed him again. He was on a roll. Or she was.

"I want you to myself on Sunday, but noted."

"Two job offers in one day, before you've actually settled into your new life."

"Crazy, right?"

"Somehow I think it's totally normal for you, actually."

She laughed. "Maybe so."

"Cheesecake," he said.

Her face scrunched up. "What?"

"A favorite food that would be cool if you know how to make it. I love cheesecake. The kind with that strawberry syrupy stuff. But I rarely order desserts in restaurants, so…"

"Cheesecake."

"Yeah."

"I think I can handle that."

"Thanks, baby."

She kissed. "Let's get wet."

He leered at her, but she just laughed and dragged him to the water.

CHAPTER TWENTY

Nell only cried a tiny bit when she waved her dad off at the airport. Naomi had come with her, and wrapped her arm around her waist and led her back to the new Honda CRV Janelle had helped her pick out. It was four years old and Naomi had paid cash. Nell had every reason to believe the vehicle would last her a long time.

They climbed in and headed home. *Hee*, she liked thinking of Wildlife Ridge as home. Tomorrow, she would go over to Bighorn Automotive and tell Jake he had a deal. She'd try out spending some hours at an actual shop and see what she thought. If she hated it—hell, even if she just wasn't loving it—she would quit and try something else.

"Hey, if you have a reason to go see your new building soon, let me know, I'll tag along."

"That would be fun, it's not a bad drive from Wildlife Ridge, only about forty-five minutes. Escrow closes next week, so I'll for sure go out for a final walk-through."

"Oh, cool, I'd love to do that with you."

"Then it's a date. I'll let you know when."

"Is it going to take a lot of work to get it fixed up how you want?"

"Not too much. But some of the other buildings I saw would take serious renovations. I'm hoping I learn enough with *this* to see if I want to tackle something like that in the future."

Janelle's phone rang, and she saw that it was Rose, so she put her on speakerphone.

"You guys on your way back?"

"Yeah, dropped him off about twenty minutes ago."

"I know it will be weird not having them so close to you anymore."

"Yeah. But we did a video call with my mom last night, and after only minor hiccups we managed to make it work."

"Good. How's Aaron?"

"I think he's good. I told him I'd stay the night tonight, so he's happy about that. He hasn't brought up my moving in with him again, instead of staying at the apartment, which is good. On the one hand, he thinks we're ready, but on the other hand, he knows I need to get settled in on my own first."

"I didn't want to ask, with your dad there, but was there a problem yesterday?" Naomi asked. "He seemed a little off for a while."

"I mentioned he didn't have a great family growing up. He was a little bothered by something Dad said, but we cleared it up. Plus, I think he feels a little weird that he's, sort of, seeking my parents' approval. He hasn't been in that situation in a long time, and he's opposed to the idea of it in general, but understands that they're important to me."

"Hm," Naomi mused. "Your parents are good people, I'm not worried about him seeing that. Or them seeing that he's good for you."

"Is he?" Nell asked. "I mean—that sounded bad. I'm in love with him, I like him, I think he's a great guy and an amazing artist. I don't think he's bad for me, but has he changed me? I don't know if that would be good or bad."

"He's good for you," Rose affirmed. "You don't need him, you're awesome as you are, but he makes you more confident. You didn't move to Wildlife Ridge for him, but I do think that being with him helped you get out of your rut and willing to make the changes you wanted to. You would have done it eventually, but I'm glad it was sooner rather than later."

"You ate a bagel for breakfast," Naomi said.

"And creamy cilantro dressing on your salad," Rose added.

"Um, what?"

Naomi laughed. "At first you were always dieting. Then, you stopped that, and you'd say you weren't really dieting, but you'd also eat shit like egg white omelets and salad with no dressing. Which, by the way, we've told you is unnecessary because you're healthy and beautiful."

"I still want to lose five pounds, but I think all the walking I'll be doing around town will help with that. And hiking; we're going to give that a go."

"The point is, you don't even think about your weight anymore, at least not that I've noticed."

Hm, that was true. "I had this little fear of becoming a spinster, in my guesthouse, maybe with a dozen cats, eating Oreos all day and ice cream all night."

"Seriously?" Rose asked.

"Kind of," she admitted.

"You're a dork," Naomi told her. "So, anyway, you're not thinking that anymore, you're more confident, you hung up on Tony the Asshole. Last night you were looking at hotels in New York City and said you wanted to go on a trip just for fun. I'm not saying Aaron gets the credit for all of that, I'm just saying he's good for you."

"Huh. Okay. I guess I can see that."

"*And,*" Rose said. "You get that goofy little look on your face when you talk about him."

"And when she sees him for the first time in a while," Naomi added.

"I don't look goofy," Janelle objected with a laugh.

"It's adorably goofy," Naomi reassured her.

"Hmph. Rose, how are you feeling about having less than two months left in Spain?"

"Oh, I'm going to be so sad to leave, but also so happy to come home. I want to see you guys, living right there, and get a cookie from Mrs. Rubinski and walk to the grocery store to see what kind of shenanigans people are up to, see my parents, maybe get a dog, maybe get pregnant, see all the fall colors."

"Hey now," Naomi said. "Back up a step or two. Maybe get pregnant?"

"We were thinking the time is right. We'll be good while we're here, but when we get home, we'll stop with the birth control."

"Aww, we'll be aunties!" Nell squealed. "I can't wait."

"I'm really happy for you guys," Naomi said.

"Well, we haven't done anything, yet."

"I'm sure you've done plenty, but making the decision is huge," Naomi said.

"Yeah. I'm not going to tell my parents until it happens, so keep your traps shut."

"Yeah, yeah," they agreed.

When they got home, she and Naomi worked on their boxes for a little while, then declared the job pretty much complete. There were some boxes left, but they were mostly things that would stay that way until they each settled into a more long-term situation.

Which reminded her, she wanted to check out the realtor in town, who's name she was forgetting but whose office was next to the hardware store. She figured even if she did move in with Aaron, if she'd bought a house first, she could always rent it out. Naomi would help her, and she thought it might be kind of fun to be a landlord.

She packed a small bag then found Naomi in the living room. "Are you annoyed I'm leaving the first night we're roommates with the apartment to ourselves?" she asked.

"Go to your man, you dork," Naomi answered, tossing a cheese puff at Janelle.

Janelle caught it and ate it with a grin. "Fine, then. I will!"

She drove her car and used the garage-door opener Aaron had given to her. The garage had plenty of space for her little sedan alongside his SUV. By the time she'd gotten out of the car, he was standing in the doorway, waiting for her. Her stomach did that little flutter thing it always did whenever she saw him again for the first time. She supposed she probably did get a goofy look, too.

"Your dad get off okay?" he asked as he wrapped his arms around her.

"And landed, safe back at home. My mother says he reported back that the town is cute, the apartment is good, your house is very nice and you're a good guy."

"So they're okay with you being gone?"

"Not yet, but they will be. They've always been okay with the idea, but the reality will take a little getting used to. They're hoping we'll meet them in Hawaii for Christmas." She tiptoed up and kissed his lips. "We have a little time to decide. Or, of course, if you had other ideas, we can discuss."

"I like that 'we.'"

"I like this we, too."

"I know you said you wanted to cook. Are you still feeling like doing that, or do you want to go out to dinner?"

"Hm. I think I'm feeling lazy. Have you tried the barbecue place yet?"

"No, I was waiting for you."

"You're so good to me."

"I keep telling you."

She laughed and went upstairs to put her bag down.

BBQ AND TAPHOUSE WAS, of course, right on Main Street, at the corner of Dragonfly Road, between the grocery store and

Wolfhound Tavern. Which meant Aaron had passed by it several times and been impressed by the scent of barbecued deliciousness coming from it. But he'd resisted going until Nell was back in town, and he was happy she'd suggested it.

While he'd waited for her to return to Wildlife Ridge, he'd finished the painting of her. It was pretty simple, her face kissed by the sun, a little bit of shade on her slightly windblown hair. Her expression serene, her eyes open and loving. He'd used a couple of photos and his memory, and thought it might be one of the best pieces he'd ever painted. He'd considered giving it to her parents. A sort of consolation prize when she'd moved away.

But…no. He was too selfish. He hadn't even sent a photo to his agent.

She came back downstairs, and he was confident the look in her eyes was represented in the painting.

She loved him. Hot damn.

He held his hand out to her, and they walked down the driveway and the empty Toad Lane. No game happening at the sports park today, he noted, as they made the turn onto Dragonfly Road.

"Let's cross the street and peek in the window of the realty office. I've been watching for listings online, of course, but I'd still like to meet this guy properly."

He wasn't fully onboard with her plan to buy a house if something suitable became available, but he wasn't exactly opposed, either. They'd only known each other four months, it was a big ask to have her give up her space and move in with him. But he also knew she'd never had her own house before, and it would be nice for her to experience that. Besides, it wouldn't be a big deal to go back and forth; it wasn't like the commute would be an issue.

The office was closed, but they looked at the listings that were pasted to the windows. Most of them were for the surrounding areas, and Denver.

When they reached Main Street, they ran into Erin Granger, who he'd briefly met at the wedding, but who had spent more time with Janelle at the bachelorette party. She introduced them to her daughter, Livvy, and her neighbor, Josh.

"I'm five," the little girl told them, unprompted.

"Wow, that's impressive," he said. "Are you in kindergarten?"

"Next year," she said solemnly. "Mr. Josh will be my teacher."

Erin laughed. "No, honey. Maybe for second grade, but first you have to go to kindergarten and then first grade."

Livvy did not look impressed with the news.

"That reminds me," Nell said. "Aaron, did you ever talk to Sandy and her friend from the elementary school?"

"Yes, we had lunch and a long talk about different ideas. But, really, they need to find an art teacher."

"Yes, they do," Josh agreed. "After your lunch with Sandy and Valerie, Val told us the ideas you guys came up with, but, yeah. The real conclusion is to figure out a way to entice someone up here to teach the class, and get the funding for them."

"We were walking to the barbecue place, did you guys want to join us?" Nell asked.

"Mr. Josh is taking us to get chicken fingers," Livvy told her.

"Oh, well that sounds lovely. You guys enjoy."

"We will," Livvy promised.

Josh and Erin said their goodbyes and headed off, while Janelle and Aaron continued down the street.

Nell gestured back toward the house converted into a doctor's office that they'd passed. "I can't quite convince myself to try the local doctor. I mean, what if we become friends? And then I have to ask them about bodily fluids. I think I'll look in Denver."

"That's what I did," he said. "I completely understand. But we're probably both silly."

She bumped his shoulder. "Please, you weren't worried about becoming friends, you were hiding from the whole town."

"Not for forever," he swore.

"Uh-huh."

They crossed Main Street and saw there were several groups

waiting on the benches out front at the Taphouse, and in the small lobby area.

"Let's see how long the wait is," Nell said. "I don't mind a little while, it smells so good out here."

They made it to the small stand and the middle-aged man who stood there.

"Hi, how long is the wait for two," Aaron asked.

The man tipped his head down slightly and answered in a low voice, "Only about five minutes for locals."

"Ah, great. Thanks." He held out his hand. "Aaron Romero, Janelle Bouchard. It's nice to meet you."

"Danny Browning, and the pleasure is mine." He shook both their hands. "My wife Fay is the cook," he added, giving a nod towards the back. "We're glad to have you here. Lots of tourists in town for this time of year, but we'll get you seated soon."

"Don't go to too much trouble," Nell said. "We don't mind a little wait."

"No trouble at all. We take care of our locals."

True to his word, they were seated less than ten minutes later. Which was good, because the smell was getting to Aaron and his stomach was rumbling. He recognized a couple of people sitting around them, but not many. The tables were covered with red-and-white checked plastic cloths and there was a basket of hand wipes at the ready. Good signs.

They were quiet as they read the menus and both ready when a waiter came by to take their orders.

"Pulled pork, potato salad and corn on the cob, please," Nell said. "And..." She ran her finger down the list of drafts. "I'll try this Colorado Native Amber Lager."

"I'll take the rib tips, BBQ beans and fried zucchini. And I'll go with that Scotch Ale you have on tap."

Their orders were deemed "excellent" and the waiter was on his way.

His phone buzzed, and he glanced at it. When he saw a photo

from CC, he set the phone on the table so that they could both look. The text read:

Too soon to get her a kitten? This is the neighbor's...

And the picture showed an absolutely enthralled Aubrey with a little ball of marmalade fur in her lap.

"Oh my gosh, she's just too precious!" Nell said.

"Completely. I'm so glad I get to be an uncle slash godfather. So much better than having my own." He gave a pretend shudder.

He sent some hearts and an admonishment that unfortunately, yes, it *was* too soon for a kitten, but she'd be old enough eventually.

When he looked up from the phone, he found Nell staring at him, biting her lip.

"What?"

She had to wait while the waiter brought their food. That was nice and fast. He picked up his sandwich and returned his attention to Nell.

"You don't want to have kids?" she asked quietly.

Oh shit. "I hadn't really foreseen it as a possibility," he admitted. "It didn't really seem like something that was in your long-term plans, either," he added. "You hadn't mentioned anything like that."

"Well. I had figured that if it didn't happen, that's fine. But I was...cautiously optimistic that if things went well between us, we wouldn't be too old to start a family if we decided to get married." She paused, then rushed on. "Not to say that we're at the point of talking about marriage or anything, I'm just saying it seemed like I could imagine us getting there."

"I understand what you mean about not being there now, but envisioning where we might find ourselves in the future. I guess I just...a long time ago, I realized there was no reason for me to have kids. I can't imagine the stress of not screwing that up."

He let loose some of his tension when she reached over and put her hand on his arm. "If that's what you decide, I would never push you in the other direction. I just think...it's possible that you made that decision when you were a different person, one who was still in a lot of pain. Understandably so. But you're not that person anymore. You worked hard on yourself to become who you wanted to be, not who your upbringing suggested you would become."

He wasn't sure he had a response to that, and she didn't seem to expect one. "Just think about it. It's like we said when we talked about Rose and Naomi and I all moving to the same town without ever having thought about it as a possibility. Sometimes, you need to step back from the situation and look at it with fresh eyes to see what is really kind of obvious."

Nodding, he took a bite of his sandwich. She was right, he *should* think about it.

And if he decided that children weren't in his future, did he really want to be responsible for Nell not giving all the love she had to give to her own kids?

It was hard to finish his bite and swallow it, even though objectively, he recognized that the meat was delicious. He glanced up to see how Nell was enjoying hers—and the one bite he'd managed turned to lead in his stomach.

"You *are* mad."

Fury had leaked into her eyes, but she shook her head. Then she nodded. She swallowed her own bite and reached out to thread her fingers through his.

"I am, but not at you. At your shithead parents. I'm *very* mad at them, and while I would never wish that tornado on anyone, it's probably for the best that there's no chance of me confronting them."

He sat with that for a minute, watching the anger bleed into sympathy. He wasn't sure that was any better. Her fingers squeezed his and she went back to her sandwich.

He found he was able to take the next bite a little more easily.

CHAPTER TWENTY-ONE

Naomi laughed when she turned and caught Nell's expression. "You don't love the mint-green paint?" she asked. "Not what you were expecting?"

"Please tell me that's on the list of things to change." They'd driven out to the triplex that Naomi had bought not far from Wildlife Ridge. The one she'd gone to look at the day Aaron had driven Janelle and Grandma to the museum and airport. In some ways that seemed so long ago, considering how much her life had changed.

The building was not in the greatest neighborhood, but not so bad that Nell had been worried as they'd driven in.

"I'll tell you about the neighborhood when we're back in the car, but here comes Brandon, my contractor." Naomi gestured to a man getting out of a pickup truck that had just pulled into the driveway.

A white man with short brown hair and a Metallica t-shirt got out and raised his head in acknowledgment, then turned back to the truck. He reemerged with a heavy-duty clipboard and headed towards them.

"Hi, Brandon, good to see you again," Naomi said, putting out her hand. "This is my friend Janelle. Janelle, Brandon Mills."

"Nice to meet you, Janelle."

"Thanks. I'm just tagging along out of curiosity."

"It's always fun to show off what we're going to do. And Naomi has excellent ideas about that."

They spent the next hour and a half going through the building in exhaustive detail, both Brandon and Naomi making a lot of notes. Janelle offered to be the note taker for her friend, but Naomi said writing it down helped her cement the details in her mind better.

They went through every inch of the interior and the exterior. Nell thought she understood most of it, but some of it was over her head. She didn't interrupt. At first she was worried about the number of things being added to the list, but then she realized that a lot of it was cosmetic. Plus, neither Naomi nor Brandon seemed concerned about the scope.

She left them on the steps to talk some more and moved to Naomi's car to call Aaron.

"Hey, we'll be heading back soon. Naomi's going to drop me off. You need anything?"

"You should go back to the apartment, not here. I seem to have gotten a bug of some sort."

"Oh no, what's wrong?"

"I'm nauseous. I don't want you to get it, too."

"It sounds like you're in pain." Like he was talking through gritted teeth.

"That comes and goes in waves."

"Baby, that's not good. Did you take anything?"

"I tried some Pepto but I threw it up."

Throwing up was not the same as just being nauseous, but she didn't say that. "Okay, we're going to stop for chicken soup, in case you get to the point where that sounds like a good idea, and I'll see what other stomach stuff they have, and I'll be home soon."

"Nell..."

"Aaron, I'm not leaving you alone like that."

He sighed. "Okay, I'll see you soon. Maybe pick up a hazmat suit."

She laughed, and was glad when Naomi headed over. She filled her friend in on the need to stop at the grocery store and they started back to Wildlife Ridge.

"So, help me not obsess about Aaron being sick. Did that all go the way you thought it would?"

"Yep, it was just as I remembered. It's going to be a lot of fun." She shot Nell a big grin.

Nell laughed. "If you say so."

"I'm glad I'll be here to actually see the progress instead of managing it from Los Angeles."

"Me too. Tell me about the neighborhood."

"Right, so I would call this area a C-plus or B-minus neighborhood."

"Jeez, you're grading them now?"

Her friend laughed. "Not just me. We call them class A, class B, etc. Your parents live in a class A neighborhood. You were in B-plus, I was in a B. The way I like to tell, more objectively than just driving through once or twice, is the grocery stores. A class A neighborhood will range from an upscale grocery store to a very nice one. B will range from very nice to nice. C might have a kind of nice to okay."

"Huh. So like Tru Value versus Vons versus Pavillions versus Gelson's.

"Exactly."

Nell frowned. "I never thought about how shitty grocery stores were in lower-income neighborhoods. That's not cool."

"No, it's not. And I can't wait to be able to make an impact in an area like that, when I have the money to make a difference."

"I never even thought about having enough money to make an impact. If I make it there, I'll attach myself to your impact-making coattails."

"Sounds like a plan. And you'll get there. You're not going to sit at home and watch TV all day, you'd go crazy."

"I went to Jake's Monday, and told him I was in for working the hours he suggested, as long as I can take vacations whenever I wanted. He just asked for a week's notice, so he could manage customers' expectations."

"Seems reasonable."

"But it's not going to be huge dollars."

"It's a continuation of what you've got going. You'll get there. And don't try to tell me you haven't started the search for an old beater car to fix up and sell for a ridiculous amount of money."

"Okay, I won't tell you that. So, you were looking for a C-plus or B-minus neighborhood?"

"I was looking for a C, but this was such a good deal with how hideous it was, and how easy it would be to fix that and bring up the value quickly."

Nell nodded. Interesting. "I'm glad I'll be able to see the progress, too."

They made quick work of grabbing some soup and then a couple of stomach medicines and were headed to Aaron's with Nell having successfully resisted the urge to check up on him during the drive.

She used the remote on her keychain to open the garage door and was only slightly surprised that Aaron didn't come to the door to meet them. Definitely not feeling well.

She dropped the groceries in the kitchen, checked the living room, then jogged up the stairs. She didn't see him in the master bedroom, but found him in the studio, sitting on the club chair, bent over at the waist.

"Oh, Aaron."

He looked up, a sheen of sweat covering his face. As she watched, his expression turned into a grimace of pain.

"Let's get you into bed," she said, moving to him.

"I think…I think I need to go to the doctor."

She checked her watch. "It's after five, I think he's closed."

"Shit."

"We can go to Bell View, I'm pretty sure they have a hospital. Do you want to try one of the medicines I brought?"

He started to answer, then grimaced as another wave of pain hit.

"I'm thinking it might be a kidney stone. Or appendix. Not a bug. If we're driving out of town, I'd just as soon go to Denver."

"Okay, we'll leave now." And maybe stop at the closer hospital in Bell View, if he got worse on the way, she figured, but didn't feel the need to say out loud.

She sort of expected him to argue, but when he just nodded, she jumped up and ran into the bedroom to throw a change of clothes for each of them into a bag and grab her purse, which she hadn't taken to the triplex, and jogged downstairs to put them in her car before helping him down.

She found Naomi sitting at one of the barstools, drinking a glass of water. "How's he doing?"

"Not great, I'm going to take him to an urgent care or the ER. I'll figure that out when we get closer to Denver."

"I'll drive."

She started to object, then just nodded. "Thanks."

The drive was normally an hour and forty-five minutes, but with Naomi pushing the speed limits a bit more than she usually would, they made great time. It still felt like forever as she watched Aaron grit his teeth against the pain. She'd checked her phone and decided it would just be easiest to go to the emergency room, so she directed Naomi to the hospital.

When they got inside, it didn't appear to be too busy, but it felt like the intake person was dawdling along at her ease, with no sense of urgency for Aaron's situation. Part of Nell knew she was being unfair, and that Aaron wasn't about to die, but she had to clench her fists to keep from saying anything rude.

They sat down to fill out paperwork, with Aaron insisting he could do it himself. Her phone rang, and she glanced at the screen. Her mother. She stood up and walked to an empty corner so as not to bother the other people in the room.

"Hey, Mom, I can't really talk—"

"Grandma's in the hospital. They found her on the floor, unconscious, and they rushed her over. Your father's on the phone booking tickets. Your cousin Mary is with her, but she doesn't know anything. She says we can wait until she has information before we make plans, but screw that."

Nell's legs had almost given out at the first sentence, but she leaned against the wall. *Grandma.* She swallowed past the giant lump that threatened to choke her. "I—okay. Shit."

"I know, baby. I'm really worried." The fear in her mom's voice intensified her own.

"Yes. I'm in Denver right now, I'll get the next flight I can." She looked over to Aaron, who was clutching his stomach and handing the clipboard to Naomi, who returned it to the front counter. Naomi was glancing Nell's way, a worried look on her face.

It was hard to think. She wanted to be here for him. *Needed* to be here for him. They'd looked up symptoms in the car and felt there was a good chance he had a kidney stone, which was supposed to be one of the most painful things a person could experience.

But Grandma...

She blinked back her tears and set her shoulders, moving back to Aaron as Naomi returned.

"Grandma's in the hospital. She was unconscious, they don't know what's wrong yet."

"Fuck," Aaron said, taking her hand.

"Oh, honey," Naomi said, moving to put a hand on her shoulder.

She looked at Aaron's pain-filled face, and she knew he'd already read the decision she'd made, because he gave a tight nod. Still, she said it.

"I have to go," she whispered, the tightness in her throat too constricted to allow for more.

"I know. It's fine." He grimaced and looked away from her.

She leaned over to kiss him.

"Go," he said through gritted teeth. "Go now."

She landed a kiss on his forehead anyway, then turned and walked away quickly, waiting until she was around the corner to wipe the tears from her face. Naomi was at her side.

"I don't want to leave him. I shouldn't leave him. He's mad. Of course he's mad! Shit!"

"I doubt he's mad. I'll stay with him, you go. You know that chances are very, very tiny that whatever is wrong with Aaron is life-threatening. With Yuki…it could be really bad."

"He's in so much pain," she whispered. "But if Grandma dies, I don't—"

"He knows you need to go. I'll stay with him," Naomi repeated. "Let us know when you hear anything, and I'll send you messages to update you from here."

"I'm so glad you're here. Thank you."

Naomi gave her a big hug. "Order a car on your phone and let's make sure there's one nearby. You have your credit card? You okay to get a ticket?"

"Yeah, I'm fine. You brought the bag I packed, you're thinking a lot better than I am. Let me see if I can fit my stuff in my purse." She left her change of jeans in the bag but managed to get her shirt and underwear into her purse, pulling her wallet out first so that it sat on the top. She gave her friend another hug as the app showed her car was only a couple of minutes away.

"Please go back to him. It will help me a lot knowing you're there."

"Okay, be careful and keep us updated."

Another big hug and they went in opposite directions. Nell only had to wait a minute before the car arrived, and she was on her way to the airport.

The next few hours were a blur with moments of sharp focus as she updated her parents from the car, got to the airport, booked her flight, and picked up some basics from one of the shops. Then she was boarded and on her way. The Wi-Fi on the flight wasn't working, so she was stuck with no updates for the entire trip, and she was a nervous wreck by the time they landed. It took everything she had to hold back her tears as she turned her cell service back on.

Her phone lit up with messages as soon as it reconnected. She fired off the same message to her parents and Naomi, first, letting them know there'd been no Wi-Fi and she had landed and was about to catch up on messages.

Her mother had let her know that they'd landed, then that they'd arrived at the hospital. Grandma was conscious but out of it. She had pneumonia and was very dehydrated, but they'd made progress on that. Her parents had tracked her flight and knew when she was landing, so her cousin should be there to pick her up.

Naomi had updated that Aaron was definitely experiencing a kidney stone and they had given him some heavy-duty pain relievers and were trying to flush it out, but if that didn't work soon, they would attempt to break the stone up with sound waves.

She felt so much relief, she had to sit down for a second. While the kidney stone sounded awful, he shouldn't be in any danger. She was super worried about Grandma, but nothing devastating had happened while she'd been in the air.

Naomi also mentioned that when it had become clear Nell was unable to send updates, she'd texted Nell's mom, and so she and Aaron were up to speed on how Grandma was doing.

She sent kissy faces to her mom and Naomi and headed out of the airport to find her cousin and get to the hospital.

The warmth of the air surrounded her, the lush greenery welcoming her home, but it wasn't enough to calm her anxiety. Her cousin waited with the car and gave her a tight hug. The fear in her eyes matched Nell's, but she assured Nell that Grandma was hanging in and the doctors were hopeful.

Hours later, she'd managed to send her parents off to Grandma's house to get some rest and make a pot of saimin. The Hawaiian noodle soup, sort of their answer to Japanese ramen, was a must for when Grandma came home, and they were all determined to act as though Grandma would be going home shortly.

When not sleeping, she was more aware now than she had been when Nell had first arrived. They'd determined that the pneumonia had made her very dehydrated, which was why she'd been unre-sponsive. The family had known she was sick, but not *that* sick. Her cousin had been going by the house to check on her and make sure she was eating, which is when she'd been found.

Nell hadn't texted Aaron yet, only Naomi. She assumed the

heavy painkillers were keeping him pretty out of it. And he hadn't texted her. The thought of how disappointed he must be in her made Nell tear up again.

She'd left him when he'd needed her. He, who'd never had anyone at his side, who'd had to do everything on his own because his family was so awful, hadn't been able to rely on the woman who said she loved him.

Would he forgive her? He knew she loved her grandmother, and hell, he was fond of Yuki, too. So maybe he would understand. *Probably* he would understand. He was a caring, understanding kind of guy.

Gah, her brain was running around in stupid, useless circles.

Grandma's hand, held gently in her own, gave a little twitch, and Nell looked up to find herself being watched.

"Hey, Grandma. Did you get some rest?"

The nod was small but there, and then her eyes closed and she was back asleep.

Somehow that little bit of contact was enough to relieve Nell. She'd get home, she'd make it up to Aaron, and somehow assure him that she loved him.

She dozed off and on and switched with her parents, aunt and uncle when they all arrived before breakfast, leaving them on hospital duty and heading to the house for some food and a bed.

When she woke up, the room was bright despite the curtains being closed. She heard the echo of Aaron's pained "go" and knew she'd been reliving the awful moment in the hospital. He'd been hurting so bad, and had turned away from her to say the words.

She checked her phone. It was later than she'd realized, and she needed to get to the hospital. Her texts showed that Grandma was more awake and responding well to her treatments. Nell had said that the kidney stone had passed and Aaron was no longer in pain.

Taking a huge breath of relief, she got up. She shot a quick text to her mom, letting her know she would be on her way soon, a thank you and hearts to Naomi, and a heart to Aaron.

He didn't respond.

She took a very quick shower, threw on her clean underwear and top, and her jeans from the day before, and headed to the door. Her parents had ridden in with her aunt and uncle, leaving her grandma's car.

When she opened the door, a car was pulling up. A man started to get out of the passenger door on the far side, and her stomach dipped.

It looked a lot like Aaron.

She squinted against the bright sun, and then began to run when she realized that it wasn't her hopeful imagination, it really *was* Aaron. Pale, and moving slowly, but Aaron.

Restraining herself from jumping on a man who'd just gotten out of the hospital, she instead melted into the strong arms that wrapped around her and held on tight. She didn't realize she was crying until he nudged her back, which she resisted at first, and he wiped her tears away with his thumbs.

"Oh, baby, is it Yuki? Last I heard, she was doing better."

She managed to pull herself together as she shook her head. "No, it's you. You're here."

"Of course I'm here. I'm so sorry it took me this long."

She choked out a laugh. "You were in the hospital!"

"Yeah, that really sucked. I wanted to be at your side."

"I was supposed to be at *your* side," she argued.

"Not while your grandmother needed you, you weren't."

"I wanted to be there for you, but I had to be here. I thought you might be mad. You sounded so angry when you told me to go."

"Oh, baby, no. I was hurting pretty bad and it was hard to even talk. I didn't want you to feel guilty about going, so I was trying to hide that. I guess I didn't do a very good job."

She shook her head again. "It was me, my mind was all messed up. I really, really hated to leave you."

"Don't be upset about that. We were pretty sure it was a kidney stone, and we were right. It sucked, I'll be staying much better hydrated in the future, I can promise you that. But I wasn't in danger, and we knew that."

"We *thought* we knew that, but we weren't sure."

"We thought right."

She sighed. "Yeah, okay, but let's not do that again."

"That I'll agree with."

She leaned back in and rested her forehead against his shoulder. "I love you."

He held her tighter. "I love you, too."

CHAPTER TWENTY-TWO

Aaron looked around his packed backyard. When he'd bought the house, the backyard space had seemed a bit large for his needs, but he'd liked the idea of the pool and hot tub. Now, it almost seemed too small.

He'd been dubious about hosting a barbecue in November in Colorado, even if the month had just started. Rose's mom had assured him that if they needed to switch to indoors, they could do so easily, and that the covered porch would be fine to barbecue under, if needed. George had gotten four outdoor heaters for the space and brought them over two days ago.

Fortunately, the weather was cooperating, and though it was chilly, it wasn't unpleasant to sit out in the sunshine and talk with the townspeople. And there were a lot of townspeople.

As promised, he was hosting the welcome home party for Rose and Ethan, who had arrived back yesterday morning. They'd invited Nell, Naomi and Aaron over for dinner the previous night and showed them lots and lots of photos of their trip. Aaron had enjoyed himself quite a bit. He felt like he'd gotten to know the couple decently well from the video chats of the last two months, but in person was better.

Plus, Aaron and Nell had been able to show off pictures of their little trip to New York City the previous week. They'd spent four days with him showing her his favorite parts of the city, the cheap restaurants he'd frequented when he'd been a student, the fancier places he'd switched to before he'd moved. She'd insisted on seeing some of the tourist places he'd never bothered to go to before. He'd grumbled a bit, but hadn't really minded. It was the first time she'd taken a vacation for no reason other than to have a good time with her partner, and he was pleased as hell to share that with her.

They'd considered going back to Hawaii, but Yuki had insisted that she was fully recovered and that as much as she loved seeing them, it was time for Janelle to branch out and visit somewhere new and just for fun. He really loved that lady.

Ethan wandered over and nodded towards a cluster of women gathered around one of the heat lamps. "I believe Mrs. Rubinski is trying to entice Anna into *accidentally* bumping Jackson into the pool so they can see him with his shirt plastered to his chest, then see him as he removes the shirt, then assure him that he can warm up by climbing into the hot tub."

Aaron choked on his beer, and Ethan slapped him on the back manfully to help it go down. "Mrs. Rubinski is the grandmotherly looking lady wearing the green cape that appears to be made out of feathers?"

"Yes, that's her. I warn you because they might turn their sights to other prey."

"Thank you. I'll be watchful."

"Thanks for hosting this, man. It's really nice to be able to get this many people together, which wouldn't have happened at Rose's mom's place. Francine probably would have insisted on renting the banquet hall at the Masonic Temple if you hadn't come through."

"Happy to help. You guys had a great trip, I'm going to have to see about getting Nell to actually make plans to go to Europe, rather than just talk about making plans."

"Yeah, Rose has indicated that might be a challenge. Nell's been in save mode for so long, it can be hard to flip the switch. Sounds like she's enjoying working at the garage, though. And the fact that she took the trip to New York is an excellent sign that she's starting to live instead of just planning to live."

"Yeah. And her old boss called again last week to try to get her to do some remote work. She's getting less polite about telling him no, but she's kind of having fun doing it."

Ethan laughed. "Nice."

Rose came over and bumped her husband's hip. "Mom's trying to talk sense into Mrs. Rubinski."

"Good. She and your dad were looking awfully cozy when they were working together to help us set up."

"I was thinking the same thing. I asked Mom if she did any dating while I was gone, and she just said she hadn't met anyone worth giving a spin lately. I tried not to gag."

Ethan and Aaron laughed. Nell and Naomi moved to join them.

"It's going very well," Nell said.

The others agreed.

"How is the building coming along?" Aaron asked Naomi.

"Really well, should be done next week, actually. Unfortunately, painting the interior is one of the last things that will happen, so the management company can't come in and take photos for listings yet, but they're pretty confident they can fill the units quickly."

"That's great," Nell said.

"Uh-oh, my mom is giving me a look, we'd better get back to mingling," Rose muttered.

They broke off, and Aaron looked around. Things seemed to be in pretty good shape. George was having what looked to be a lively discussion with Tom Romano. The mayor was now involved with the group that included Francine, Mrs. Rubinski and Anna, along with a couple of other ladies of varying ages. All of whom should know better. But he trusted Francine to see to that.

Jackson was checking out the grill with Jake, who had promised to handle those duties.

It reminded him that the last person to work the grill had been Nell's dad. She'd invited her parents, but her mom wasn't ready to come for a winter visit. Aaron had gotten a chance to get to know Andrew and Dana pretty well in Hawaii. Nothing like a family crisis to really bring people together, he'd learned. At least, with the right kind of family. He wouldn't have hated them coming for a visit.

CC and Beth were showing Aubrey off to Naomi and Erin Granger, whose daughter Olivia was enthralled with the baby. His goddaughter appeared to be equally enamored of the energetic Livvy.

He wondered if it would be wrong of him to go in and get a piece of the strawberry cheesecake Nell had made. She hadn't said anything, just made it while he was working, and he'd come down to her taking it out of the oven. He hadn't said anything either, but he was pretty sure that she knew the kiss he'd given her, the one that had lasted about ten minutes, was a thank you.

She'd given him so much, just by coming into his life. Opened his eyes to the family he already had, then readily shared her family and friends. Baked a cheesecake just because it would make him happy. It was almost hard to remember how alone he'd been eight months ago. Not lonely. He hadn't been unhappy. But he hadn't even known how happy he *could* be. Until Nell.

David Zeigler, the local realtor they'd finally met, opened a fresh beer and came to stand next to Aaron, which was probably a good thing, before he convinced himself that stealing a slice was reasonable since she'd essentially made the dessert for him.

"I'm beginning to think Nell's not really serious about buying a place."

"Well, you'd have to talk to her about that." Though Aaron kind of agreed. But the only places that had come up for sale in town in the last little while were completely wrong for her, anyway. They'd found their rhythm for spending most of their time at his house, but also hanging out with Naomi at the apartment, as well as him staying home so the ladies could have time together now and then.

David only harrumphed in response. He was currently giving Naomi the stink eye, and Aaron suspected he was more insulted that she had no interest in using his services to build her real estate empire than he was about Nell not buying a two-bedroom house that hadn't been updated since the fifties.

The party wound down several hours later, and Aaron and Janelle waved Rose, Ethan and Naomi off, after the group cleanup was accomplished very quickly.

He turned to Nell and pretended to collapse.

She laughed. "It was a long day, but a good one."

"Yes."

She leaned into him, as was her habit, and he wrapped his arms around her, enjoying her weight against his chest. He kind of just wanted to stay like this for an hour, but he'd had something on his mind all day…and he was ready to act on it.

"Come upstairs with me," he said. "I want to show you something."

NELL HAD an idea about what Aaron wanted to show her upstairs, and she was ready for it, though she was surprised when he opened the door to his studio instead of taking her to the bedroom. They'd stayed up late last night with their friends, and hadn't made love when they'd finally gone to bed.

But there were two very comfortable club chairs on the far side of the room that she'd mentioned wanting to try out one of these days. She put her hands on his waist and gave a little push, then another as she began to work his belt loose.

"Oh, well. That wasn't actually—"

He broke off when she reached into his pants and took him in hand. She smiled and continued to edge him back until his legs hit the seat of one of the chairs, and he sat down. She lifted her dress teasingly high, but not high enough to show anything as she slipped her hands under and drew her panties down her legs.

He groaned. Then he lifted his hips and shoved his pants and shorts down to his knees. She helped, grabbing them and pulling them free, then tossing them aside.

Somehow he was holding a condom, which made her smile. Her man was always ready for her. She kneeled in front of him and took him into her mouth, her hands going to fondle his balls.

He pressed up into her, then relaxed into her ministrations, one hand lightly sifting through her hair, the other holding tightly to the chair arm. She hummed.

"Fucking hell, I love when you do that."

She smiled around him and continued her play.

"Touch yourself, since I can't reach you," he said.

Ooh, that sounded like a good idea. She reached under her skirt and worked her clit lightly, teased her finger through the slickness that had gathered until her hips began to rock. Then she sat back and brought her finger to her lips, before changing her mind and offering it to him, instead.

He drew her finger in, licked it clean and apparently decided that was enough. "Come here."

She stood, turned around, then watched him over her shoulder as she lifted her skirt to sit on his lap. He put his hands to her waist to guide her. She reached between her legs and positioned him, then sank down. He filled her up, and she couldn't move for a minute, enjoying the feeling, his legs flexing under her thighs, his hands wrapping around to hold her to him, her dress covering them.

She lifted the skirt up to give her more room and draped her legs over the arms of the chair. They both moaned as that dropped her even lower. She used the leverage to move up and down as he teased her breasts through her dress, his lips roaming her neck, his hot breath ragged in her ear.

"So hot," he murmured. "Love you like this."

"Mmmm," she moaned. She wanted to say more, but he did something, canted his hips somehow, and touched that place inside her that set her off. She increased her speed and reached down to finger her clit again.

"Go off, baby," he encouraged, his fingers twisting her nipple, just enough.

She couldn't resist. She cried out and gripped the chair arms as she shattered. He groaned and she reached down to caress his balls. He squeezed her breasts and gasped out his own release.

Letting her hands fall to the sides, she leaned back, head against his shoulder. After long minutes, he nibbled her earlobe then readjusted her so that she was sitting across his lap. "That wasn't actually what I wanted to show you," he said.

"No?"

"No. But no complaints."

She smiled. "Good. What did you want to show me?"

"It would help if you opened your eyes." She'd snuggled down and was resting her head against his chest.

"Oh. Fine."

She did so, and thought about tracing the grin that stretched his lips wide, but couldn't summon the energy to lift her hand.

He used his head to gesture to the room.

She rolled her head back and looked. An easel had been set up in front of the door, so that you would only see the back unless you came fully into the room and turned to face it.

The painting was *her*.

But it was a her that was so beautiful and so filled with love that she immediately felt tears prickling the backs of her eyes. The painting showed only her face and hair, her eyes bright, her smile pleased.

"Wow."

"You like it?"

"I—it's amazing. I think…is that how you see me?"

"Every day."

"Aaron, it's incredible. I'm so honored."

"I want to do a series. Of you. You when we fell in love," he said, pointing to the canvas. "Of you when we get married. Of you holding our baby."

She gasped and turned back to him. "Aaron. Are you sure? You know I love you, and I'll be with you without needing that."

"I'm sure. I'm sure that I want to see you as a mom, see the love that you would bring to a family. Our family."

"Oh, baby." She took his face into her hands and met his gaze, knowing that he was seeing the same love shining through her eyes as she was seeing in his. Knowing, because he'd shown it to her in the painting. "I want that, too."

"Can I give you a ring, then?"

She sniffled back her tears and smiled. "Yeah, you can do that."

He reached over and pulled a velvet box from the drawer in the side table. She caught sight of condoms in the drawer, as well, and laughed, then clapped her hands in giddy excitement as he opened the box and pulled out a ring.

"I mentioned to your mom that she seemed pretty attuned to your style and maybe she could help me pick something out. She said that you had always loved your grandmother's ring, and Yuki gave it to her when we were in Hawaii, just in case. She sent it to me."

"Ooh, I *have* always loved it! And they gave it to you and didn't give me any hints at all!"

"We can get you another one if you'd like."

"No, this is what I want." She held out her hand, and he slipped it onto her finger. A perfect fit.

"You're what I want," he said. "I'll do everything in my power to make you happy for the rest of your life."

"I already am." She wrapped her arms around his neck and kissed him. "I already am."

Finding Forever
(Fully Invested Book 3)
By KB Alan
(Available now)

When Naomi moves to Wildlife Ridge, she has high hopes for her new town, her real estate business and being close to her best friends. When her contractor does a runner, she's stuck with his brother who agrees to fill in, but isn't at all happy with the situation.

Tempers flare until they can get a handle on their working relationship. And until they start to notice how much they have in common. Can Jason convince Naomi that his initial jerk reaction wasn't about her, and that, given the chance, he can be *all* about her?

Chapter One

"Happy New Year!"

Naomi clinked her champagne glass with those of her friends. She, Rose and Ethan had come to Janelle and Aaron's party a little bit early, so they could have a private toast before the other guests arrived.

Janelle had wanted to start a new tradition with her fiancé, adopting that of her mother. Every year, Dana Bouchard hosted an open-house style New Year's Day party. This would be Janelle's first year not attending, and Aaron had encouraged her to start her own tradition. Their tradition. Naomi had attended the Bouchards' party several times, and was glad that Nell was going to give it a go.

Last year, Rose had been in Colorado for the holiday, and Naomi and Janelle had done a video call with her from the Bouchards' house. At the time, they'd never expected that only one year later they would all be back to living in the same city. Rose had been engaged, but now she was married and *Nell* was engaged.

This was the first time they'd invited men to join them in the early celebration, and Ethan and Aaron were welcome additions to the group. Naomi didn't feel like a fifth wheel, not most of the time. She and her best friends had spent too many years together for her to feel left out with them, and the guys were good for her girls. She was thrilled that her friends were so happy, and Naomi looked forward to helping Janelle plan her wedding.

Ethan raised his glass again. "To Rose, Naomi and Janelle. Thank you for making us family."

Damn, it was like he'd seen inside her heart, Naomi thought as she raised her glass again. Aaron pulled Nell in tighter too him, and Naomi suspected he'd been touched by the toast, as well.

"To family," Aaron echoed.

They clinked glasses again and drank.

"Can you tell me more about this tradition, Nell?" Ethan asked.

"Sure. My grandmother Yuki's parents were Japanese, first generation born in Hawaii. This is a Japanese tradition. We serve ozoni, which is a soup that has a little cake of mochi in it. It's for luck—something about how the mochi stretches means longevity."

"The soup is good," Rose said. "Nell made a pork version and a shrimp version that you can choose from."

"She'll put a mochi cake in your little soup bowl, and you can have a second serving, but only if you have thirds. You have to eat an odd number of mochi cakes," Naomi added.

Aaron nodded. "Odd number. Got it. There's lots of food here, does any of the rest of it have rules?"

"Nope, just the mochi," Nell said. "I may have overdone it on the food."

"I don't think that's possible," Ethan assured her. "Half the town was talking about coming. They enjoyed the barbecue in November."

Half the town of Wildlife Ridge would be about eleven hundred people, so not a lot when talking about towns, but definitely too many when talking about a party. Naomi knew he was exaggerating, but she was wondering how many people really would show up. The party in November had been to welcome Rose and Ethan back from their six months living in Spain, so the guest list had been heavily tilted towards Rose and Ethan's families.

Janelle and Aaron were both newcomers to the little town in Colorado, though. As was Naomi. Sometimes she had a hard time believing that she'd moved from Los Angeles to a town where the total population was about half the number of students that had been enrolled in her first year at UCLA. It was kind of crazy. But it was cool, too.

She actually knew her neighbors. The lady at the bank addressed her by name and sincerely meant it when she asked how the progress on her building was going. If she passed the postal woman on the street while heading to the grocery store, she would let Naomi know if there were packages for her that day.

When she'd first moved, she'd intended to live in one of the units of the triplex she'd purchased and renovated in Bell View, the town about forty-five minutes away. But then she'd gotten several excellent rental applications and decided she'd be an idiot to turn down the good tenants paying even more than she'd originally calculated in rent. And she liked Bell View well enough, but she liked Wildlife Ridge more. So she'd asked Ethan if she could stay in the apartment in his building until she found something to buy there.

He'd tried to give her a deal on the rent, but she'd insisted on paying standard price. The cost for the little two bedroom apartment was only a little more than half what she was charging for the two-bedroom units in her own building. Still, she didn't want to be in an apartment forever, so she was going to have to figure out her next moves.

"Naomi, when does the work on your new project begin?" Ethan asked. "Pretty soon, if I remember right?"

"Yes, next Monday."

"That's exciting," Rose said, and raised her nearly empty glass again.

"I think so. I'm not planning on going into the business of renovating buildings, but it'll be a good opportunity to do it again so soon after mine, and cement the relationships I started with the contractor and the other vendors. Even if I never again work on someone else's project like this, it will be more good practice and education for my own stuff."

"This is the multi-unit your friend from college bought?" Aaron asked.

"Right, a sorority sister. She and her husband moved to Colorado Springs years ago, and when she heard about me buying my triplex in Bell View and renovating it to hold for long-term rentals, she contacted me. Said she'd been interested in getting into being a landlord and a friend had pointed her to this building, which isn't far from mine. She thought it was a good deal, but was intimidated by how much work is needed to bring it up to speed. I thought she just wanted advice, but it turns out she wants to hand that whole side of it over to me, and not take over until it's time to rent out the units."

"And she'll pay you decent money?" Nell asked

"Yes."

"Then it sounds like a good deal. I'm excited for you, though I don't love you making that commute so often."

"Please. Driving the highway here, where sometimes you don't even see another car for half an hour, is almost a pleasure."

"Ha, true," Janelle agreed.

The doorbell rang, and Janelle and Aaron went to greet their first guests.

"How much work is there to do?" Ethan asked as he, Rose and Naomi made their way to the living room to claim seats.

"Brandon estimated about twelve weeks."

"And you liked working with him."

"Yeah, we did well together. He didn't get pissy when I asked questions and he showed up and kept things mostly to budget. He had a good crew. I appreciated you going over with me a few times, Ethan. It was good to get a second opinion that everything was as it should be."

"Happy to do it, and happy to do it again, if you need me, though it looked like you had everything completely under control."

Rose waved her glass at Aaron so that he would bring a full bottle when he returned. "You're in full construction mode now that you finally get to tear our house apart," she told her husband.

They'd bought a house on Dragonfly Road, the same road as the Salmon Springs apartment building where Naomi was staying, but on the other side of Main Street, in an older development. Naomi agreed with Ethan that it needed almost a full teardown to become the house that he and Rose wanted.

Aaron returned with the bottle and filled their glasses as Janelle ushered Rose's parents into the room. Funny how they'd come together, even though they'd been divorced for nearly twenty years, Naomi thought. She raised an eyebrow at Rose, who shrugged and drank from her flute.

Naomi suspected that Rose was indulging in the champagne a little more than usual because she and Ethan were going to start trying to have a baby in the new year. Her heart warmed at the image of her friends cuddling an infant this time next year.

Jin and Cal, who owned the antique store in town, joined them in the living room.

"This is so fun," Jin said. "I haven't had ozoni in years."

"You've been holding out on me," Cal complained.

"How long have you two been married?" Naomi asked.

"Six years," Cal said. "And Jin's mom does make a lot of traditional Japanese food, although not sushi, which is what brought us together."

"Wait," Ethan said, laughing. "I haven't heard this story. We've even gone to sushi together, and you didn't mention this. Spill."

"It's not a big deal. We were mutual friends with someone on Facebook. I had gone to college with her," Jin said.

"And I'd worked with her at my previous job," Cal added.

"She posted asking for the best sushi place in Pittsburgh," Jin said.

"And someone answered with this spot near campus that only survives because kids are too broke and vehicle-challenged to go farther." Cal popped a shrimp dipped in cocktail sauce into his mouth.

"I've seen that happen," Naomi agreed. "A subpar eatery that students swear is the best thing ever, and is total crap. I think it has something to do with them finally gaining their independence, but not much of it. And their brains still forming."

"Total crap exactly describes this place," Cal confirmed. "A couple of people were agreeing with the madness, so I went on to gently redirect. I mentioned my favorite place, but the kids were sticking to their guns and insisting that the college joint was better *and* cheaper."

"I think one of the diehards was actually her sister, who was still a college kid. She didn't take kindly to her suggestion to big Sis being criticized. Hopefully she's gotten choosier since then. And less defensive." Jin picked up a handful of nuts from the bowl on the coffee table and tossed a couple into his mouth.

"Anyway, Jin came on and was a little more blunt in his assessment of that place, and backed my selection," Cal continued. "Which I appreciated. We had a little back and forth, friended each other, stalked each other's accounts, and met up for sushi one week later."

"Eight weeks from then we moved in together, and we got married on the six-month anniversary of that Facebook post."

"Awww," Naomi and Rose said at the same time.

"Anyway, the point of all of that was that I've never been with Jin's family on New Year's Day, and he's never made soup in his life, so this is a first for me."

"Well, I'm ready for mine," Naomi said, and moved back to the kitchen, most of the group following her.

Aaron was standing in front of a large pot of boiling water, long tongs in his hand. Nell was dishing up soup in small, colorful bowls, then holding them out to Aaron, who fished out a mochi cake and added it to the bowl. Naomi asked for the pork and waited for her mochi, then dug in. The soup was delicious, and the cake chewy and stretchy, exactly as she remembered. Now she could really start her new year.

"Just like your mom makes," she told Nell, who beamed.

She managed not to make a joke about Aaron manning the pot of boiling water as she waited for the others to get their soup.

<hr>

When Naomi slipped out a couple of hours later, there were a lot of people in the house. She'd had her ozoni as well as plenty of other delicious foods, and was feeling pleasantly full. She made sure that Naomi didn't need any help and was pleased to see that Aaron had clearly shed his early reputation as a hermit and was fully participating in the hosting duties.

She'd considered driving, as the snow had been falling fairly heavily when she'd left her place, but she had her good boots, down coat, hat and scarf. And she was trying to embrace the idea of not driving if she was only going somewhere within town. A huge change from her life growing up in Long Beach, California, and then in Los Angeles as an adult.

It had been a little bit surprising how well she'd taken to living with the snow. But she didn't have to shovel it and it was just so damn pretty. She looked around as she cleared the open gate at the end of the driveway and continued on.

The mountains rose up all around her, sheltering the small town in its tree-filled valley. Rose had told her that Wildlife Springs had been a logging town way back in the day, but effort had clearly been made not to denude the town. Still, there weren't so many trees that she had bad camping vibes of the horror movie variety.

Some of the housing tracts were surrounded by what she would consider forest, and then there were the single houses and cabins out in the actual woods. She could maybe see herself in one of the housing tracts, but no way was she moving out into the damn forest. For one thing, the housing tracts were plowed as soon as the snow fell, and she was pretty sure that wasn't the case for the more out-of-the-way properties.

A ray of sunlight broke through the gray clouds and sparkled off the snow on one of the mountains. She actually stopped to stare, it was so beautiful. Sort of like watching the sun sparkle on the waves of the ocean, but different. Everything was a little bit different here.

Where she'd grown up, it was all traffic and people and businesses and noise. She didn't mind that. It was all she'd known. But she was starting to get used to rarely seeing more than two cars in a drive-through, not having to stop at a single stoplight the whole length of town—because there were none—and the predominant background sound being birds and the wind in the trees instead of cars whooshing by.

Speaking of cars, David Ziegler tooted his horn at her as he turned into the parking lot for the house that had become his real estate office, across the street. The fact that she recognized his car, and him—and had known the horn was a greeting, not a complaint —showed her she was getting used to being here after only four months.

Of course, in this case, recognizing the car was easy. David liked to think of himself as an artist. She supposed she couldn't argue otherwise, as his artwork was skilled. His hobby was to paint his car, once a month, to look like an animal. He'd scrape the job at the end of the month, spend a day or two working on the new artwork, and debut the art on the first. She had to admit, the car looked cute as a mouse. The whiskers were impressive.

The storm clouds seemed to be lightening up as the day progressed and she wondered if they'd see stars tonight. That was something she wasn't sure she'd ever get used to. Back in California, she could have driven out to the desert to see the stars, but who ever bothered? She'd gone on a small retreat with some of her sorority sisters to an AirBnB out in Joshua Tree once, and the sky had, indeed, been spectacular. But here, anytime the clouds were clear you could see the stars so clearly, it was spectacular.

She went up the steps to Salmon Springs, then held the door open for Mrs. Rubinski, who was coming out. The older woman was wearing a kelly-green puffy jacket, forest-green snow pants and lime-green knock-off Ugg boots. Naomi didn't even blink, as this was typical wear for the woman who had retired from teaching about a hundred years ago.

"Hi, Mrs. Rubinski. Are you walking? Can I drive you somewhere?" Yes, she thought, the small-town infection was taking her over.

"Thank you, Naomi, but I'm fine. I'm just meeting my friend Sharon for a walk. She's Mayor Romano's mother, you might not have met her yet."

"I don't think I have, though I've met Shirley and Tom." The mayor and her husband were frequently seen out and about.

"Sharon and I have known each other since sixth grade," Mrs. Rubinski told her. "We've decided our New Year's Resolution will be to take a forty-minute walk every day, rain or shine. We figure if it's really bad out, we can walk up and down the halls in the building here."

"That's smart," Naomi said as a car pulled into the lot.

"There she is now. You go on inside and shut the door so Ethan doesn't have to pay to heat the stairs."

Naomi bit her lip. "Yes, ma'am. You ladies enjoy your walk."

She headed inside to the second-floor apartment she and Nell had rented when they'd moved to Wildlife Springs. The sound of

Mr. Houston in 203, calling for his dog Ellie, made her smile. Ellie was a cutie and Naomi couldn't resist the tiny creature.

It was all quiet, however, when she went into her place. Janelle had moved in with Aaron after he'd proposed in November, and Naomi had turned the second bedroom into an office. Heading there after she shed her winter gear, she opened her laptop.

When she'd renovated her triplex, she'd made extensive notes so that she could build a template checklist for all future renovations. She didn't want to have to reinvent the wheel if she did this again. Which, she now was.

She pulled up her notes and started on her template.

When the phone rang an hour later, she was pleased with what she'd come up with. Checking the screen, she saw that it was her mom.

"Hi Mom, Happy New Year."

"Hi, baby. How are you doing out there in white land?"

Naomi laughed. "Do you mean the people or the snow?"

"Yes."

Naomi laughed again. Her parents had known she'd planned on leaving Los Angeles for some time, so they hadn't been surprised last June when she'd announced that she'd made her decision and was moving to Colorado in September.

They'd known for years that she was working towards the goal of living in a lower cost of living city, where she could manage her buildings and invest in more real estate, eventually living off the passive income.

"I'm doing good. Nell had a party at her and Aaron's place, so we all got to have our ozoni like her mom makes. And our champagne toast. The neighbors and community were only slightly skeptical of a tradition and food they'd never heard of."

"I'm glad. I'm working on prepping your father for us to go out there for the wedding. I'm still annoyed we didn't make it for Rose's. I may need you to call him and tell him how much you miss him, after the invitations go out."

"Yes, ma'am. I start on renovations for Shelly's building on

Monday. I might call Auntie June today and butter her and Uncle Derek up before I start with the construction calls next week."

"Call them, but you know they're happy to help."

"I know. What's going on with everyone else?"

She'd flown home for Christmas, which had been an interesting experience—to be back "home" without her own place. She'd stayed one night with her younger sister, Eleanor, in her new condo. Nora had been excited to play hostess and proud to show off her space. Her sister had spent years studying and busting her butt to get a good promotion at a law firm and was beginning to see the rewards.

She'd also spent a night with her older brother, Marcus, and his wife and twin boys, who were three. He and his wife, Honey, had flown to Jamaica to visit with her family the same day Naomi had returned home to Colorado. She loved that, as a dentist, Marcus could make a schedule that allowed for such a three-week trip. One of these days, she planned on joining them. She'd only met Honey's relatives at the wedding, but would enjoy getting to know them better. She'd set the goal in her travel budget and was working her way towards meeting it, slowly but surely.

Of course, she'd spent the last two days—Christmas and the next —at her parents' house. The first time she'd spent the night with them since moving into her apartment her junior year of college. It had been a little bit strange, helping her mom fill the stockings late at night while sharing wine, but still feeling the thrill of waking up on Christmas morning and knowing Dad would be making his Santa shaped pancakes. The bedroom she'd shared with her sister had been turned into an office, so she'd slept in the room that had been his brother's, now a guestroom.

"Marcus and Honey won't be home until the sixteenth. He says the boys are having a blast. They have a ton of cousins to play with."

"The flight was okay?"

"Mostly. They had that layover in North Carolina, so they were able to run around the airport for a bit and stretch their legs. Your father's trying to grab the phone from me, so I'll go. I love you!"

"Love you too, Mom."

She chatted with her dad for a while then hung up and went to make dinner. Her late New Year's Eve was catching up with her. She'd gone on a date with Vic, who lived in the building next to her triplex. It had been a second date, and the chemistry hadn't been strong, so she hadn't expected it to go late. But they'd been having a great time talking about their favorite book series, which had led to their favorite movies, and they'd ended up chatting until two in the morning. Unfortunately, they'd agreed that the chemistry thing wasn't about to change, and there would be no more dates.

Still, the dinner at a decent restaurant, with a cheerful midnight kiss, hadn't been a terrible way to spend an evening.

She checked the dating app on her phone. Louis Delgado had been chatting her up for a few weeks. She wasn't sure about him, but it was time to either move forward or cut him loose. Giving him the address for Shelly's building, she arranged to meet him there after her walk-through with Brandon on Monday.

Find purchase links for Finding Forever at
www.kbalan.com/books/finding-forever

To join KB Alan's newsletter, visit www.kbalan.com/newsletter

ABOUT THE AUTHOR

KB Alan lives the single life in Southern California. She acknowledges that she should probably turn off the computer and leave the house once in a while in order to find her own happily ever after, but for now she's content to delude herself with the theory that Mr. Right is bound to come knocking at her door through no real effort of her own. Please refrain from pointing out the many flaws in this system. Other comments, however, are happily received.

www.kbalan.com

To join KB's newsletter, visit www.kbalan.com/newsletter

facebook.com/kbalan

twitter.com/KB_Alan

instagram.com/authorkbalan

bookbub.com/authors/kb-alan